THE EXPIRATION DATE

"I love that rush, when he folds me into his arms and I can let out a sigh of relief, knowing that I'm safe there. Always."

— MICHELLE POELKING

First paperback edition June 2024

Cover design by Alt 19 Creative

www.authorlesliemcelroy.com

Paperback: 979-8-9889757-6-2
Ebook: 979-8-9889757-7-9

To my readers who have their walls up.
I hope that someday those walls will be obliterated
By a love that will never back down and never expire.

AUTHOR'S NOTE & CONTENT WARNING

Dear wonderful reader,

I am so honored that you wanted to dive into Aidan and Haley's world and love story. For the majority of the book, I have written it to be lighthearted and full of comedic, awkward and swoony banter. However, there are some heavy topics mentioned such as alcoholism, abuse, anxiety and depression. The story also contains adult language and explicit sexual scenes. If you prefer to keep their love story closed-door, please skip chapters 26 & 27.

XO, Leslie

THE EXPIRATION DATE

A NOVEL

LESLIE MCELROY

1

Haley

It's official.

This is the worst date ever.

I don't know why or how Rachel convinced me to go on a date with this guy. I mean sure, he isn't bad to look at, meaning he is extremely hot, but his personality is all wrong. We have absolutely nothing in common. He is a professional surfer. Californian born and bred. Total babe. It's like looking at a Ken doll. Unfortunately, based on our conversation so far, it seems like college were the best years of his life. He hasn't stopped talking about his frat boy days and all the fun he had hazing the incoming freshman. A real gem of a human being, this one. My face hurts from plastering on a smile for the past half hour and nodding as if I have any semblance of interest in what he's talking about.

"So what about you? What do you do, Kaley?" he asks.

"Um, it's Haley. I'm a writer," I respond, a little annoyed that he messed up my name for the fourth time this evening.

His eyebrows shoot up and he nods. "Oh really, for like a newspaper? Or?"

"Um, well actually I should have said I'm an aspiring writer. A screenwriter actually. You know Nora Ephron?" By the blank look on his face and the slow nod he gives me, I can tell he has absolutely no idea who my idol is. Figures. "Well anyway, I would love to write movies like hers. You know *Sleepless in Seattle, You've Got Mail, When Harry Met Sally?*" Again, no indication of familiarity with any of these iconic films. Does this guy live under a rock? I clear my throat and add, "But, um, right now I'm working as a personal assistant for an actor." This of course piques his interest. That little fun fact about me always piques everyone's interest.

"Oh really? That's gnarly. What actor?"

"Um, I can't really disclose that information. You know. Privacy reasons." This is when my life becomes less interesting to people. I dangle the bait in front of them and then I take it away almost immediately. But according to my contract, I cannot disclose who my employer is. Even though technically the whole world knows who he is.

He nods nonchalantly. Yeah, this date is going super well. Granted I haven't been on a date in a few years, but I know when a date is sinking. This one is like the fricken Titanic.

"Oh hey, I see some of my bros from the beach over there. Excuse me. I'll be right back." He flashes his perfect smile my way before he heads to the opposite side of the restaurant.

I give him a half hearted smile as he walks away, then pull out my phone from underneath my black cloth napkin and hurriedly text Rachel.

> Why in the world did you set me up with
> this guy? He is a total dud, Rach.

Eric?? Um, because he's hot and you need to get out and socialize with people. And did I mention he is hot?"

I roll my eyes and type back:

I will admit that he is hot but we have NOTHING in common. There is nothing of substance here.

Oh there is definitely substance there ;) I had a sneak peak the other day at the beach when I set this up for you.

Rachel!!

LOL. OMG Haley don't be such a prude. You need this. You need to get over your asshole of an ex once and for all.

My heart twinges a little at that last line. Rachel knows me well enough now after three years of being roommates and coworkers. She knows about my past with men. Correction: one man. She's right that I need to get out more, but it's safer for my heart to stay at home. The fictional men I write about and read about will never break my heart.

Well, I am coming home soon. Remind me to never let you set me up on a date again. Don't wait up for me. I'll see you on set tomorrow morning. XO

Ugh fine. Your loss. XO

I hit the side button on my phone and watch my screen go black. *You need this. You need to get over your asshole of an ex once and for all.* I close my eyes tight and try to erase those words in the gray boxes in my conversation thread. Is it possible for words to echo off a screen? Is it possible for someone's name to still haunt you after three years?

After telling Eric I have to leave (my roommate had an emergency apparently), I grab an Uber and head home. I have a busy day at work tomorrow and to be honest, there was nothing else to talk about with him. If I know anything about myself, it's that I do not casually date. I don't want to waste my time playing games or trying to figure out if it is going to last. Or thinking that it will last forever, only to be blindsided with a truth I never wanted to know or never saw coming.

The apartment is already dark when I close the door behind me. Rachel did leave the stove light on, and I glimpse a spoon on the counter covered with a Post It.

There's Ben & Jerry's in the freezer. I know you need it. XO-R

Smiling, I open the freezer and pull out the pint of chocolate chip cookie dough. As I take off the lid, the notification ring sounds on my phone. A Google alert.

BREAKING NEWS

HOLLYWOOD'S GOLDEN BOY GONE BAD: INEBRIATED AIDAN STONE HEADS OUT OF A DOWNTOWN L.A. CLUB WITH TWO WOMEN!

"Dammit, Aidan." Now I need this Ben & Jerry's more than ever.

2

Haley

The next day I head into set. I am so glad Aidan didn't have an early call time today. I was able to get a decent run on the beach this morning. I find Rachel near craft services. She has to be here at an ungodly hour since she is one of the makeup artists on this film. Her red hair is of course curled to perfection and her makeup is flawless. How does she manage to look like this all the time? Since I moved in with her, there have been maybe a handful of times that I've seen her without makeup on and even then, she looks flawless. She notices my approach and grins. "Good morning, sunshine. Did you find my treat last night?"

I repeat the words I texted to her: "Never again."

"I know, I know. You made that extremely clear last night. Never again will I try to help your sex life."

I let out a small chuckle, "Oh my goodness, Rach. My sex life is fine."

She snorts. "Okay, I'd say not hooking up with anyone in three years is nowhere near fine. Just trying to help a sister out."

"How do you know I haven't had a one night stand or two?"

"Um, because I know you, Haley, and that's not you. And it's a damn shame if you ask me. No-strings-attached sex is the best way to go. Less of a chance of getting your feelings hurt."

"Well, that's just not me, Rach. Not judging anyone that can do that. I think people get their feelings hurt either way. You're lucky you can separate your feelings from sex." Rachel shrugs and grabs a banana. "Thanks anyway, Rach. I promise I'll be fine."

"Oh, there's no doubt. You are nothing but a strong woman, Hales, especially with everything you've gone through." Rachel grabs a giant croissant and places it on a napkin alongside her banana. "So, I know your best friend's wedding is coming up. What are you going to do for a date? Wait, you're not going alone, are you? With him there?"

My stomach drops. I lean against the table. The wedding is coming up quickly and I don't know what I'm going to do. I still haven't responded to Anna's official RSVP. I feel like a terrible Maid of Honor, but I want to wait to check the box that says plus one just in case that plus one does miraculously pop into my life before the wedding. Mr. Perfect has unfortunately not made an appearance.

My phone buzzes and the screen flashes *Mom*. "Hold on, I have to take this...Hello?"

"Hey sweetie. How are you?"

"I'm good, Mom, just at work. What's up?"

"Well I am just trying to help Anna out and call to confirm with her bridesmaids their plus-ones. She said you haven't responded to her RSVP yet. She knows that *you* are coming, but are you bringing a date or not?"

God forbid the Maid of Honor show up to her best friend's wedding alone, while the groom's Best Man is her ex. It has been months of my mom and Anna asking me the same question over and over and I can't take it anymore. So I spontaneously pull a little white lie out of my ass to put an end to this conversation.

"Yes, Mom, I am bringing a date to the wedding! He's my new boyfriend, okay? So just stop asking!"

Yup that just came out of my mouth. There's no take-backs on that one. I hold my phone away from my ear as my mom starts squealing with joy about my out-of-the-blue news. It was very out-of-the-blue. I don't have a date. I don't have a boyfriend. I don't even have a semblance of a man in my life.

Well, that's not true. There is one man that my life basically revolves around, but he's my boss and that would be a definite no. Not to mention he is completely out of my league.

I don't know how I am going to pull this off.

"Oh my goodness! Haley Girl! Why didn't you tell me sooner?! Why did you put your mother through this agony of worrying about her daughter who is all alone out in L.A.? Who is he? What is his name?"

I start tapping the side of my thigh and my face turns hot from lying to my mom. I never lie to my mom. Mainly because I am a terrible liar. But my guilt always gets the best of me.

I clear my throat. "Um, Mom, I can't say right now. I'll tell you more about him later." Yeah, later. After I have the time to think about how I am going to fashion an imaginary date—no not date, *boyfriend*—out of thin air.

I glance over at Rachel. Her mouth is agape and her eyes are wide. She whispers, *What are you doing?"*

I press my fingers against my eyebrows and squeeze my eyes shut. "Uh, Mom, I gotta get back to set. My boss needs me. I'll call you later, okay?"

"Okay, I love you sweetie."

"Yeah I love you too. Bye." I press the red icon on my screen and sit in a nearby director's chair. I cover my face with my hands.

"You're screwed." Rachel says plainly.

"Ugh, I know I am. What was I supposed to do?"

"Um, not lie about having a date, or a boyfriend for that matter."

"She wouldn't stop pestering me, okay?" Ever since Anna announced that she was getting married, my mom – and Anna too, I might add – asked me almost daily if I was going to bring a date. I know they are trying to distract me from what happened and trying to make me feel less alone. Ironically, it's become a constant reminder of how alone I actually am. "I had to say something. She was driving me crazy."

"Okay, I get it. But, girl, where are you going to find a date in two weeks? As we discussed five minutes ago, I've known you for three years and I've never seen you bring home a man or even go on dates."

Rachel already knows why my focus has not really been on a man. Ever since my ex-fiancé dumped me, I have basically sworn off men to protect my heart from ever going through that again. Part of the reason I moved out to Los Angeles three years ago was to get away from the drama that ensued after the whole situation with Robert. There were way too many stares. Way too many whispers. Way too many memories that slapped me in my face everywhere I went. I needed to get away. I needed to find myself without someone by my side. I needed to focus on work.

"Well I've been a little busy. Aidan's schedule is so insane. Especially since he has landed a lot of blockbuster roles. Managing his day-to-day has kind of consumed my life. And that's totally fine with me. I didn't come out here to find a boyfriend or even love. I came out to L.A. to pursue my career."

"As a personal assistant?" Rachel jokes.

"Haha, very funny." Rachel knows full well how much I want to pursue my dream of becoming a screenwriter. As I told my blind date last night, I want to be the next Nora Ephron. I want to write the next *Sleepless in Seattle, You've Got Mail,* or even better, *When Harry Met Sally.* I want to revive the magic that those movies brought into my life and the lives of so many viewers over the years. In the meantime, I have to work my way up the business and play the game for a little bit. I need to establish myself and get some experience on movie sets and network with the screenwriters, directors and producers. This whole opportunity fell into my lap courtesy of Rachel. While she was working on a movie, one of the newer actors on set said he needed a personal assistant. His schedule was getting more and more hectic since he was booking more roles. I had just moved in with Rachel and was struggling to find something that had decent pay to keep up with the ridiculous rental rates that California had to offer. She said that this actor was desperate and needed to hire someone quickly who was trustworthy and not a total nutcase.

Who was that actor? None other than Aidan Stone.

AKA one of the hottest up-and-coming actors. AKA the universe's most eligible bachelor. AKA probably the most good-looking man I've ever encountered in my life.

AKA my boss.

AKA off limits.

I have been working for Aidan for close to three years. I know his daily schedule like the back of my hand. I am his girl Friday in almost every aspect of his life. I coordinate every travel arrangement, book his flights, arrange transportation and any accommodations he may need (which is not many...he's actually pretty laid-back). I manage his schedule, including any upcoming appearances and meetings. I coordinate with his agent, Chris, and his publicist, Samantha. I also work with producers and directors on behalf of Aidan. The only aspect of his life I'm not directly involved with (not that I want to be) is his love life. He was dating an actress, Natasha Davis, who is now the star of a very popular vampire series. They were together a full year, but about six months ago, she dumped him for one of her co-stars. Aidan was devastated. I think he really did love her.

It's official.

Love sucks. Even when you are a famous movie star.

Lately, Aidan's been dating a new woman every week, as if he's swiping right on every single profile that pops up on a Tinder feed.

Although I work exclusively with Aidan and am basically his

extra limb, I try to stay out of the spotlight as much as possible. I hide my face from paparazzi anytime they spot Aidan and me together, which is a rare occurrence anyway. I don't want anyone to speculate anything because that would never happen. Not in a million years. I haven't even told my friends or family who I actually work for– only Rachel knows. That would lead to too many complicated and invasive questions, and my job is to make Aidan's life easier.

Whenever I have downtime, I work on my own romantic comedy screenplay. It's pretty strong and I hope to pass up the ranks. I'm just not sure how to do it. Do I approach one of the screenwriters and ask them to read it? Do I chat up the producers on set? Try to find an agent? Truthfully, I am too scared to try any of that. Also, the one thing about my screenplay that I can't quite figure out is the happily-ever-after. There is a mental block and the root of it leads back to what happened with Robert. Even though the story I'm writing is fictional, I want what the male lead does or says to win the girl back to feel real and genuine–everything that Robert ended up not being. It is hard to write about something that I haven't experienced myself. I don't know if I ever will.

"So, what are you going to do?" Rachel asks, breaking me out of my own head.

At that moment, my phone dings with a calendar notification:

MEETING WITH SAMANTHA & CHRIS AT 1:00 p.m.

I check the time: 12:30 p.m. It takes about thirty minutes to get to Samantha's office.

"Um, I don't know right now. I've gotta run to a meeting with Aidan's publicist and agent. See you back home?"

"Yeah, see you later."

As I turn to leave the set, I run right into a rock-hard body and drop my phone in the process.

3

Aidan

I have the worst headache anyone could possibly have. My temples are pounding at an ungodly level and after looking in the mirror this morning, noticing how bloodshot my eyes were, I decided to wear my black Ray Bans to mask any indication of the night I had. I barely had time to run my hand through my hair before leaving my apartment. I haven't touched up my beard in days. I am the walking epitome of a mountain man at this point. After getting a text from both my publicist and my agent about a meeting today, and a screenshot of a headline they both received at midnight last night, I know I'm in for it.

I am about to hit send on a text when a body slams against me, followed by an "umph." I look down and see my personal assistant, Haley Swann, who is now bending down to pick up her phone.

"Whoa, Hales, are you, okay? Why is it that you're always running into me?"

Her cheeks turn the slightest bit pink and I smile at the way she gets flustered.

"Oh my god, Aidan, I am so sorry. I didn't see you there. I was just heading out to the car so we can head over to Samantha's for your meeting with her and Chris." She adjusts her blue-light glasses as she looks up at me.

"Yeah, I was just about to text you that I was heading that way as well. How could I forget? Our calendars are synched, remember?"

She gives me a small smirk as I extend my hand out to have her walk in front of me.

Haley has always been real with me. Since I became an actor, she is probably the only girl who treats me like a normal person. Other than the first time we met, I have never seen her act differently in my presence. She has always been unapologetically herself. I appreciate that about her. Today, though, she does seem a little distracted. Is it because of me and last night's headline?

As we exit the studio, I am almost blinded by the intense sunlight. This is not helping my throbbing head. I see that my driver's car is parked and ready to go. When we climb into the car, I notice there is a coffee waiting for me in the cupholder. Haley is an angel sent from heaven. I'm about to say thank you, but the wrinkle in between Haley's eyebrows is very prominent. She is obviously worried about something. Probably me. I'm making her life a living hell, I know I am. I'm surprised she hasn't quit on me after my behavior these past six months. I'm sure she's applied for other means of employment and is too nice to tell me. That's the thing about Haley, she is the most genuinely nice person I've ever met. Genuine is hard to come by in L.A., let alone this industry.

"So, how has your morning been, Hales?"

The crease between her eyebrows almost disappears as she looks at me. "It's been okay. Kind of weird, but okay." She immediately looks back at her phone and I don't press any further.

We listen to Leon Bridges on the drive. I doom-scroll on Instagram and look at all the terrible comments that accompany the photo from last night that US Weekly so generously tagged me in. Nothing happened between me and those two women. I went home by myself. The shitty thing is–the photo doesn't tell that story. It only confirms the picture the media has painted of me. A picture I want to tear up and throw in the trash bin. I click the side of my phone and look over at Haley, who is looking out the window. *I wonder why her day has been kind of weird.* By some divine intervention, there is not a ton of traffic and my driver pulls up to the curb with a couple minutes to spare.

Haley and I walk into my publicist's office, Johnson & Associates. Samantha Johnson is the best in the business and has been for the past twenty-five years–part of the reason I wanted to work with her. She was a trailblazer in the industry when she started her own public relations company when she was thirty years old. Samantha's larger than life personality is reflected in her appearance, as she almost reaches my height with her stilettos and loves to wear bright neon suits and dresses. On all occasions, her bleached-blonde hair is styled perfectly, her lipstick pristine and her nails manicured. Despite her feminine appearance, she didn't make it to where she is without a very dominating energy–she takes no prisoners. Even though she is almost twice my age, I don't want to ever cross her. She scares the hell out of me sometimes, but I will never admit that to her.

"Ms. Johnson will see you now."

I open the door to Samantha's office and gesture to Haley to walk in before me.

Samantha is on the phone with someone. "Well, tell your client that wasn't a part of our contract." She holds her finger up to Haley and me and then gestures for us to sit down.

Haley takes her usual place in the chair located in the back corner of the room. I told her once that she could sit next to me, but she said she never wants to be in the line of fire with Samantha. Honestly, I don't blame her. I don't want to be in the line of the inevitable fire that is heading my way in about a minute. I hear the door open and my agent, Chris, walks in. I stand up and shake his hand. Instead of sitting in the chair next to me, he backs away and stands next to Haley in the back of the room.

Sam hangs up on her call and jumps right into the meeting without so much as a greeting. That is one thing about Samantha, she knows how to get shit done. She's always professional when she is dealing with clients and their own publicists, but she is a no bullshit type of person and since she has a tight schedule, there's really no time for small talk with her. I appreciate her approach, and I suppose being a woman in this industry has been difficult for her and she has definitely fought many battles to be one of the best publicists out there. That's why I chose to work with her, because I know that she will always have my career's best interest at the end of the day.

"Okay, the main item on the agenda is the upcoming premiere of your movie in NYC next week and then you jet off to do a European tour a few weeks after that. Ms. Swann, do you have everything booked for those trips?"

Haley adjusts her glasses and looks at her phone. "Yes, I do. Everything is set. Flights, hotels, car service. All of it. I am forwarding all of you the information as we speak. And obviously the driver is ready for the premiere next week."

"Excellent. Now, the next matter." Samantha's hard gaze turns to me and she flashes her phone in my face. It displays a photo from last night. *Dammit.* "Your dating life."

Ugh. I knew this was going to come up. I furrow my brow and pretend ignorance. "What about my dating life?"

"Well, Aidan, you haven't been with anyone officially since Natasha. When was it that you two broke up? Six months ago?"

Why should this matter? I clear my throat, hopefully signaling to Samantha that I don't want to talk about this. "Just about, yeah."

Unphased by my discomfort, Samantha stood up, crossed her arms and continued, "You know how important image is for public relations. And that old adage, 'All press is good press,' is fading fast.

People are speculating about your love life. You've been spotted with numerous women these past six months. Last night I even got this Google Alert saying something to the effect of 'Aidan Stone spotted with two women leaving a club' but you have not brought any of these women to any press event, have you?"

"No," I mumble.

"You have obviously not started a true relationship with any of these women."

"So?"

Samantha starts walking around her desk; the sound of her stilettos fill the silence. "So, you are America's Sweetheart, Aidan. You don't want to be seen as a playboy. You want to be wanted, even desired, but in a classy way. You are the upstanding guy in all of the movies. Young boys are looking up to you, young girls are looking at you as their perfect example of how a guy should act. I know it's a lot of responsibility, but it comes with the territory of being a famous actor–and an actor who, I might add, has generated quite the Instagram following. I just want to make sure we maintain the 'good guy' image because I know that you are–also, it's the brand you have established. You are my favorite client, and I say that sincerely." She leans against the edge of her desk and crosses one foot over the other.

"Thank you."

"But your personal presence on social media has been minimal these past six months. Everything has been through tabloids. We need to change that. We need to take back control."

Is a guy not able to process a breakup at all? Are we just supposed to move on to the next "love of our life"? Because that's who I thought Natasha was before she pulled the rug from under me and started screwing that asshole from her new hit TV show. Doesn't Samantha know that every time I see a tabloid with those two on the front, I want to rip it up or throw my phone across the room? Those women were my way of trying to move on. It may not have been the healthiest way possible, but I needed to take my mind off the whole situation. All those women just wanted their fifteen minutes of fame, anyway. I knew they were not going to last. They knew I wasn't looking for a serious relationship. For once in my life, I was just having a good time... and now I'm being punished for it. Unfortunately, I do have a conscience and I do actually care about my fans, and I know the huge responsibility that comes with that. I haven't tried to find my next girlfriend because I really want to focus on my career.

"I get it, Sam. I just needed some time to blow off steam. To heal. To try to get over the girl that proverbially ripped out my heart." Sam starts to respond, but I hold up my hand. "With that being said, I want to maintain the trust I have with my fans and I know that a lot of that trust is based solely on image and what is *perceived* to be true." I sigh. "So what were you thinking?"

Sam exhales, as if she is about to deliver the worst news ever. "Well, I know it's short notice, but I think you need to bring a date to the premiere next week and you need to make it seem like you are absolutely smitten with this person. I am not going to lie to you, Aidan– studios don't want to be associated with negative press. And if their main star, such as yourself, is galavanting around L.A. with someone new every week, they will find someone else who is not going to attach drama to their name. Do you understand what I am saying?"

My chest constricts. I can feel my ears getting hot as I process what Sam is telling me. It is like I am a puppet and society is controlling the marionette strings. I feel completely out of control. "So you want me to find a fake girlfriend in less than a week."

"Immediately if possible. We need to get pictures of you two together at various locations around L.A. and NYC to make this seem legitimate. Like you said, people want to believe what they perceive to be true."

I place my hand on my forehead and then rub my temples. "And how do you expect me to find someone trustworthy enough not to talk to the press and leak that this is all fabricated to help with my image?"

"Funny you should say that. Both Chris and I have come up with a list of potential fake girlfriends for you," Samantha says proudly as she reaches over her desk, grabs a paper and hands me a list of A-list actresses who apparently would be willing to fake-date me. How flattering. Although these women are undeniably famous and beautiful, I don't know any of them well enough to trust them with this task. I shake my head as I am reading. My stomach is in knots. How is this even going to work? Even if I do pretend to date one of these women, there has to be real chemistry between us to truly make this believable.

Who can I really trust?

Then I hear a pen hitting a notepad and my gaze naturally drifts toward my trusty personal assistant of three years, who is frantically scribbling down all these notes. Suddenly, I know the best solution to my problem. It may be crazy. Or it may be totally genius.

I hand back the list to Samantha. "This isn't going to work."

"Of course it is. These are all A-list actresses who would look great by your side."

"That's not the problem."

Samantha narrows her eyes at me. "Then what is the problem?"

"I don't know any of these women. I don't trust them. Just because you are deemed an A-list actress, doesn't mean you have good intentions or a good heart. Trust me." An image of Natasha flashes into my mind. I shake my head to get rid of it, as if my brain is a fricken Etch A Sketch.

Chris chimes in from the back of the room. "Okay, Aidan, so what is your suggestion?"

"Haley could do it." I glance back at Haley, and her brown eyes are round with surprise. Shit, she looks mortified. I mean, can I blame her? I just dropped a completely outrageous solution to my problem. But I trust her with pretty much every aspect of my life, so why not go all-in and trust her with this, too? I know she would be discreet about our little secret.

Samantha laughs. "Haley? Like the Haley who is sitting right there, looking like she just saw a ghost?" Samantha points her finger toward my assistant, who does in fact look frozen like a statue.

Chris chimes in. "Yeah, I don't know about this, Aidan. She's your assistant. Won't that send the media the wrong message?"

"What wrong message? People date their coworkers all the time. How is this any different?"

Haley still isn't saying anything. I've overstepped. I should have talked to her first about this. She is definitely going to quit on me now. I can't have her quit. She is the best assistant I could ask for. I clear my throat. "Haley? Are you okay?"

She gives the slightest nod.

Yep, it's official. She is going to quit. She's probably calculating all the ways she could escape this room, run out the door and never come back.

Samantha isn't giving in so easily. "Aidan, I'm really not sure about this. Why her? People don't even know who she is."

"So? Maybe the fact that I date people who aren't in the industry can be seen as endearing and relatable. Maybe people will finally see that I am just like them—a fucking human being who can fall for anyone in this world. It doesn't matter if they're famous. And to be honest with you, it's all about trust. Look, Samantha—Haley has been my assistant for close to three years. And I really don't trust anyone else. I know she is going to keep it professional. And no one outside the industry knows her role in my life. She has been nothing but discreet and we can use that to our advantage."

"How so?"

"Haley's not going to draw any negative attention to us. She will draw enough attention because of the mystery of who she is. The press will finally shift their focus from my recent behavior and because she is not in the limelight all the time, will help protect the fact that this whole relationship is just for show. Plus, with Hales by my side for a while, I won't be bombarded by screaming women, and let's face it, sometimes men, out on the street. I'm sick of being swarmed everywhere I go, and maybe if I have a 'girlfriend' those superfans will back off and respect that I'm in a relationship. I need things to calm down on, and this will simultaneously restore and strengthen my 'good guy' image, as you put it. It will look like I'm in a committed relationship."

Samantha leans back in her chair. "What about after you stop this little arrangement? What then?"

"We can cross that bridge when we get there. For right now, with your outrageous suggestion, this is the only solution that I am comfortable with. That is," and I look back at Haley, who finally looks up into my eyes, "if Haley is willing to do this for me."

Samantha sighs and directs her attention to Chris. "What do you think about this plan?"

I glance over at Chris, who has been my agent since I moved out here, and his arms are crossed. But then he gives a little nod and his demeanor relaxes a little. "Surprisingly, I think this could actually work. I think people seeing you in a relationship, and honestly with someone who is not an actress, could work in your favor. We always see these couples that starred in romantic comedies end up together but then their 'love' never lasts." He winces, as if realizing what he just said. "Sorry man."

Yep, that one hurt. That's basically what happened to me and Natasha. We starred in one of the biggest romantic comedies of the year. Then after a while, the love obviously fizzled out... for her, at least.

"Anyway," Chris continues, "I think if you want to continue on the path you're on and you want people to see you as a serious actor, having a stable girlfriend would benefit your career. You can turn over a new leaf. It not only shows that you're now in a committed relationship, but also that you've moved on from the Natasha fiasco."

Good, he is on my side. Now, I need to make sure that Haley is also with me.

Samantha clasps her hands together and places them against her lips as she thinks about this proposal. Her gaze shifts toward Haley.

"Ms. Swann. What do you think? Are you willing to do this for Aidan?"

I look back at Haley again, and this time she is actually blinking. That's a good sign.

"Um." She looks at me again. "I need to talk to Aidan before I agree to this."

"Of course," says Samantha. "In the meantime–" She reaches out and grabs the list of A-list actresses from me– "I will keep this on hand if we need it."

As Haley and I stand up from our seats, Samantha adds, "If you can let me know as soon as possible, that would be in your best interest Aidan. The NYC premiere for your movie is *next week*. I look forward to hearing from you."

4

Haley

"I'll think about it."

Those were the last words I uttered to Aidan.

I felt ambushed. I never thought in a million years that Aidan Stone, THE Aidan Stone, would ever suggest to fake date ME of all people. Samantha clearly had others in mind and I don't understand why he would choose me. I mean the guy dates, or rather sleeps with, Brazilian supermodels for gosh sakes.

The next morning, I change into my workout clothes and take out all my intrusive thoughts and insecurities out on the beach. I dig my feet into the sand as hard as I can, hoping that all the doubts in my body will escape through my soles. I blast my running playlist, hoping that Taylor Swift or Rihanna will get me through this grueling 6 mile run. Clearly, I have a lot to think about. *"Look what you made me do"* indeed.

With every stride, I attempt to drown out the questions impeding my brain. *Why me? How the hell would this work? How would this be believable? I am a struggling writer and personal assistant and he is unmistakingly the hottest actor in the world. There is no way. The press would chew me up and spit me out. I wasn't made for this. I'll just go back to being on the sidelines. Being invisible is my specialty and I'm not about to give up that superpower.*

Somehow through the blasting music, I hear a muffled, "Haley?"

I break out of my negative thought spiral and see what would be best described as a 6-foot 1 Greek god incarnate. *Is he running toward me in slow motion? Shirtless, glistening, with every muscle on his body on full display with every twist of his damn torso?* And with his cute little English bulldog puppy, Ginny, alongside him. Geez the dog is overkill.

I quickly glance around and notice multiple women lower their sunglasses as he runs toward me. Then they lock eyes with me. Me, the woman who is definitely the color of a lobster, despite slathering on sunscreen, with frizzy, sweaty hair in a sloppy bun. Yeah, I wouldn't believe it if I saw it either, ladies. Trust me.

He is a real heartstopper. Unfortunately at this moment, I am no longer immune to the phenomenon that is Aidan Stone. I'm glad that I have the excuse that I've been running to cover up the fact that my heart is racing.

"So you like to run too, huh?" He takes out his earbuds and readjusts his hat, revealing his longer-than-normal brown locks. I don't see him in a hat all too often and it certainly is a sight to see. It starts a reaction in my body that only occurs when I think someone looks hot. Sexy, even. And of course he wears his hat backward. Every woman's weakness. Well, maybe not every woman, but it certainly is a weakness of mine. He has no business knowing that, though.

Playing it cool and unphased, I finally take out my earphones and nod, feeling my loose bun bop against the back of my head. Still out of breath, I answer, "Yeah, I uh, took up running when I moved out here." I hurriedly pull out the monstrosity of a bun and redo it, so it hopefully looks somewhat presentable.

Aidan just nods at me. God, he must be questioning his earlier proposition. I know I would. I know what I must look like right now—extremely red, sweaty and no makeup. The only thing I put on my face was sunscreen and even that is seeping into my eyes, causing them to burn a little. The only sound I hear is Ginny breathing. Her tongue is hanging all the way out and it looks like she is smiling up at me. I love Ginny. Any time I cross paths with her, she has always been so sweet to me and never shows any aggression.

I break the awkward silence. "Geez, how long have you been running? She looks wiped out. Poor puppy dog." I bend down and pet her ears, and her leg twitches with enjoyment. She licks my arms, out of love but also probably because of the sweat permeating out of my pores.

"She loves you. She usually doesn't show this much affection toward others. Especially women. She's a little overprotective in that department."

"Dogs have amazing intuitions. You should listen to her."

"Oh, I am." There is a sultry intonation in his voice. Almost as if he is flirting with me.

I purposely keep my eyes on Ginny, terrified of looking into Aidan's ocean-blue eyes. Ginny knows I am stalling and finally lies down, causing me to stand and look up at my boss's flawless face.

"And to answer your question," Aidan says, "We've gone about six miles. You?"

"About the same." I can't help but notice how sculpted Aidan's body really is. There is this notion that the pictures of celebrities are all photoshopped. This man is definitely not photoshopped by any means. I feel like Emma Stone in *Crazy Stupid Love* where she goes up to Ryan Gosling and touches his abs. Only I'm not nearly brave enough to pull off something like that without being a total creeper. Not that I'm not interested.

"Impressive," Aidan says.

I'd say.

I shift my weight to the other leg. "I, um, needed to think about a lot of things this morning."

Aidan reaches behind his neck and rubs it. "I'm assuming one of those things is my proposition?"

"Maybe." I'm not about to tell him the whole truth–that his proposition is the ONLY thing I've been thinking about.

"So have you made up your mind?" Aidan asks, sounding almost eager.

I huff, half-catching my breath, half-exhaling out of mere shock to be in this position at all. "Um...yeah."

"And...what is your answer?"

I nervously fumble with my earphones. *Am I really about to do this? Am I about to crawl out of my introverted safe space of anonymity and be exposed for the world to see? To criticize? To completely laugh at the idea that I could ever get a man like Aidan Stone to date me?* I squint as I look to the ocean and my stomach clenches at the many scenarios and outcomes going off like fireworks in my brain.

Out of nowhere, a frisbee hits my shin and breaks my chain of intrusive thoughts. Before Ginny can completely destroy the poor toy, Aidan grabs it from her line of fire. A couple of little kids, maybe around eight or nine years old, run up to Aidan and are completely star-struck. I have witnessed this happen many times before, but always from a distance. This time is different. I am inches away from what can only be described as the magic that is Aidan Stone.

"Oh my God! You're Aidan Stone! We are huge fans! Can you sign our frisbee please?"

Aidan squats down to their level and smiles. "Sure, guys. Do you have a marker?"

"I think my mom does! Let me go check!" one of the boys

excitedly yells as he runs back to his mom. She lowers her sunglasses and looks over to where we are standing. She smiles and rummages through her large, straw beach tote and finds a black Sharpie. Her son grasps it from her and joyfully bolts back toward me and Aidan.

Aidan stands back up and leans into me slightly. "Can you hold onto Ginny real quick?" When he places the leash into my hand, his fingers brush against mine and goosebumps appear all over my body. And I don't hate it. Instead my body is betraying me and craving more. More of his voice. More of his touch. I watch Aidan as he basically creates a core memory for the boys. I can see their eyes light up at the sight of their favorite superhero signing their frisbee. In the three years I've known him, Aidan has never turned down an opportunity to meet and interact with his fans—no matter how busy he is. Especially when it comes to children. I smile at the pure happiness emitting from the boys' faces, and that is more than enough for me to make my decision. That and the fact that Aidan is the nicest guy on this planet.

"Have a great day, guys! Have fun!" Aidan clasps the black cap onto the marker and hands it and the frisbee to the boys.

"Thank you so much! You too!" The boys run towards the one boy's mom and resume throwing their frisbee.

I look down at Ginny and see that she is also beaming at her owner, almost as if she is completely captivated by his presence. *Join the club, girl.*

"Sorry about that, Hales. I just..."

"Couldn't say no to a couple of sweet kids? How dare you." I jokingly smile as I give Ginny's leash back to him. He holds onto the handle of her leash and scratches the material. He really thinks I am going to say no. I need to put him out of his misery: "My answer is...yes..."

"Oh Hales, you are such a lifesaver! Thank you." It appears he is closing in on a hug. Absolutely not. I'm afraid of what might happen to my body if he touches me with half his clothes off. It's possible I would spontaneously combust.

I stick out my arm to stop his advancement and my hand collides with his bare chest. His rock-hard, glistening bare chest.

It's confirmed. Definitely not photoshopped.

I retract my hand as if I just touched a hot stove. "But I think we need to talk about this more. Can we go somewhere before we head to the studio, to discuss the terms of this whole... deal? I don't really want to talk about this with eyes glaring at us everywhere we turn." I know this is going to be my new reality soon. I'm just not quite ready for that attention yet. I open and close my hand to hopefully dispel any remnants of Aidan Stone's body from its memory. Not sure it will really work, but it's worth a try.

"Sure. There's a nice diner close by that I like to stop at some mornings. The owner of the diner is a sweetheart and she is very protective of me and respects my privacy. Plus, I usually go early in the morning and all the old folks in there don't know who I am, so we shouldn't be bothered. I'll drop you a pin so we can meet there, if that's okay?"

"Sounds good. Meet you there."

"Great. See you there, Swann." Aidan smiles at me and turns his hat the other way around, covering his dark brown locks again. He says, "Come on, girl," causing Ginny to happily follow her best friend.

Apparently, I am more than willing to follow Aidan's lead, too. Otherwise I would have said no to this absolutely preposterous proposal.

5

Haley

The door chimes as we walk into this old fifties-style diner located on the pier. It smells like fresh coffee, buttermilk pancakes and bacon. Probably my favorite breakfast combination, with the exception of pancakes. Waffles are the better choice.

"Welcome in! Sit anywhere and we'll be right with you."

"C'mon." Aidan nudges my elbow. "Let's go to that table over here. It's my favorite. And the waitress will be discreet. I've known her for years."

I follow Aidan to a small booth in the corner. He's turned his baseball cap around so now the bill half-covers his face. Although I don't think anyone would recognize him anyway. Most of the demographic here are elderly people probably upwards of eighty years old. One of the diner patrons at the bar reads a newspaper. At another table, two men bicker about the upcoming NFL season and which one of the L.A. teams is superior, the Chargers or the Rams.

A sweet lady, probably in her sixties or seventies, walks over toward us with a huge smile on her face. "Why hello hun! How are you doing? I was wondering when you were going to stop in. Haven't seen you in a while, sugar."

Aidan flashes the widest smile and gets up to bear-hug our waitress. She looks miniscule and frail compared to him. "How are you doing, Mabel? It's nice to see you. I know, I've been very busy."

"Yeah, very busy sleeping with every hussy in LA."

Damn, the gumption on this woman to call him out like that. She is my hero.

Aidan grins. "Fair enough. You know you are my number one, Mabel," Aidan says as he sinks back down into the booth.

"You flatter me, sugar, but I'll believe it when I see it." She winks at me and I let out a guffaw. I slap my hand to my mouth to stifle the sound, but I can't resist. This lady has no boundaries. Something that I always pride myself in having. I possess the Hadrian's Wall of boundaries.

At the sound of my hyena-like outburst, Mabel finally looks over at me. "Oh I should've reigned it in – I didn't even realize you had someone with you."

"Now, Mabel, when have you ever reigned it in?" Aidan teases.

"Oh you hush. I'm sorry sugar, what's your name? I don't remember seeing you in any of the tabloids these past six months. Are you one of Aidan's little minxes?"

Aidan places his right hand over his eyes and rubs his temples out of embarrassment.

My face hurts already from smiling so much in the span of two minutes. "Um, no. I am..." Actually, I don't know how to answer this question. "I'm, well, I'm Aidan's..."

"She's my girlfriend, Mabel."

There it is. It's out there. Mabel is the first to know. Well, I guess fifth to know, seeing how Samantha, Chris, Aidan and I already knew about this whole "girlfriend" thing. Suddenly, I feel tingly all over. I don't know if it's a title I'm ready for.

Mabel slaps her hand over her mouth. "Oh! Now *I* am embarrassed. Me and my big mouth. I don't know what the word 'filter' means. Never have been good at it. I didn't mean to call you a minx. Actually you seem really genuine and sweet. I have this ability to read people and sense their auras. Yours sends all the good vibes." She turns her attention to Aidan. "About damn time honey, I was worried you let this L.A. culture influence you to the point of joining the dark side."

"No dark side for me, Mabel. I can promise you that."

"Good." Mabel smiles at me. "Now what is your name, sugar?"

"My name is Haley, ma'am. It's so nice to meet you." I reach out and shake Mabel's hand, which is covered in wrinkles and with turquoise rings on every finger.

"It's a pleasure, Miss Haley. I'll let you look at the menu, darlin'. Sugar, do you want your usual?" She places her delicate hand on Aidan's shoulder.

"Yes, Mabel. But you don't have to put it in right away. I'll wait for Hales to decide."

I place the menu down and beam up at Mabel. "Actually Mabel, I'm ready."

Mabel takes out her notepad and pen from her apron to take down my order.

"I would like a Belgian waffle, two eggs over easy, bacon extra crispy if possible, hash browns, and a coffee please."

But Mabel doesn't even click her pen. "No need to write this one down." I see her smile a little. Why is she smiling? Did I order something weird? "I'll put that in for you right away. Wow, I think you found a keeper, sugar. Someone who is beautiful *and* loves food? That's a rare find here in Los Angeles. Be back soon with your coffee."

Aidan gathers the menus and puts them at the end of the table near the window. I can tell he is humored by something.

"What?"

He shakes his head slightly, and yet he is still smiling, "Nothing." He clasps his hands together. "So, Haley."

"So, Aidan." This is weird. I've never been alone with Aidan in this type of setting before. We usually exchange information through text, emails, calendar updates or on our short walks on set in between shooting a scene. We have never sat down and eaten a meal together. I am freaking out! Why in the world did I agree to do this? My knee starts to bob up and down and there aren't enough breathing exercises in the world to aid in stopping it.

I must be zoning out because when I glance back at Aidan, his face is concerned.

"Hales. Are you okay? You look like you're going to pass out."

I notice Mabel coming back with our coffees. I plaster on a smile and say, "Yeah, I'm fine. I promise."

Mabel plunks down two sturdy diner mugs. "Here you go hon. Would you like any cream and sugar?"

Before I have a chance to answer, Aidan pipes in, "Yes, please Mabel, thank you."

"Sure thing. Be back with your food shortly."

I clear my throat and finally look up at Aidan's gentle blue eyes. Somehow, for the split second our eyes meet, I feel calmer. "So, you brought me here to talk about the terms of our agreement."

"Yes." Aidan exhales. "Look, I sincerely apologize for throwing you into the catastrophic mess that is my life. But, when Samantha was telling me that I had to go out with those random women, I don't know–I just felt like I was finally over it. Over acting like an absolute jackass."

Jackass? This much was true. "Acting like I could have any woman I wanted because I knew that there would be some women waiting for their opportunity to get with me."

That is also true. I'm sure he has a revolving door spewing out women almost every night.

He continues, "I guess deep down, I wanted to get back at

Natasha. I was so hurt. I kind of lost track of myself, to be honest. But you always make me feel calm and safe, and you know me better than anyone. I trust you completely. That's the only reason I suggested you to fulfill this role, so to speak."

I know he already said that in the meeting, but it's kind of nice to hear him say how much he trusts me. I do know pretty much everything there is to know about him, professionally that is. The only personal stuff I know about him, honestly, is from the news alerts and headlines I read on tabloids–which, to his credit, I shouldn't take much stock in. There is something inside me that wants to give him the benefit of the doubt these last six months, because I have this intuition about people and Aidan honestly seems like one of the good ones. I think that's what surprised me about his behavior after the breakup. He never seemed like a womanizer or really a drinker for that matter. What he's saying now makes me feel better–I *was* right about him.

Mabel returns with the cream, sugar and our food. Thank God, I'm starving. I guess I did run six miles this morning, so my stomach was bound to yell at me at some point. Which probably contributed to me looking like I'm going to pass out. (That and the fact that my boss wants me to fake date him.) When I look across the table, I notice that Aidan has ordered the exact same thing as me. Or rather, I ordered Aidan's usual order. *That's why Mabel reacted the way she did.* Instead of pointing anything out, I unroll the silverware from the napkin and place them beside my plate.

"I want to preface this next statement and say that at any point, you can always back out of this arrangement. And, I want you to know with total certainty, this will not affect anything at all with our working relationship."

I pour about half the small carafe of cream into my coffee mug. I can feel my eyebrows narrow in on each other. "How can you say that?"

"What do you mean?"

I scoff, "Aidan, you can't know that it won't affect our working relationship! Are you kidding me? I mean what will this entail? Because if we have to act like we are dating for real, that means we have to like...do stuff." I nervously cut my waffle into tiny pieces and drizzle a mountain of syrup over it.

Aidan raises his eyebrows and smirks. "That's presumptuous of you."

Horrified, I quickly swallow the bite of waffle I'd jammed into my mouth a second earlier. "Oh my God! No! Not that! Ew..."

Aidan shifts a little in his seat and crosses his arms, still with that stupid, dangerously cute smirk on his face, clearly enjoying this show of absolute embarrassment.

"I mean not ew," I fumble for words. "I don't think it would be ew. Not that I've thought about it at all." I slap my forehead, then cover my face with both of my hands. *For the love of God, please stop talking, Haley.*

I hear a rumble from across the booth. *Is he laughing at me?*

"Are you seriously laughing at me right now?"

"How can I not, Hales? You need to calm down. And for the record, that is not the 'stuff' that we would have to show the world. In fact, I think showing the world us having sex would probably be frowned upon." Aidan starts cutting his own waffle.

My ears suddenly turn hot and I guarantee they are reflecting how much they are on fire right now. The real embarrassment stems from thinking of me and Aidan having sex–it makes me shiver, and not in a bad way. My whole body warms to the idea, probably because I haven't been with a man in three years. Sad, I know. Pathetic, maybe. I just haven't trusted anyone since Robert. I guess Aidan and I have the trust issue thing in common. Although his way of dealing with it has been the complete opposite of my method: absolute celibacy.

I swallow. "Okay, well then we need to lay out some ground rules."

"Sounds perfect to me. Hey Mabel! Can you come over here real quick?" Aidan waves her over.

"Are we seriously going to ask a 70-year-old woman for advice on what the ground rules should be for fake dating?"

Aidan gasps. "First of all, Mabel is a young 70-year-old woman. Second of all, she thinks we are *really* dating, remember? So asking her about tips on fake dating will seem suspicious and she would probably tease me from here until eternity. Finally, I need a pen. We are going to write down the ground rules."

"Okay, old man. On a napkin, really? Why not on Google Docs or Notes or something and we can share it with each other?"

"I prefer the term old-fashioned."

Mabel comes over. Her silvery hair is up in a disheveled bun and wavy tendrils are sticking out in all directions.

"Can I borrow a pen for a little while, Mabel? I promise I'll return it."

"Sure, sugar." She reaches into her indigo apron, pulls out a pen and hands it to Aidan. "Don't lose it though. That's one of my favorite pens, you know."

"I wouldn't dare lose it." Aidan grabs a napkin from the table dispenser.

Mabel's sweet eyes meet mine. "How's the food, hon?"

I take a bite of the bacon, which was cooked to extra-crispy perfection. "So good, Mabel. Thank you."

"Be back a bit to check on you love birds." She winks at Aidan and he winks back.

Aidan clears his throat, clicks the pen, and smooths out the napkin. "All right, here we go. Let's start with the basics: holding hands and hugging. I would say definitely, right?"

Even though my hands get clammy at the thought of holding Aidan Stone's hand in public–or anywhere, for that matter–I answer, "Right, of course. Continue."

"Okay... um, kissing?"

"No!"

"Hales..."

"Aidan..."

"Why not?"

"Because you're my..." I lower my voice to a whisper. "My boss."

"Hate to break it to you, Hales, but if you agree to this whole arrangement, I am not going to be your boss throughout the time we're perceived as 'together.' We need to put our working relationship aside for right now and remove those boundaries. Just for a couple weeks. And remember, I'm an actor. Kissing someone without catching feelings is basically second nature to me at this point in my career." *Yeah, easy for him to say. That's not my career.* "It's my job to make chemistry happen on screen. But the only way to do that is to actually play the part, right?"

The more he talks about it, the more I open up to the idea. He's right. He does this for a living, and if I think of it from that perspective and pretend that we're acting in a movie, maybe it won't be so weird.

I sigh. "Okay, fine. Kissing can be a possibility. But only," and I point a finger at him, "only when deemed an *absolute necessity*. Got it?"

"Got it." Aidan continues to scribble the parameters of our partnership down on the diner napkin. Then I see him write down the letters S-E-X and before I can protest, he crosses it out and writes "ABSOLUTELY NOT" in all capital letters. *Oh thank God.* That would definitely complicate things, even more than they already are.

"All right, Ms. Swann," he says in a very professional, no bullshit tone. "Please read over this agreement. If you agree to all the terms laid out, please sign and date at the bottom."

I study it once more, even though I saw him write down the whole thing.

"Looks acceptable. I agree to these terms." I take the pen out of Aidan's hand. Right before I sign my name, I think about the other predicament I put myself in. The whole *I have a boyfriend and I am bringing him to my best friend's wedding.* Yeah, that one.

"Wait," I say. "Since I am doing this for you, would you mind doing something for me? If not, that's totally fine. I understand if it's too much exposure for you and you probably think it's a stupid idea and it won't even..."

I feel his hand on mine. "Woah, Hales, slow down. Of course I would do anything for you. I would do it anyway, even if you weren't helping me out in the first place."

That surprises me a little. Actually, a lot. *I would do anything for you.* We've never been close, and I think what I am about to ask him is going to cross all sorts of boundaries that I never thought that we would cross...ever. Then again, I am agreeing to fake-date this man. I guess the least he could do would be to return the favor. Besides, all of my family and friends are going to see the tabloids and social media posts anyway.

I slide my hand away from his and clasp my hands firmly in front of me. "So, remember a couple months ago, I asked for some time off for Labor Day weekend?"

"Yes. You said that you had some kind of family event?"

"Right. Well, it's not just some average family event. I mean technically Anna isn't even family. But she kind of is...sort of..." I am rambling again. My goodness, I've never been like this around Aidan before. The only time I could remember being frazzled in his presence was when I first met him. Other than that, I've always acted normal. I mean what is normal really? Focus Haley. "Anyway. My best friend from childhood, Anna, is getting married in the Hamptons and I might've told my mother and Anna that I have a date to bring to this wedding. Well, more so like I have a boyfriend, who by the way is coming with me to this wedding. So, I figured since we are already going to be all over the internet because we are 'dating,' I was hoping you'd be willing to..."

"Yes."

"I...I didn't even finish my request."

"Yes, Haley Swann. I would be honored to be your date to your best friend's wedding. No, excuse me, boyfriend."

"Are you sure? Because I know that people will be all over you asking you for your autograph and to take a selfie with them and whatnot. I mean you're Aidan Stone, big-time movie star."

"I've never been more sure of anything in my life. And don't worry about people asking me for autographs or pictures. I'm used to those types of requests, Hales. You know that. For that weekend, I'll be Aidan Stone, regular ol' boyfriend to the incomparable Haley Swann." Aidan raises his mug and takes a drink of his coffee.

Why does he keep saying stuff like that to me? It's like he is reciting lines from the most romantic movie ever. He's probably just getting a head start in talking to me without my walls up. And Aidan is hardly any regular ol' anything. How can the man who was deemed People Magazine's Most Sexiest Man Alive be so modest?

I fold and unfold my napkin. "I know you are used to it. That doesn't mean you should *have* to deal with it."

"Thank you for saying that." Aidan grabs a couple sugar packets from the small black container at the end of the table and begins fiddling with them. Almost like *he* is nervous. "But I am more than willing to take on the attention to help out the best assistant in the world. Besides, you are already helping me out on a much grander scale. This is literally the least I can do for you. If anything, this will make our dating situation seem more legit."

My cheeks turn hot and knots start to form in my stomach. Suddenly, I am the one who is getting nervous again. And then I ask him the question that has been eating me alive since his insane proposal. "Are you sure this is going to work? I mean, how could anyone believe that a guy like you would ever end up with a girl like me?"

Aidan smirks his signature smirk. The one that makes women and men scream out of pure hysteria and causes them to become weak in the knees. Unfortunately, my body is reacting in the same way, minus the audible scream. I am screaming internally for some reason, inexplicably craving his attention, even though I fully have his attention at this moment. Is that the Aidan Stone effect? He reaches across the table and takes the pen from my hand, the pen that

I've been involuntarily tapping against the table. I guess my nerves aren't as hidden as I thought. He pulls the napkin across the table over to him and raises an eyebrow. "Any changes?"

Before he signs, I blurt out, "I think there needs to be an end date. When is this relationship going to expire?"

"Well, I think we should give it until the day we come back from New York. The negative press should be off my ass after a couple of weeks of being madly in love and completely devoted to a new girlfriend. We can even take extra pictures of us doing things together, so we can release them for a few more weeks after our 'expiration date,' if that's what you want to call it."

I nod in agreement, still trying to process the situation that is my life right now. "So we get through the premiere and the wedding, and then when we get back to L.A., everything goes back to normal."

I think I notice Aidan's jaw tighten a smidge before he answers. "Yes. Everything will go back to normal. Our contract will expire effective upon our return to L.A."

The next thing I know, Aidan is signing our impromptu contract. He's in. He's all in. He slides the napkin and pen back over to me. "What do you say, Swann? Do we have a deal?"

Before my mind can convince me that this idea is absolutely insane, my gut takes control. I grasp the pen and sign my name. "Deal."

Aidan swipes the napkin from me, takes out his wallet and puts it in the main pocket. He winks. "For safekeeping." In one smooth move, he takes out a credit card. Mabel is on her way to our table and without looking at the bill, he hands Mabel his card.

"Thanks, sugar. I'll be right back."

I pull out some cash from my small belt bag, "Wait, Aidan, let me pay for my half."

"Not in a million years, babe. My mother taught me that a man always pays for his girl's meal."

Well, that does it. I guess I'm his girl now.

6

Haley

The week building up to our trip to New York has been a whirlwind. Samantha suggests that we start going on little "dates" around L.A. She's going to hire a photographer to take our photos so we have some to release for a possible later date if needed; plus, she's sure the paparazzi will naturally find us. They're always on the lookout for Aidan.

To say this feels awkward would be a massive understatement.

The first time Aidan tries to hold my hand, I flinch–obviously forgetting that for the time being, he isn't my boss and I'm not his assistant. We are just sitting outside at Urth Caffe under a big green umbrella, drinking lattes, when he reaches over for my hand. It sends a stupid amount of shock through my body and the knots being tied in my stomach are, honestly, ridiculous.

Aidan leans over the small bistro table and whispers into my ear, slightly tickling me, "Relax, Hales. Sam's cameraman is across the street. Play the part, remember?"

I exhale and repeat in my head: *Play the part.* I force a smile and give into his hand touching mine. Our fingers intertwine. Before he retracts back to his own seat, just when I think I'm free and clear, Aidan sneaks in: "You smell amazing, by the way. Pomegranate, right?"

At that moment, I wish I had the supernatural ability to hide the redness filling my face. When Aidan leans back into his chair, he has that same smug look on his face that he had at the diner. He needs to stop giving me that look since it is also igniting those damn butterflies to start flapping their wings in my gut.

"Why are you blushing?" he asks, knowing very well the answer.

I rub my cheeks, contributing even more to the redness. I must look like a fricken tomato at this point. "You make me nervous."

His lips press together, stifling the ego boost I just gave him. "Well, then, I guess we are going to have to practice more so you get used to me touching you, Swann."

Yeah, like my body will ever get used to Aidan Stone touching me in any way, shape or form. Fat chance.

For more "practice," Aidan suggests we dive into the deep end. Our next "date" is at The Grove, a massive shopping center in the heart of L.A. By now, Aidan knows that coffee is my love language, so any excuse to get some is enough convincing for me.

Still, I am not prepared for the chaos that ensues. Word somehow gets out that Aidan Stone is in the vicinity and within minutes, clicks and flashes of cameras are everywhere. People stare and point and scream Aidan's name. The mayhem when we walk out of La La Land coffee shop is, quite frankly, insane. The paparazzi are ruthless. They clearly don't know what the term "personal boundaries" means. Aidan calmly leads the way down the sidewalk, holding my hand so tightly, I think my fingers will turn to mush by the time we reach a clearing. "Aidan over here

Aidan! Who is with you? What's your name? Are you dating? Aidan!"

My heart is beating out of control. *What did I get myself into?*

After the paparazzi finally back off a little, Aidan smiles down at me. "You did great, Hales. I know that was a lot." He finally lets go of my hand.

I flex my fingers in and out to ensure the function is still there. Then I get a weird sensation, like something is missing, and suddenly I know exactly what is missing: Aidan's hand glued to mine. I quickly wipe the thought out of my mind.

A moment later, his hand goes somewhere else entirely–around my waist. My heart fricken jumps as if Dr. Frankenstein sent electric currents through my body, trying to awaken whatever is dead inside of me. There is no denying it: whatever was dormant for the past three years is definitely awake now.

Nerves bundle in my stomach as I ride the elevator up to my hotel room. The nerves have been a constant resident since we got off the plane at JFK, knowing that the big reveal of our relationship will be tonight at the premiere. The only ease I feel is from being back in New York: a familiar friend that I desperately needed to revisit. Aidan offered for me to stay at his apartment– "You know, to help with appearances'," as he put it. Stubbornly, and truthfully out of fear, I insisted that I stay at a hotel a couple of blocks away. I've been getting more comfortable around Aidan in my new capacity as his fake girlfriend, but not comfortable enough to stay with him in his apartment. An apartment, I might add, that overlooks Central Park.

I am mentally running through all the tips and tricks Rachel has taught me for the past three years about applying makeup. I need to look worthy of being next to Aidan on that red carpet. I really hope we can sell this whole charade. After several attempts, the lock turns green and clicked. Pushing the door open, I am instantly bombarded with racks of dresses. No, not dresses–gowns. My jaw drops at the gorgeous couture that fills nearly the entire hotel room. On the bedside table, I see a huge bouquet of red roses and a small note. I pick up the note and read:

Thank you for agreeing to this insane idea, Hales. I had Bree (the stylist who helps my mom get ready for premieres when we are in NYC) come by with plenty of dresses to choose from. I know you were worried about that. Oh and there might be a few more surprises heading your way. ;) See you later–A.

What other surprises? The nerves return in full force as my phone buzzes. Rachel. I sweep the "answer" bar on my phone.

"Hello?"

"Hey girlie! Are you ready for tonight?"

"Not even close, Rach." I plop onto the massive king bed. I told Aidan I would be fine with a standard hotel room. But nope. He had to get the fricken presidential suite. "I have no idea where to start with my makeup and apparently there's this stylist who is supposed to help. I don't know. I'm so nervous. I wish you were here to help me get ready."

"Well, maybe you should open your door because there may be something out there that I sent over to help."

What? I literally got to my room not even two minutes ago. I didn't see any package. Plus, the front desk would've likely fielded a whole receiving-packages situation. And then I hear a knock.

"Oh, Rach. This may be whatever you sent me. Hold on." Without looking through the peephole, I open the door.

Standing there is none other than my sassy, red-headed roommate herself.

"Oh my god. You're the surprise??" I pull her in for a hug. "I am *so* happy and relieved you're here!"

"Me too. Aidan flew me out. He said he could tell how nervous you were for this event. Plus, I haven't been out here in a while. This is going to be so fun! This is kind of your *Pretty Woman* moment, sans the whole hooker thing and oh my heavens...look at these beauties."

Rachel strides in with her two suitcases, one filled with what I assume is all the makeup in the world. She runs her fingers through the rack of gowns. "Aidan has good taste."

"I don't know if it's necessarily Aidan who has good taste. I think Bree has good taste."

"Who's Bree?"

"The stylist who dropped these off."

"Well either way, these dresses are spectacular. So we have a few hours before Aidan picks you up for the premiere, right?" Rachel asks.

"Yes. He should be here around 7 p.m. He said that it is okay if we are fashionably late for these things. I think the movie is showing at 8 p.m. so there's a whole hour of red carpet and interviews that he has to do before we even sit down. I need to wear the comfiest possible heels out of these insane options." I gaze down at the rows of stilettos. I am definitely going to fall on my face like Agent Gracie Hart in *Miss Congeniality* after she gets her own makeover. Then out of the corner of my eye, I see some blush sparkly heels with more of a block heel. They are still outrageously tall, but the block heel will help my balance substantially.

"These are the ones, Rach. Okay, I need to pick out a dress."

Across the room, Rachel is hurriedly texting away with a goofy smile. Normally I would investigate the texting-and-goofy-smile combo, but I don't have time for that right now. I continue, "This movie is a romantic comedy, so I feel like I need to go for a romantic dress, what do you think?"

I hear the message send and Rachel says, "Sounds great. Sorry, that was Aidan texting me."

My smile flattens. "He changed his mind. I knew it." A sliver of disappointment finds its way into my stomach, replacing the nerves that were there before.

"Oh no honey, he is not canceling on you at ALL," Rachel

reassures me. "I was just checking to see what color his suit is going to be. I figured it would be classic black. That's easy for us because now we can pick whatever dress we want. And yes, I agree. We need to go the romantic route–but Hales, I think you should show off your body a little bit. If you are going to be next to the sexiest man alive, then you need to exude at least some sex appeal." She gently paws through the racks, shaking her head, pursing her lips. I can mentally imagine her saying, *No, no, no, no.* And she gasps, "This is it!"

I look at the gown she picked out: a long, form-fitting, silky red gown with a very long slit. "Um, I am going to veto this one."

"Why? It's super sexy. And what color is more romantic than red?"

"It's a little *too* sexy. The slit would go all the way up my leg and practically show my underwear. "

"And that's a bad thing?"

"I would look like Jessica Rabbit in this dress."

"Hey, Jessica Rabbit is hot. All the men would practically drool all over you. Aidan included. "

"That's not really the vibe I'm going for. I'd rather not look like a cartoon character. Sorry."

She huffs a little, "Fine." She puts the Jessica Rabbit dress back on the rack. I shake my head. I know for a fact that Rachel could totally pull that dress off. Not that she needs help with the whole "guys drooling over her" department. She is so beautiful that sometimes it's intimidating to go anywhere with her. Especially since I look like a troll most days.

Then I spot it. The perfect dress. "Rach."

She looks over and shrieks, "This is totally it! Sexy but sweet. Just like you, Hales. Aidan won't know what hit him."

Aidan

I fiddle with the blue box in my hands. I told Rachel not to have Haley wear any jewelry because I have a surprise for her. After passing by Tiffany's earlier, I got the idea to surprise Haley with earrings to wear to the premiere. I knew exactly which ones to get her because they just reminded me of Haley. I wanted something that was simple and elegant. After talking at length with the sales associate about Haley's personality, she pointed me towards a pair of platinum, drop earrings with small, round diamonds.

This is the perfect opportunity for Haley to wear them. It's honestly the least I can do to make up for my behavior these past six months. I know that it hasn't been easy for her, dealing with me and the messes I've made, and there are no words to describe the amount of gratitude I feel for Haley right now in my life. I am lucky to have an assistant like her.

I place the box in my jacket pocket and glance down at my watch: 7:00 on the dot. I try to keep my head down in the hotel lobby so that no one recognizes me. Maybe they won't even recognize me now, because lately I've been rocking a full beard and longer hair than usual. In the past three hours since I dropped Haley off at her hotel, I contacted my favorite barber to help clean me up a bit. He didn't shave off my entire beard, but I don't look like Tom Hanks from *Cast Away* anymore. (Yeah, it was getting that bad.) Now I look like my same old self; the only difference is that my heart isn't the same old heart. Tiny pieces have broken off and I've become a little more jaded.

The elevator dings and the doors open. I adjust my suit so the sleeve covers my watch. Rachel emerges from the elevator, hauling a large tote bag over her shoulder. I teasingly look at my watch.

"Wow, it took you the whole three hours to help Haley get ready?"

"Ha ha very funny, Stone. I definitely didn't need most of my supplies. Haley's gorgeous all on her own. I just highlighted her beauty."

"You didn't make her look like a Stepford wife, did you?" Even though I know Haley wanted Rachel to do her makeup for this event, I still want her to look like Haley. Personally, I don't think she needs any makeup, but I didn't want to push back.

"Um, you have seen my work on set, right? Do any of you all look like Stepford wives? Including yourself?" Rachel crosses her arms and sticks out her hip to one side.

I smile. "You're right." I place my hands in my pockets. "So, is Haley on her way down, or...?"

"Yes, she should be. Here, speaking of highlighting beauty, I need to put a little powder on your face."

Rachel reaches into her tote and pulls out some sort of powder and large brush. Geez, this is the part of my job that I hate. The makeup. Not that I am too much of a man to wear makeup, I know that it's part of my job and it helps me look good on screen. But the time it takes to do makeup baffles me. To her credit, Rachel is the very best in the business.

"There. Now you are camera-ready and you look almost as beautiful as our girl." She pats me on the chest and wiggles her eyebrows. "Well, I am off to meet up with some old friends for drinks. If for some reason you want to show Haley a good time tonight, that wouldn't totally be a bad idea, if you catch my drift, Stone. Have fun."

With that, Rachel strides out of the hotel. Her comment makes my face get hot. If I recall from that little napkin burning a hole in my wallet, showing Haley a good time is strictly off-limits.

The elevator dings again and my heart starts to palpitate at an ungodly speed.

Haley steps out and walks towards me. She is wearing a flowy, off-the-shoulder lavender gown. Sparkles appear on the fabric with every step that Haley takes. The neckline dangerously shows off her cleavage, and her shoulders are bare. The bodice wraps tightly around her ridiculously small waist and then fabric cascades down and out.

At that moment, I want to throw out all of those damn cardigans and oversized t-shirts she wears to work on a daily basis. Nothing will ever compare. She was made to dress up like this.

After taking in her perfect figure, I notice her hair, which is down, curled and cascading down one of her shoulders. She is stunning. Not that she isn't beautiful with that messy bun of hers, but seeing her like this adds a new layer to Haley that frankly leaves me speechless.

And then my gaze rises to her face. Her perfect, absolutely breathtaking face.

Rachel was not wrong. She only highlighted the best features on Haley... which are all of her features, apparently. Haley's lips are the prettiest shade of pink I've ever seen. I've never noticed how full her lips are, until now. The top of her eyelids are side swept with black eyeliner that curves up on the outer corners of her eyes. The jetblack offsets her brown eyes so they appear lighter than ever before, like a dark honey color. She has a very old Hollywood look to her. Classically beautiful.

And my favorite part: she is still Haley. She doesn't look like anyone else but herself.

Mental note: *text Rachel to thank her.* Haley is an absolute knockout. She is more gorgeous than any other woman I've ever been with.

She finally reaches me and one of her eyebrows furrows a bit. "What's wrong?" she asks, looking down at her gown and fidgeting with her hair.

I finally snap out of the temporary trance her presence put me under. I clear my throat. "Uh, nothing's wrong. You just look..."

"I know, I probably look ridiculous in this gown and if you have changed your mind, that's okay, I completely understand..."

I better intervene before she runs away like goddamn Cinderella. "Hales, stop..."

She looks up at me. I luckily get a closer look at her striking eyes and notice they have flecks of gold in them. She mostly wears her blue-light glasses, which obstruct me from seeing the true color of her eyes. They always looked dark brown to me before. "Nothing is wrong. You look beautiful."

Her cheeks turn even more pink. She seems flattered, which makes me smile. She clears her throat and says, "Thank you..." Then her eyes scan my entire body and I swear her cheeks turn a darker shade of pink. "You look very handsome yourself. You finally shaved, mountain man." She reaches up and touches the thin layer of scruff on my face. "Man, I was really looking forward to walking next to Grizzly Adams on this red carpet."

My cheeks hurt from smiling so much. I don't remember the last time I felt this way. Completely mesmerized by someone, even when they are making fun of me. "Sorry to disappoint, Swann."

"In all seriousness, Aidan, you look great. The scruff look suits you. Cue the swooning from fangirls and fanboys alike." She glances past my shoulder to the limo outside the lobby doors. "Well, shall we?"

"Hold on. I feel like something is missing." I say.

She immediately gets that cute worried look on her face and starts patting down her torso. I pull out the blue box from the pocket inside my jacket. When I open it, the diamonds reflect off her eyes, and her mouth falls open.

"Aidan. You loaned out a pair of earrings for tonight? You didn't have to do that."

"I didn't get them on a loan. I bought them...for you. I figured these would go perfectly with what you're wearing." Haley meets my eyes. Her eyes are round with disbelief and I think I see some tears build up, but she blinks them away really fast.

"You seriously didn't have to..."

I take the earrings out of the box and place them in her hand. "I know I didn't have to. I wanted to. Seriously, Hales, there's no amount of flowers or jewelry or anything that I could give you that would repay you for doing this for me. Do you like them?"

"I love them, Aidan. Thank you." Gently, she puts on the earrings. Just as I thought – they look perfect on her.

I reach out my arm for her to take, and she slowly slides her hand around my elbow, sending a complete shock wave through my body. At that moment, I know this whole arrangement is going to work. Haley was born to be seen. Born to be admired. She deserves the world to know her name.

8

Haley

My knee bobs up and down the entire limo ride. I don't think I am cut out for this. I was comfortable being behind the scenes. Never in the photos the paparazzi takes of Aidan. I always just blended in with the background, and I was okay with that.

"Hey," Aidan says softly, putting his hand on my knee that won't stop moving. I look at him. His soft blue eyes are concerned. "You don't have to do this...I can tell my driver to turn around and we can figure out another arrangement. I know it's a lot. I kind of threw you into this because I needed a quick solution, but if you have any doubts, let me know, please."

His hand is still on my leg and my lips part. I have never before felt this kind of reaction from anyone's touch.

"I'm fine. Let's do this." I move my leg out from underneath his massive hand. Internally, I am actively shouting at my small stomach-flips to go away...indefinitely. They are no longer welcome!

"I'll be right by your side. There may be times where I have to let go of your hand because they want to do quick interviews, or they may want photos of me by myself, but I promise that I won't leave you behind."

As I nod, the limo comes to a stop. I take a deep breath and say, "I trust you."

Aidan gives me a side smirk, revealing the sexiest dimples and smile-lines around his eyes. I've never been close enough to his face to notice his perfect imperfections. He has the perfect amount of stubble on his jawline. This is a much better look than his full-out mountain man beard he was rocking since he broke up with Natasha. He used to be clean-shaven. I think this version is better.

"Hales?"

"Huh?"

"You ready?" He holds out his hand. I take a deep breath and put my hand in his.

"Here we go."

"Oh and remember," he adds.

I look into his blue eyes and suddenly lose my breath all over again.

"We are madly in love." He winks and flashes one last smile before pulling the door handle.

***

The second we climb out of that limo, cameras are flashing, causing me to see white spots all over. I probably look like a deer caught in the headlights.

"Aidan!"

"Aidan, over here!"

"Aidan, who is with you? New girlfriend?"

My eyes blink at an uncontrollable rate. *How does he do this all the time?* I feel his hand tighten around mine as he pulls me further onto the red carpet. Once we are out of the initial chaos, Aidan turns his head to look at me, clearly seeing how flustered I am. He pulls me closer so I am in his nook, right in the side of his chest. I feel his hand slide down to my waist and it rests perfectly at the crux of my waist and my butt.

This isn't helping my flustered state. It's only amplifying these butterflies in my stomach.

While still smiling at the cameras, Aidan lowers his chin so his lips lightly brush the side of my face. It's so loud around us that I barely make out what he says in my ear, "Relax. I got you. Don't worry, Hales."

I didn't realize until this moment how much he relaxes me. No one else in the world does that. That thought makes me smile. Cameras flash more and more. *This is an act.* I need to act like we are dating and falling in love.

Just keep smiling, I remind myself. Even when Aidan has to step away for interviews, I keep a smile plastered on my face. The press call out to me:

"Hey sweetheart! You got a name?"

"Are you and Aidan a couple?"

"Hey Aidan's date, over here!"

Anytime I feel the slightest bit overwhelmed, Aidan's eyes seem to find mine. It's like he has a sixth sense whenever I feel uncomfortable or out of my element– to be honest, is the majority of the time I am on this red carpet. I'm starting to feel disoriented with all the yelling and the flashing of the cameras. I have to remember to breathe. I probably look like a puppy dog following Aidan around. He is busy signing autographs on movie posters or People magazine or really any body parts fans want him to sign his name. He takes a few selfies with crazed-out fangirls who practically faint in his presence.

One of the last interviews Aidan has to do is for E! News. *Thank God this is almost over.* I can't wait to hide in the dark theater and recover. My introverted self is craving much-needed alone time after this whole event. I am twiddling with my fingers in front of my gorgeous lavender gown when a question cuts through all the noise: "So, Aidan, who is this mysterious girl you brought with you to the premiere?"

Aidan turns toward me and gestures for me to come over. *No. No. No. No. No. No.* I shake my head slightly to ward off his request. My body has gone into some sort of paralysis as a defense mechanism. It's like I am malfunctioning. Too much socialization and spotlight for me. *Why in the world did I agree to do this? I am not a part of this world. I am an imposter in a lavender dress.*

He holds a finger up to the interviewer and walks–no, more like saunters– over and whispers to me, "This is my last interview. I think it's time that the world met my girlfriend." He grabs my hand and before I have a chance to protest, leads me over to where the reporter is patiently waiting. Other reporters from various networks are huddled behind the E! News reporter, anxiously awaiting Aidan's response.

Aidan flashes his superstar smile and says, "Well I guess the cat's out of the bag now, isn't it John? This is my gorgeous girlfriend, Haley Swann."

At that moment, I know my life will never be the same. My name will be printed on all the tabloids, posted on Instagram, X... everywhere. There is no hiding now. It is one of those moments where there is so much chaos and noise all at once, that everything becomes a blur. It is like all the voices are muffled and they start to sound like the grown-ups on Charlie Brown. Microphones are being shoved into my face and cameras are clicking at a wild rate. I do my best to force a smile and make it seem natural. Even though nothing about this whole scenario–hell, about my life right now–is natural. Aidan must sense that I am getting lost again because he waves to the crowd and wraps his free hand around my waist once more to lead me toward the theater entrance.

"One more picture, Aidan, please! With Ms. Swann?"

Aidan leans down and asks: "Trust me?"

For some inexplicable reason, I nod. How is it that deep down, I know that Aidan will always protect me? Even before I was pretending to be his girlfriend, my gut told me that I could trust Aidan with anything.

He slowly bends over more and touches his lips to my cheek. So innocent. So sweet. And yet the crowd whoops and hollers, acting like we are in the middle of a steamy makeout session.

It is the reaction from my body that I'm not expecting. The shivers that travel across my entire body are nearly too much to bear. And yet, I find myself wishing that his lips would stay in that very spot for a second longer. *Snap out of it, Haley!* Aidan is only doing this for the cameras so the world will be convinced that we are a legit couple.

Once we escape into the theater, Aidan pauses. "You look absolutely stunning, Hales. And you did so good out there. You're a real natural." He places his forehead to mine, causing a genuine smile to escape my lips.

9

Haley

"The film was amazing, Aidan, really."

"Thanks Hales, that means a lot coming from someone who has never watched my movies." He opens the door to the limo, snickering in the process. He turns toward the flood of paparazzi for one final shot before following me into the car.

I scoff as he shuts the door. "Okay, you are being dramatic. I haven't watched your last film. I've been a little busy with my boss's schedule. He's been quite demanding lately."

"Fair enough." He laughs a little. "Again, I'm sorry I've been such a pain in the ass lately."

"Aidan, I was just kidding. It's fine."

"It's not. But you're sweet for saying so." He scoots closer to me in the limo. Did he forget we're not in the public eye right now? No one except the driver can see us.

I don't think I'm ever going to get used to Aidan being so close to me. His cologne is honestly the most delicious, masculine scent I've ever smelled. I am keenly aware of all things Aidan. My proximity to him for the past week has made it impossible for me not to notice these small things about him. How when you actually look closely, his eyes have the smallest hint of green in them, rendering them teal instead of ordinary blue. How he has the most pronounced jawline I've ever seen in my life, even under all the stubble. He has lines by the outer corners of his eyes that deepen when he smiles, which has actually been a lot this past week. I don't think I've ever seen him smile so much, even when he was with Natasha. I wonder what has changed? Maybe he has relaxed, knowing that the perception of him will become more positive thanks to our little agreement. I mean that's the point, right?

I cleared my throat. "So, I just want to thank you for having a stylist help me get ready and for flying out Rachel to help with my makeup. I wouldn't know the first thing to do with that. At least I didn't look like a troll next to you tonight. I looked somewhat decent."

"You were more than decent, Hales. You were gorgeous. Are gorgeous."

A wave of heat rises from my toes to my cheeks, exposing my absolute shock at that statement. There's no way he could truly think so, not after dating Natasha Davis. He is obviously just making me feel better.

"Thank you," I manage to say. "So, are you dropping me off at the hotel?"

"I wish we could be done for the night. Not quite yet. I won't hear the end of it from Samantha if I skip the premiere after-party. I mean, unless you're not up to it. I totally understand if you want to turn in. If I had the choice, I would go back to my apartment and sleep."

"No it's okay, Aidan. It's part of our deal right? How is it going to look if you show up to this after-party alone? The whole point of this is for you to be seen with your girlfriend to get the negative press off your back. I think you would hear more from Samantha about that than if you didn't show up at all."

"Yeah, you're right. That is the whole point." There is a flicker of sadness in Aidan's eyes. I can't help but wonder why he repeated that line back to me. His attention is now on the driver. "Hey, Raul. I'll AirDrop you the address for this after-party."

"Sure thing, Mr. Stone."

After about a ten-minute drive, we arrive at our destination: 48 LOUNGE. Before we walk in, Aidan lingers outside for a moment. "Hales, I promise I'll stay by your side for the whole time, unless I'm pulled away for a moment. But if that happens, I'll come find you as soon as I can. Okay?"

"Okay." I am a strange mix of pure exhaustion and high-strung nerves.

Aidan takes my hand and we walk inside. A bright purple hue illuminates the walls, contrasting with the champagne leather couches and bar stools filling the entire space. The two large chandeliers provide more of a glow than actual light. Everything is dim, romantic even, and I can't help but be grateful there are no fluorescent lights hanging above us. They would surely highlight all my flaws, especially next to my fake boyfriend.

Rows of champagne flutes wait for us at the bar. Aidan grabs two and hands me one. We clink glasses and each took a sip. To be honest, I'm not a huge fan of champagne. Wine, yes–give me all the wine. Maybe it's the bubbles I don't like.

"Hey, man!" One of Aidan's male co-stars comes over to chat.

"Hey Dominic," Aidan says, bumping his fist. "This is my girlfriend, Haley."

I put on the biggest smile I can muster, even though I am freaking out internally. I can see the headlines now in my head: *Who is this imposter posing as Aidan Stone's girlfriend? Doesn't she know that she doesn't come close to reaching the beauty standard of his ex-girlfriend? Who does she think she is?*

Although here at 48 LOUNGE we aren't inundated with a never-ending line of paparazzi and media, this whole scene seems so much more intimidating. And then she makes her entrance, and I think I know exactly why it begins to feel more claustrophobic.

Natasha Davis looks more stunning than ever. Between the end of the premiere and the after-party, it appears that she's changed her entire outfit. She is now wearing the shortest cocktail dress I've ever seen– it's practically glued to her body, just like Isaac Sommers, who Natasha left Aidan for six months ago. Maybe I should've changed my dress. I can totally see why Aidan was with her. Natasha's caramel skin and long, sleek dark hair match her equally dark eyes. Her legs are super toned and on full display except for the sliver of fabric covering the uppermost part of her thigh. She looks like a damn siren. Drawing men and women's attention with her mere presence. How are regular women like me supposed to compete?

Without notice, I feel Aidan's hand make its way around my waist and pull me in closer. His eyes don't drift from his male co-star. It's like he just *knew* that I was starting to feel insecure. If there is any indication that he registers Natasha's presence, he hides it masterfully.

You need to play the part, Haley. Hold his hand or something. Act like your life depends on it. I exhale and place my hand on top of his. His gaze finally breaks from Dominic – a handsome man in his own right, I might add, but nowhere near as handsome as Aidan – and he looks at me and smiles. He leans down and whispers in my ear, "You're doing great, Hales. Don't worry about anything else in the room. Or anyone else."

After an hour or so, I'm starting to get more comfortable. Aidan is seriously the life of the party. You would think he was in a fraternity at UConn and not a drama nerd. People are naturally drawn to him, and I can see why. Besides the obvious factor of his looks, it is his genuine character. The way he pays attention fully to the person talking to him. The way he actually laughs when someone says something amusing. The way he just holds space for people. It is really a sight to see. Now I understand why directors want to work with him— it's not that they're going to get high box office sales solely based on his sex appeal.

Aidan told me he had to go talk with the director of the film for a second. It's the first time I've been alone all night, but I actually feel remarkably secure. I find an empty seat on one of the many couches and I'm sipping my second drink of the night— white wine this time, not champagne. I usually don't drink, so unfortunately I am already feeling a little bit of a buzz. Maybe that is the factor calming me down: alcohol. Then a voice sends a shiver down my spine. And not in the way that Aidan's voice does. A bad shiver.

"Hi. I don't think we've met."

I turn towards the high-pitched voice and there in front of me stands none other than Natasha. Great. Of course she doesn't remember me. How could she recognize someone whose daily wardrobe usually consists of Converse, jeans, cardigans and blue light glasses? I am a real Cinderella over here. She doesn't even have the courtesy to extend her hand out toward me with her introduction.

I stand up from the couch and extend my hand, because my parents raised me to have manners. "Actually, we have. I'm Haley. Haley Swann."

Her brow wrinkles in confusion. "I totally pride myself on remembering people's names. I'm sure I would've remembered you if we had met before. Haley, is it?"

Is this girl serious? Maybe she didn't pay attention to Aidan's lowly assistant who was trying to break up their makeout sessions in order to get Aidan back on his schedule for the day, or the assistant who Aidan had daily rundowns with in his trailer while she was sitting on the couch scrolling through her Instagram and laughing at whatever DM she received.

"Yes. It's Haley. I was Aidan's assistant. For about three years?"

"Oh yes! Haley. Wow, you look..." She scans my entire body. I start to hunch over a little, closing in on myself– what I do whenever I feel insecure or less than. I hate being the center of attention or under a microscope in any way. "...different. I didn't even recognize you."

Obviously. "Yup." I sip my drink and catch a glimpse of Aidan across the room. His eyes meet mine and I can see his gaze drift quickly to Natasha and then back to me. His eyebrows furrow slightly. I know how much she hurt him. I was there for the aftermath of their breakup. She wasn't. Ironically, *she* is actually the reason I am even standing next to her right now.

Her lips purse at my short answer. I have no intention of giving this woman what she wants: a certain reaction out of me. She wants to catch me off-guard. To make me feel uncomfortable. I am not going to lie, she is succeeding in one aspect: I am definitely becoming uncomfortable in her presence. But no damn way am I letting her know it.

"I've never seen you at a premiere before. Aidan must have been desperate for a date to have to take his assistant."

I'm speechless. *Wow. Okay, is that how you want to play it?*

She takes a drink of her cocktail and then something must click in her train of thought because she says, "Wait, you said *was* his assistant. What does that mean? Did you get a new position or something?"

"I *was* his assistant, but not any longer. Because we are dating now."

Natasha chokes on her drink and some of it spills on her dress. *Serves her right for saying that about Aidan.* If anything, the only reason Aidan was "desperate" was because of her. After she broke his heart, he acted in ways I've never seen from him before. I never pegged him for a womanizer, but that's the path he went down. All because of her. I was right to call her a siren. She lures men to their undoing.

Natasha slaps her hand to her mouth. She's laughing. "There is no way that Aidan would ever go out with his assistant. He strictly dates A-list actresses. I should know."

Okay, now I am pissed. What the hell is wrong with this woman? Her uncouth behavior has no bounds and it doesn't seem there is a genuine bone in her body. This is dangerous territory. Natasha has a lot of pull with the tabloids and media companies. If the past six months has taught me anything, it is that the media loves Natasha. If she expresses doubts that Aidan and I are really dating, they will eat it up. *You need to do something, Haley.* Desperate times call for desperate measures.

I know what I have to do. And I also know that I need liquid courage. I down the rest of my cocktail and place the empty glass on the small table in front of me. "Well, on that note, it was a real treat talking to you, Natasha."

I bee-line toward Aidan. When he sees me, his eyes light up and he flashes his perfect smile. I graze my hand across his back and hold tight to the other side of his torso. My god, it's just pure muscle. Natasha is one crazy girl to leave this man.

He looks down at me, "There you are, babe." Still not getting used to that, no matter how many times we practiced this past week. "This is the director Peter Hastings. Peter, this is my girlfriend, Haley."

"Girlfriend, huh. Isn't she your...?"

"Assistant. Yeah, but we had to keep that under wraps for a little while. She isn't my assistant anymore. It's going to be a bitch to find a replacement as amazing as her. But we couldn't hold off any longer. I wanted the world to know that she is mine."

It is confirmed. There is a rollercoaster operating at warp speed in my stomach. *I wanted the world to know that she is mine.* He says it with such conviction that I almost believe him.

Peter's hand reaches out for mine. "It's a pleasure to formally meet you, Haley. I always saw you around the set, just never got a chance to meet you."

"It's a pleasure to meet you, too." Even though Aidan apparently wants the whole world to know that I am his, there is still one crucial person that needs to be convinced that he is mine. "Um, Peter, can you excuse us for just one second?"

"Of course. I'll see you around, Aidan. I'll call you about that script, okay? I think you'll be perfect for the role."

"Thanks. See you, Peter."

We step away, and Aidan finally turns his attention completely to me. He knows something is wrong immediately. "I saw you talking to Natasha. Is everything okay?" He glances quickly in her direction, as do I. She is already talking to the media and people are taking so many pictures of her. It looks like a fricken lightning storm.

Instinctively, I place my hand firmly against Aidan's cheek and turn his attention back to me. "I think she's onto us." I search his face and I can see his worry crease take up residence between his eyebrows. He starts to turn his gaze toward his ex once more, but again, I turn his face back to mine.

Am I really going to do this?

It's out of necessity, right?

"Do you trust me?" He gives a small nod. I slowly move my hand from his cheek to the back of his head and before I fully comprehend what I'm doing, I pull his head down toward mine and bring my lips to his.

I expect to give him a quick peck, just long enough for the cameras to catch us in our public display of affection.

That's what is expected.

Maybe it's the liquid courage. But deep down, I know that in order for this to be believable, I have to go all in. Just like he did in the diner when he signed the contract without hesitation. So I linger against his lips for much longer than I originally intended. Exploring his mouth slightly with my tongue. My body starts to vibrate all over, and not just because I am kissing my boss. But also because I have never felt a kiss like this—ever. Heat radiates through every single inch of me and ignites a spark I never intended to light in a million years. I press my free hand against his chest, where I feel his heart racing. Through his button-down, his warm skin feels so comforting against my cold hands. He isn't letting up–at all.

My nerves get the best of me. I start to break free, but am unsuccessful because his hand presses firmly against the small of my back and his other hand cups my own jaw. He is *really* kissing me back, exploring my mouth in turn and pressing his body harder against my delicate fingers. His massive, calloused (probably due to the insane amount of hours he puts in at the gym) hand migrates from my jaw to the back of my head, gently pulling me closer to him while also tugging my hair a little. *He is really selling it.* He's gotten quite good at kissing women and making it seem real. I was hoping he would be a bad kisser, to make this whole situation easier on myself.

Spoiler alert: he is not. At all.

"Look at that, Hollywood's Newest Hottest Couple!" someone from the crowd shouts, causing us to finally break from our kiss. I look up at Aidan, expecting him to smirk due to the fact that maybe I am a little rusty. In my defense, I haven't kissed anyone in three years. Give a girl a break. Or I expect him to look completely disgusted. Or anything other than what I actually see. He looks almost *excited* that I kissed him. The only thing that breaks our eye lock is the light of a camera flashing.

After I blink from the flash, I lean in close to him and whisper, "Necessity."

I expect him to be relieved, or amused. But for some reason, the look of excitement dims from his face. He repeats through a tight jaw, "Necessity."

10

Haley

It is pouring.

Hard.

The day after the premiere, Aidan and I go on another pseudo date, which consists of walking around Midtown, ice cream cones in hand and talking about the new movie he's working on and how physically demanding the role is. It is amazing how attuned I feel to the cameras clicking and phones held up facing our general direction. But even with all of the distraction, I feel more attuned to Aidan. Talking with him has always been easy, but everything has always been about business. Now, it's like we're gathering pieces of each other and putting together the full puzzle that makes up our lives.

As we cross the street to enter Central Park, we both feel droplets fall from the eerie gray sky that has gradually become darker since this morning.

"We should be fine," Aidan assures me. "We are really close to my apartment in case the sky opens."

And boy does it. Aidan breaks out into a full-on sprint and drags me along with him. We finally make it to his apartment building. We jet past Aidan's sweet doorman, who greets Aidan with a welcoming smile and tips his hat toward me. I give a small wave and smile back, then step into the elevator after Aidan. As Aidan presses the button to his floor, which is outrageously high, I can't help but wonder how many women have followed Aidan up this elevator and greeted his doorman in a similar fashion.

Chills run up and down my body as a result of the rain, but also because I am about to enter Aidan Stone's apartment. This is entering *very* personal territory. This was never part of the plan. This is why I opted to stay in my own hotel. To avoid situations like this.

I am soaking wet from the deluge outside. *Great.* The only available piece of clothing I always carry in my belt bag for emergencies is a pair of underwear. And not the sexy kind either. Like boy-shorts underwear. At least they look like shorts. It could be worse. It could be a thong.

We finally reach Aidan's floor. As we walk down the hallway toward his apartment, I say, "Seriously, Aidan. I can go back to my hotel. I think that might be better. I don't have any extra clothes here and I am drenched."

He chuckles. "I do have a washing machine, you know. And towels. Plus, I have something for you to borrow in the meantime. I don't want you to go out in this storm. I already told Raul to go home for the night, so you don't have anyone to drive you. Your hotel is close, but it's not that close to walk out in this storm."

Aidan finally unlocks his door, turns the knob and pushes the door open. The security system starts to beep and he puts in his code discreetly. I lower my eyes so as not to see the numbers, rubbing the sides of my arms to generate some sort of heat.

"Oh wait," Aidan says. "Why am I hiding this from you? You need to know this information just in case I'm not with you."

"There's no need, Aidan," I say, trying to contain the water that is dripping from my hair into my just as soaked, if not more, shirt. "I don't think I'll ever come here without you."

"You never know. Anyway, it will be easy to remember."

"Well it's not smart to have something easily remembered as your code. My dad, who worked in IT for years I might add, would be so disappointed in you."

"Haha smartass. I meant that it will be easy for *you* to remember. Ready?"

"Fine. Tell me." I pull out my phone and open the Notes app. A common practice at this point in our relationship.

Aidan suddenly looks away from me to the ground, as if he is afraid to look me in the eye. He clears his throat. "It's 012991."

My breath catches as I process what I just heard. I examine his pink face, and then he looks back at me and now it's my turn to avert my eyes. I click the side of my phone and clear my throat. "Yeah, you're right. That will be easy for me to remember." Thank God Aidan hasn't turned on his lights yet, because no doubt my cheeks are bright red. *Why would he have that day as his code?*

Aidan smirks a little, gestures for me to step into his apartment and finally turns on the light.

My jaw drops. Massive windows in his living room reveal the stunning city lights. It feels like I am in a fishbowl, even though I know no one can see me. The rain is still pounding down on the street below. Soon thunder rolls in. Lightning streaks across the sky, illuminating the harsh outer lines of the buildings. I look to my right and see a beautiful chef's kitchen. Black stainless steel appliances, a very expensive coffee machine, double oven, the works. He has huge couches, probably to accommodate his massive build. Clean, sleek, classic. Just like Aidan.

"Here you go. I know this may be a little big on you but it's something for you to wear while your clothes are in the wash. And here's a towel."

In the time I was admiring Aidan's apartment, he's already changed out of his own drenched clothes and dried off. I've never seen his hair look this unruly. Boyish. Innocent. Unguarded. It's kind of cute. *Wait, what am I thinking?* My cheeks get warm again, and it isn't because we are in his warm apartment. He holds out a gray shirt to me and I unfold it. A UConn basketball t-shirt. I smile because I know how much of a UConn basketball fan he still is. I take the towel from his other hand and scrunch it into my hair. "Thanks."

"No problem. Um, if you want to go change, my room is down that small hallway and to the left. There is an ensuite in there, if you want extra privacy."

"Thanks." I make my way down the hall and find his room. His bedroom is just as big as his living room. A massive California king bed, perfectly made. I switch on the light to his bathroom and close the door behind me. Glancing in the mirror, I am instantly mortified. My hair is covering most of my face. It's like I am looking at an image of that scary girl from *The Ring*. Not cute. *Why do I even care if I look cute?* My clothes are clinging to my body for dear life. I inch my jeans off my legs and peel my shirt off my torso. I'm just gonna have to wear my soaking bra. I am *not* going braless in Aidan Stone's apartment. No way.

I dry off the rest of my body and try my best to dry the heck out of my bra so it won't soak through the borrowed t-shirt. I replace my wet underwear with the dry boyshort ones from my purse. They look like spandex. Not too bad, considering I wore spandex playing volleyball in high school and that was deemed appropriate. I pull Aidan's UConn shirt over my head and it falls mid-thigh. I look naked under this oversized shirt. Yep, this is exactly how I want my boss to see me. Almost naked. Wonderful.

I pull out my phone and text Aidan.

Hey do you have any shorts I could borrow?

Almost immediately, I hear the door to the bedroom open. Drawers open from his dresser and he is fumbling around. There is a small knock on the door. "Hales, I'm leaving some basketball shorts out here if you want them."

"Okay, thank you." I wait to hear the bedroom door close before I open the bathroom door. I pull his shorts on. But once I let go, they immediately fall to the floor. Perfect. This isn't going to work. Boyshorts it is.

I pick up my dripping clothes and tiptoe back down the hall toward the living room. I can smell coffee brewing. On the kitchen island, a candle flickers. It smells like fall—my favorite time of year. The rain is still coming down hard outside. I watch Aidan reach for a couple of mugs out of the cabinet. As he sets them down, he turns his head and his eyes wander down the length of my body. I involuntarily pull the shirt down further. I feel so exposed.

Aidan clears his throat. "Um, I made some coffee. Help yourself to some creamer in the fridge. I know how much you love a little coffee with your creamer," he adds, smirking, exposing his prominent dimples. He reaches for my wet clothes I'm still holding . "I'll go put these in the wash for you."

"Thanks." I hand him my clothes and when he disappears down the hall, I throw up my hair into a messy bun to try and tame whatever frizz is going to develop in the next few hours. I open his fridge and notice my favorite creamer in there: oat milk creamer, specifically the oatmeal cookie flavor.

When Aidan walks back into the kitchen, I hold up the carton of creamer. "Oatmeal cookie is your favorite flavor, is it?"

Shrugging, he says, "So what if it is? Are you judging?"

I snort. "Not at all. I also happen to love the oatmeal cookie flavored creamer."

"Well you know what they say, great minds."

I filled my mug a little over halfway with creamer and add a little bit of coffee to top it off. I hand over the creamer to Aidan so he can pour whatever stingy amount he wants to put in his own mug. Sure enough, he pours in just a splash and fills the rest with coffee. I shake my head as I take a sip of mine. *Oh my god this is the best coffee I've ever had.* "Tell me: why is it that I am the one fetching you coffee every day when you are perfectly capable of making coffee all on your own?"

"Well, you are my assistant. Isn't that kind of the whole point of your job?"

I walk past him and bump into him slightly. "Who's the smartass now?" I say as I plop onto his couch. Good lord this is the most comfortable couch. I guess being a world famous movie star has its perks.

"I'm kidding. I honestly just don't have the time in the morning." Aidan sits next to me. Uncomfortably so. "You know how L.A. traffic is, and I like to get in a workout in the mornings if I can. I just don't have the luxury to sit and make coffee and a good breakfast. I'm almost always on the go. Especially with early call times."

"Oh I know all about those."

A flash of lightning illuminates Aidan's apartment. Thunder claps, and suddenly the lights go completely out. The only thing that is preventing it from being completely dark is the flicker of the candle on the island. The city was black.

"Shit. Hold on." Aidan places his mug on his coffee table and darts off the couch. As I pull one of his blankets over my legs, I watch his silhouette move across the room. Every curvature of his body is emphasized in this light. There is no hiding anything. There are glimpses of his statuesque figure. All the hard outlines of his muscles. I want to give all the kudos to his personal trainer. Did I mention he has a lot of muscles? I guess he has to be that built to portray a superhero with superhuman strength on the big screen. I am thanking my lucky stars that he can't feel how hot my ears are getting. I'm sure my cheeks match the color of cherry chapstick. He reaches towards the middle of the island and grabs the only lighting we have in this entire apartment.

11

Aidan

Shit. This cannot be happening. I carefully bring the candle over to the coffee table so we can make out each other's faces in this blackout. Without the humming of the fridge, my apartment is eerily quiet. The only sounds are horns blaring from the frustrated drivers below. It's probably chaos out there, which is why I am immensely happy that I am stuck inside with Haley. She always disrupts the chaos with her presence. Part of the reason I love her as my assistant. *Like* her as my assistant.

When I sit back down, I see a slight shade of pink on Haley's cheeks. "Are you hot or something? You looked flushed. Hopefully this blackout doesn't last too long and the AC will come back on." I look down and notice that Haley has also draped the blanket from the back of the couch over her bare legs, which is a shame. No one should cover up legs like hers. *Why am I fixated on her legs?* "Um, maybe taking off the blanket might help, too."

"I'm fine." She secures the blanket over her legs and drinks more of her coffee. I could swear she turns even more red. I love that she can't hide the way she feels around me. I can read her like an open book.

"So..." I start.

"So?" she responds.

"Maybe since we don't have any other form of entertainment and we're stuck in this apartment, we can get to know each other a little better before we drive out to the Hamptons tomorrow afternoon."

Haley adjusts slightly into the couch. "Okay, what do you want to know?" she asks hesitantly.

"Where did you grow up?"

"Cold Spring. A small town outside of Manhattan."

"Any nicknames I should know about?"

"Um, well Hales, but you already know that. My mom calls me Haley Girl."

"Just your mom? What about your dad? Does he have a cute little nickname for you?"

Something shifts in Haley's demeanor. She breaks eye contact with me. I don't know why but when she does that, it aches me to my core. "Um, my dad used to call me Haley Girl, too." Her eyes become very watery as she grazes her slender finger around the rim of her mug.

"Used to?"

"Yeah, he died about four years ago. Inoperable brain tumor."

Instinctually, I reached out and touched her hand. "Oh, Hales. I'm so sorry."

I couldn't empathize with her at this moment, unfortunately. My dad is an absolute ass and the most despicable human being on this planet. If he died, I don't know if I would truly miss him. I know how fucked up that sounds but when you grow up with an adulterous, alcoholic father, and a mean alcoholic at that, who used to beat on your innocent, sweet mother for forgetting to iron his button-down shirt and slacks for court the next day, it forces you to evaluate who you want to keep in your life and who you truly care about no matter what. I wish I knew Haley's grief. I wish I knew this type of love from a father. I don't give a damn if I ever see my father again.

After wiping a glistening tear from her cheek, Haley responds, "Thanks. He was my favorite person in the whole world. I miss him every day. I mean no disrespect to my mom. I love her to death, but I just had a bond with my dad that was very special. He was the dreamer in the family and really encouraged me to keep writing. He saw how much I loved it and how much I studied film and we would have in-depth conversations about the scripts themselves. My mom is definitely more practical. She always checks if I am okay with money, that my job is stable enough to support me. Not that she doesn't support my dream of becoming a screenwriter, but she doesn't want to see me fail. It's a tough industry, I am finding out. My dad is also the reason why I love romantic comedies. We used to watch them all the time together. He told me that I should be with a man who treats me like I am his whole world. That's how he always treated my mom—like she was his whole world." Haley raises an eyebrow and takes another sip of her coffee. "Anyway, enough about me. What about your parents?"

Here we go. "Well, my mom is great. Maybe you'll get to meet her at some point while we are in the city. She lives here now. She moved here a few years ago from my hometown in Connecticut. I guess my mom is how your dad was. She is very supportive of my acting career and fostered it throughout high school and college. I remember the moment I realized I wanted to be an actor. It was actually in high school. I took a theater class and thought I was going to hate it because one, I was more into athletics than anything and two, my dad always thought my interest in the arts was 'stupid and impractical' as he put it. He wanted me to follow in his footsteps and pursue law. He went to Yale and that was the expectation since before I was born. And there was no room for deviation from that plan. Now, my dad –

he didn't know the definition of the word grace. It wasn't in his vocabulary and it certainly wasn't in his philosophy of being a parent. I will never forget when I didn't get accepted into Yale, the disappointment in his face was a sight that could break a kid's spirit. It almost broke mine, but luckily, my mom is my guardian angel. She always sees the beauty in things that could be perceived as ugly or as failures. My father's disappointment didn't end there –when I announced I was majoring in theater, I was basically blacklisted as far as he was concerned. He didn't speak a word to me for a solid six months."

"Wow, Aidan, I am sorry. That really sucks." Haley reaches out and grabs my clenched hand. I didn't even realize that my hand was in a fist. I guess my dad really brings out the anger inside me. A real Bruce Banner over here. But Haley's touch is the magic bullet and I relax my hand. She retracts her hand a little too quickly if you ask me, then says, "Well, your mom sounds like a real sweetheart. Your dad..."

"Sounds like a real asshole. Yeah, I know."

She lets out a small laugh of relief that I was the one to say it.

"So." I notice my leg is jiggling and stop it. "This wedding we are going to, who is who? I want to be prepared and be able to remember who everyone is."

"Well, the bride is my best friend from childhood, Anna. She is honestly like my sister, I swear. We have gone through so much together and she is my ride-or-die."

"Hold up, you're saying I am not your ride-or-die? You know, Hales, that's a little hurtful since we are in love and all." I give her a smirk. I don't know if I am imagining it, but it looks like she is blushing again.

"Sorry, lover boy. Anna is my one-and-only ride-or-die. Anyway, she is marrying Dan. They have been together for like a gazillion years. Since middle school. Theirs is a love that makes people jealous, and I get it. They are so cute it is sometimes nauseating, even for someone like me who loves romantic comedies. I am her Maid of Honor, so I may have to ditch you to do Maid of Honor duties."

"No problem. I'm a big boy, I can handle myself. Okay, Anna, Dan. Got it. Who else do I need to know about?"

Her eyes avert from me once again. "Well, my mom is going to be there because she is like Anna's second mom. She's also going to stay in the house where we're staying. And um, Dan's best friend, Robert, will be there. He's the best man." Her voice cracks at Robert. There's a connection there that she isn't telling me. Reading her expressions is easy, but sometimes getting information out of her is so difficult. But it makes me want to know her even more. I want to know all her secrets.

Since she is not offering up the information herself, I egg her on a little. "And other than being the best man, I get a sense that this *Robert* has some sort of significance in this whole ordeal."

Oh shit. She is definitely crying now. The light from the candle reflects off the tears rolling down her face. Without hesitation, I reach out and wipe the tears from her cheek. She flinches a little at my touch but didn't fully retract. Progress.

She sniffles and laughs. "How could you tell?"

"I have no clue." I realize my hand is still on her cheek. For some reason, I don't want to break our connection, but she finally does it for me when she shifts away and wipes whatever is left of her tears away with her own hand.

"He's my ex...fiancé."

"You were engaged?"

She nods and looks at me with a hint of embarrassment. "Hence me needing a date for this wedding. I can't face him alone."

"What happened?"

She shrugs and blurts out, "He just broke up with me."

Who in their right mind would break up with the sweetest girl I've ever met? What the fuck is wrong with this jackass? I already hate him and I haven't even met him.

I hear her sniffle again, "Can we please change the subject? So, I've been curious..."

Oh God, I don't know where this is going.

"What exactly happened with you and Natasha? I mean, I didn't want to pry when it happened. It wasn't my business. But in the spirit of getting to know each other, I thought I should know more about this."

"I guess it's only fair...Um, I honestly thought everything was going fine. Great actually. I even bought a ring."

Her eyebrows rise to an alarming height.

"Yeah. I know. Joke's on me right?"

"Aidan..." She no longer looks surprised. There is another expression on her face that I am definitely getting used to seeing as of late. Pity.

"You don't have to say anything." I clear my throat. "Anyway, I thought everything was going great and then, maybe a couple of months after she started that vampire show, she told me she wanted to break up. I was completely shocked. We had just taken a vacation together and she seemed happy. I guess I'm not as good at reading people as I thought. Now, she is with that guy, Isaac something-or-other." I look down. I know his name. It's Isaac Sommers. I'm just being petty about it. "It hurt and I wanted to block out the noise. The media. The critics. I wanted to lose myself for a little bit. I realized that even if you do all the right things, treat people exactly the way they should be treated – in her case like a fucking queen – it doesn't matter. People are going to hurt you no matter what."

I feel a hand on my cheek now. "It does matter." I look into her eyes. There are gold flecks in her dark brown eyes. Twice. That's how many times I've had the privilege of witnessing this beautiful trait about her. Her eyes are my favorite thing about her. Second to her being an absolute sweetheart.

She repeats, "It does matter. What you say and do matters. Not just because you are the center of attention in this world right now. Not just because you are one of the most famous actors on the planet. Not just because you are my boss and I am trying to butter you up right now." She smiles, and so do I. Her hand is still on my cheek and she leans in closer. The closest she's ever been without anyone being around to document it. I feel this pull in my gut that I haven't felt in a woman's presence in a long time. The feeling of anticipation. "But just as a regular human being, it matters. Trust me." I reach up and touch her hand that is still on my cheek. "And just for the record, I never thought much of Natasha. You deserve better, Aidan."

The knots in my stomach are getting bigger and harder to stifle now. Since Natasha, I have kissed a shit-ton of women and not once have I been as nervous in their presence as Haley is making me feel right now. Ever since Haley kissed me at the premiere afterparty, I have wanted to put my lips back on hers. Desperately. I have wanted to run my hands through her hair and kiss her soft lips over and over again. But I don't know if she feels the same. And the last thing I want to do is take advantage or make assumptions.

Then I notice her eyes are fixated on my own lips and she is biting her bottom lip. As if *she* wants me to kiss *me*. I hope to god that I am right. I lean in. Her breath hitches and her eyes flutter shut. I am mere millimeters from her lips... when suddenly the lights come back on.

Damn it.

12

Haley

Was Aidan about to kiss me?

In his apartment?

Without the paparazzi taking our photos or anyone else around to witness it?

Maybe he just wanted to practice. I do still get a little jumpy any time he touches me. Granted, I was the one who kissed him at the premiere afterparty, but that's only because Natasha was doubting the validity of our relationship. I had to. Right?

Now, I can't help but feel a little ache when his hand leaves mine and he backs away.

He reaches for the remote on the coffee table and hands it to me as he gets up from the couch. "Here, go ahead and pick something for us to watch. I'm gonna make some popcorn. You down?"

Still flummoxed by the almost-kiss, I warily say, "Sure." My hand brushes against his in the remote hand-off and my body is electrified. "You don't care?"

"Nope. Whatever you want. Maybe a Nora Ephron one. She's your favorite writer, right?"

I nod. He remembered? I recall sharing that fun fact about me back when I first got the job, and it never came up again. And why would it? We were strictly business. He was my boss. I was his employee. That was it. Up until about a week and a half ago.

Aidan rummages through his pantry for the microwave popcorn. He bends down to look on the bottom shelf and I catch myself staring at him. He is rocking some gray sweatpants that accentuate his sculpted...*Haley, snap out of it!* What is wrong with me? We are not really together. He is your BOSS! It's all a ruse. It's not for real.

But then why does it feel like it's real?

I shoo away the butterflies infiltrating my stomach, turn on his Roku TV and select the Netflix app. I type in the search bar *When Harry Met Sally*—my personal favorite. *You've Got Mail* is a close second. There are loud pops coming from the microwave and the smell of buttery goodness.

"Water?" Aidan calls.

"Sure! I should probably switch to that if I ever want to sleep tonight. Speaking of sleep, it actually looks like the rain has died down and now that the lights are back on, maybe I should head back to the–"

"You're not going anywhere, Hales," he says. More like demands. He brings over a large bowl of popcorn and a glass of water. "I don't want you to be wandering around the city at night."

"You do know I'm a big girl, right? Plus, I'm practically from here, so I'm not scared of the city at night. I know my way around."

"I didn't mean it like that. I just meant– I want to make sure you're safe. You're staying." He sits on the couch and places the bowl of popcorn in between us. He winks at me. "That's an order, Swann."

"Oh, you're ordering me around now? I thought we are taking a pause with the whole me-being-your-assistant-thing during this fake-dating period." I grab a handful of popcorn and shove it in my mouth.

"We are...pausing."

Is Aidan Stone flirting with me? A tiny part of me wants to reciprocate (the part that hasn't been in a romantic relationship in a bit and needs to brush up on her flirting skills) but I brush it off and say, "Well, I was going to stay whether or not you told me to or not. I love this movie. Any opportunity to watch it, I take it immediately. You've seen this, right?" I scoot all the way over to the end of the couch and pull the blanket over my body.

"Do you think I live under a rock? Of course I've seen this movie. This is probably my favorite romantic comedy of all time. Billy Crystal. Meg Ryan. The storyline. The directing. The acting. Brilliant."

My mouth is agape.

He looks over at me and starts laughing before he puts his own fistful of popcorn in his mouth. "Why are you looking at me like that, you goof?"

"I guess I'm just surprised you have a favorite romantic comedy. Or that you watch romantic comedies at all. It's my favorite, too." I stretch my arm as far as it can go to reach the bowl of popcorn.

"Now, what kind of actor would I be if I didn't try to watch the best films of all time?" He does have a point. "You know you can move closer to the middle of the couch if you want some popcorn. I don't bite."

I know this is true. I don't know why I feel so nervous all of a sudden. I've sat next to Aidan countless times, but it's always been in a professional setting or at events for work. Never when I'm basically half-naked. In his apartment. Late at night.

I scooch a little closer to the bowl. "Satisfied?"

"Immensely." He smirks and presses play.

The next hour and a half fly by. As the credits are rolling and I'm drying my tears (because yes, I cry every time at the end of this movie, even though I've seen it more times than I can count), we got into an argument about the whole premise of how men and women cannot remain friends after they have sex. I am on the side of Billy Crystal. I firmly believe sex changes everything. It complicates things. Aidan is on Team Meg Ryan. He says it doesn't make a difference.

I point at him. "You cannot separate your emotions for a person you sleep with. I guess that's why I've never been involved in a one-night stand."

Aidan's eyes grow very wide. "Never?"

I shake my head. "Never."

"Wow, that's surprising."

"What's that supposed to mean?"

"Nothing." He gives me another one of his iconic smirks and raises his eyebrows in an accusatory way.

"You can't make a comment like that and make a silly face like that and say it doesn't mean anything. Spill, Stone." I readjust my position on the couch so I am cross-legged, fully facing him. I realize I scooted closer and closer to him as the movie was playing. I don't know how that even happened. I felt like every time I wanted more popcorn, the bowl was just past my reach. I am probably only a foot away from him now. The only thing separating us is that damn bowl of buttery deliciousness that is, unfortunately, empty.

Aidan seems to inch a little closer. "All I meant was that it surprises me you haven't had any one-night stands. I guess I've had my fair share and it's just rare to hear someone say they've never experienced that. It must be nice. I am happy for you. Especially if you believe that sex changes things. That means you've protected your heart. Lessening the chance of it ever being broken."

I raise an eyebrow. "A lot of good that did me. I have definitely still experienced heartbreak and let me tell you, I am not a fan." I take a drink of my water. As I am swallowing, I hear, "So what's your number?"

I nearly spit out the entire contents of my mouth and start coughing. Why does Aidan Stone want to know my number? What can he possibly do with that information? "I beg your pardon?"

"What's the number of men you have slept with? Hey, don't look at me like that. This is pertinent information to know. I don't know, what if Anna decides to quiz me on something like that? I know you girls talk. If we want our relationship to seem legit, I need to know pretty much everything, Swann."

I wipe my mouth one more time. I know he is super serious when he calls me by my last name. And the truth is, he's right. People may ask questions and for both our sakes, we need to make sure our relationship seems as real as possible.

"Okay." I point a finger at him. "Now when I tell you, you cannot laugh or judge me."

His warm hand encompasses mine. "I would never laugh or judge you. Especially not when it comes to something as personal and intimate as your sex life, Hales."

My insides warm, starting from my fingertips and cascading all throughout my body. *Why does that keep happening? God, this guy is good. No wonder the entire world is in love with him. His charm is irresistible.*

I cannot believe I am about to tell my number to my boss, the-one-and-only Aidan Stone.

I haven't been this nervous in a long time.

I take a deep breath and upon my exhale, I whisper, "One."

"One what?" Aidan takes a drink of his water now.

I look back up at him and repeat, "One".

I see the dots connect in his brain and he slowly gulps down the water. "One?"

"One."

"How is that possible, Swann?"

"Geez Aidan, you are making me sound like some sort of freak. And you promised you wouldn't judge."

"I'm sorry. I am not judging you at all. I don't know Hales, I just figured it would be higher."

"And why would you figure that?"

Now Aidan is looking away and there is a slight tint of pink on his cheeks. Is Aidan Stone blushing? "Because you're you."

I'm speechless. What is that supposed to mean? I am too chicken to find out, so I reach for the remote and gesture to the TV. "Up for another one? How about *You've Got Mail*. Let's make it a Nora Ephron marathon."

"Wait, don't you want to know my number?"

"No, need. I already know it's up in the hundreds," I say matter-of-factly.

Aidan hits his chest as if I struck him with a bullet. "Ouch, Hales. Damn, is that what you really think of me?"

How can I not? In the three years I've known Aidan, I've seen him date Natasha and "date" a slew of other women these past six months. God knows he is a fricken heartthrob. All the girls at UConn were foaming at the mouth just at the sight of him, I'm sure. I bet he was the prom king, captain of the lacrosse team or insert whatever sport in high school, and now living in L.A. there is undoubtedly a line of women happy to entertain him for the evening. I've seen the premieres and the photos of him getting practically bulldozed by adoring fans.

"Is it not? Ok, maybe in the fifties." I try to hide a playful smile as I press the "Ok" button on the Roku remote. A picture of Tom Hanks and Meg Ryan graces Aidan's flatscreen.

"Well, well, look who is judging now. Not even close, Swann. Why would you think my number is so high? Is it because of my dashing good looks and charming personality? Is it because I am an international movie star and I just can't control myself when women throw themselves at me?"

"Okay, lover boy, what is it then? Thirty-five? Twenty?"

Aidan moves the empty popcorn bowl to the coffee table and drapes part of the blanket over his own legs. "You'll find out soon enough. Let's just watch the movie." The lines around his eyes deepen and his dimples are on full display.

"You're not going to tell me? How is that fair? What if someone asks me what your number is?" I start yawning as I check my phone. *Midnight?!* How did it get so late?

"They won't. They'll be too embarrassed to ask. Trust me. Let's start the movie since you are already yawning, old lady. You're giving Mabel a run for her money."

"It's midnight. I'm hardly an old lady!" I gruff as I pull the blanket even more over my body. Now it's just my head peeking out. "Fine. Let's watch Tom Hanks and Meg Ryan hate each other, then fall in love."

I press play and snuggle back into the couch. Even though I am covered with this blanket, I get goosebumps when I realize how close I am to actually laying my head on Aidan's shoulder. It's mere centimeters. He smells so clean. I can feel his body heat radiate, like my own personal heater. I've never felt so comfortable in a stranger's house so quickly in my life. Then again, Aidan is hardly a stranger. But for some reason–maybe it's the candle, the coffee, the blanket, the conversation–this apartment feels like home.

13

Aidan

We didn't see Tom Hanks and Meg Ryan fall in love. Haley fell asleep somewhere on my shoulder at about the point when Meg Ryan was commenting on how much she loved New York in the fall and I followed suit shortly after Tom Hanks and Meg Ryan were discussing *Pride and Prejudice* and Starbucks.

It's raining again. I slowly raise my arm to check my almost dead Apple watch. Already 7:30 A.M., but it seems earlier since the sky is covered with dark clouds.

Haley is cuddling with me. I haven't cuddled with a woman since Natasha. But even then, it didn't feel this comfortable. Whenever Natasha and I would fall asleep in each other's arms, she would always let go at some point during the night and retreat to the opposite side of the bed.

Not Haley.

She stayed put all night, apparently. I woke up to her slight snore. It's the cutest snore I've ever heard. Her leg is draped over mine and her arm is wrapped around my torso, hand clutching my t-shirt. It is then I notice my hard-on. Jesus Christ, she cannot wake up to the sight of my hard dick under my sweatpants. She is going to freak out and never want to be next to me again. I need to get up now, but I don't want to wake her. This is perfect. She is perfect.

When she walked out last night from my room, wearing my t-shirt and close to nothing else, with her hair in a mess, I almost exploded. Her legs are long and toned and just goddamn amazing to look at. *OMG Aidan, snap out of it! This arrangement isn't real.* The whole reason she is in my apartment is because we are pretending to be together, and also I wanted to protect her from the rain and the creepers she might've encountered if she tried to walk back to her hotel last night. I'm about to be perceived as one of those said creepers if I don't get off this couch immediately and handle this situation.

I carefully slide my trapped arm out from under Haley's torso and inch off the couch. I cover her back up with the blanket and place a pillow under her arm that was draped over me. She won't suspect a thing. I grab my phone from the coffee table and plug it into the charger in my kitchen. Maybe I should order from Ess-a-bagel. One thing about Haley is the girl can eat. She is like one of the Gilmore Girls with food. That's always refreshing about Haley.

After ordering two everything bagels with cream cheese, I make more coffee for Haley and place the mug on the coffee table. Damn, she looks so peaceful. I don't want to wake her up. I'm sure the smell of coffee will do that for me.

I write her a note and set it next to the coffee and head toward my bathroom to jump in the shower.

14

Haley

I smell the heavenly scent of coffee.

A little disoriented, I wake up from the best night of sleep that I've gotten in a while, which is surprising since I usually can't sleep well anywhere except for my own bed that has the perfect pillow, the perfect mattress, the perfect duvet. Yet here I am on Aidan's couch, waking up from the most restful sleep. I don't remember finishing the movie last night. Aidan must have covered me up and slept in his bed. Oh God! I hope I didn't snore. I've been told that I snore in my sleep when I am sleeping really hard. A wave of embarrassment rushes through my body. At some point during the night, I must've removed my hair from my messy bun because now it is down and in a ratty mess. It is probably sticking up on all sides. I do my best to tame my tresses with my hands so it doesn't look like I went through a wind tunnel or was a part of a fricken rock music video.

I glance around the apartment. *Where the heck is Aidan?* Maybe he went on a run or something.

I take a sip of the steaming coffee that Aidan must've made for me, and that's when I notice a post-it note.

Good morning. I ordered bagels. Delivery man should be here soon. I paid ahead of time. I left money for the tip on the kitchen island. I'm going to shower. Be out in a bit. :) Aidan

Oh good, I am starving. I hear a knock at the door. Perfect timing. With my stomach gurgling, I grab the cash from the island and open the door without looking through the peephole.

The mid-fifties woman standing in the hallway looks oddly familiar. It's something about her eyes. I feel like I've met her or seen her before, which is weird because I haven't been back to NYC in three years.

"Hi!" I blurt. "Um, we've already paid for the bagels, but here's the tip." I extend my hand with the cash out to this woman, who now looks at me with amusement covering her entire face. Her eyes scan my whole figure–from my crazy hair all the way down to my bare legs and feet.

"Hi. Is my son here?"

Now, I want to crawl into a hole and never come out. The familiar eyes make perfect sense. How could I be so stupid? I look down and process that Aidan's mother is meeting me when I am half-naked. Wearing her son's oversized UConn t-shirt that is covering a fraction of my upper thigh. *Great first impression, Haley.* This has to be my most embarrassing life moment to date. She must think I had sex with her son. Oh my God. Does she think I'm just another one of those girls who want to sleep with her son for funsies? Just because he is Aidan Stone? I can only imagine what she must think of me right now.

Her brow wrinkles. "Are you okay, honey?"

"I...I...I am okay. Hi, Mrs. Stone, come on in. I am so sorry. This isn't what it looks like. I swear." Flustered, I reach out my hand as I close the door. "Hi, I'm Haley. Haley Swann. I'm your son's..."

"Girlfriend." I hear Aidan proclaim as he walks into the living room, smelling absolutely amazing. Like cashmere and rain. He must've trimmed his beard a little. I'm glad he didn't shave it all off. He's wearing gray sweatpants and a dark teal shirt, which brings out his perfect blue eyes. He has a huge smile on his face as he embraces his mother. "Hey Mom."

"Oh my boy. It's so good to see you!" She turns her attention toward me and I notice how miniscule she seems next to Aidan. I wonder if his dad was a fricken center for a basketball team. "You said this young lady is your girlfriend? Your name is Haley?"

"Yes, ma'am." I nod as I awkwardly pull Aidan's shirt down to try and cover my legs. I must be the color of a beet because Aidan's smirk will not leave his stupid face. Is he enjoying this? What a punk. "I'm Aidan's girlfriend. And I am sorry for..." I gesture to my just-rolled-out-of-bed-but-defintely-did-not-sleep-with-your-son-even-though-it-looks-like-I-did-look.

"It's okay, sweetie. I know you two are grown adults." *Sweet lord! No that's not what happened, I swear!* "Have we met before, because I swear you look somewhat familiar? And I know I've heard your name before."

"Well, I am...was...am Aidan's..." God, can I not form a full sentence today?

Aidan came to my rescue. "She *was* my assistant, Mom. But we're together now, so we're still working out the kinks to our new situation, I guess." He shrugs and puts his hand behind his head, as if he is also a bit nervous about our new *situation*.

There is a flicker of recognition in his mother's eyes, even though we've never met before. "Ah yes, the famous Haley!" She pulls me into a hug. Did I mention I am still pantless? "It's so great to finally meet you. Aidan hasn't stopped talking about you since you started working for him."

My eyes shoot directly to Aidan, and now he is crimson. I press my lips together to stifle a laugh. I've never seen him so flustered before. He's been talking about me?

"He goes on and on about how amazing you are," his mom continues, as if answering my thoughts.

"Well, she's been such an amazing assistant," Aidan interjects, rubbing the back of his neck. "I don't know how I would get through my days without her."

I tuck my hair behind my ear and smile. "Just doing my job."

She holds onto my hand and her eyes twinkle with gratitude. "Thank you for taking care of my son out there in L.A. It keeps a mother's mind at peace knowing that her child is safe and okay. Also, thank you for putting up with him these past few months, especially with all of his shenanigans." She gave her son an accusatory look. "Wait, something doesn't add up, how long have you two been dating?"

"Um, a few weeks. It's really new, Mom."

"Aidan Miles Stone. Do you mean to tell me that you were running around with multiple women WHILE you were dating Haley?! I saw the tabloids. Shame on you. I know I raised you better than that."

I have to intervene because Aidan looks like he's going to pass out. I think I catch a glimpse of how he looked as a little boy when he got scolded by this woman in front of me. "No, Mrs. Stone."

"Please call me Ellie, dear."

I give a quick smile. "Ellie...That was all a ruse. We didn't want anyone to know about this–" I point between me and Aidan frantically. "–yet. So, he had to be seen with those other women so that no one would find out about us. We weren't sure how everyone was going to take it. But I guess everything turned out fine and now we can really be together. Out in the open. For everyone to see."

I pull the best fake smile I can out of my ass and try to be as convincing as possible in front of this sweet woman. I walk over and wrap my arm around Aidan's ridiculously muscular torso and tilt my head against his chest. I feel Aidan's massive hand wrap around my own waist and tug me tighter toward his body. My pulse is racing. He's pretending too. He's such a natural. I'm sure she can see right through me. Silly me for thinking drama class was stupid in high school. It could've really come in handy right about now.

"Yeah, Mom, just wanted to make sure Haley was ready for our relationship to be out there in the world." *Yeah, something like that.*

"Oh thank God," Ellie says. "I love you sweetie, but if you would've started seriously dating one of those bimbo model types, I would've had to say something. You already know how I felt about Natasha."

What? I look up at Aidan and see his jaw tighten. So his mother didn't approve of Natasha. Maybe a mother's intuition that she was going to be bad news. Interesting. For some reason, I can't shake the hope for her approval of me to stand the test of time. I don't know why that matters to me so much. It's not like I'm ever going to see her again.

There is a knock at the door.

"That must be the bagels. Excuse me." I hurriedly make my way to the door and answer it, obstructing the view into the apartment as much as possible. Even though I am not technically supposed to act like his assistant right now, I still have this overwhelming need to protect his privacy in some way. "Thank you! Here's your tip! Have a great day."

I set the bag of bagels on the island counter. Gosh I am starving, but I have to get rid of my horrid morning breath as soon as possible and change back into my clothes. "Um, will you both excuse me for a second? I'm going to run to the bathroom."

As I shut the door of Aidan's bedroom behind me, I exhale. Alone for a moment, I can relax. I turn to the bed, and noticed that Aidan has my clothes folded and ready for me on his bed. *That's sweet.* His thoughtfulness is something I noticed about Aidan right away and in the three years since – even during his "shenanigans" – it has never faltered. He has an innate ability to be kind to others. He treats everyone on set like they are just as important as the CEOs of the media companies and studio execs. No matter how famous he has become, he remains the same sweet Aidan Stone.

I scavenge around Aidan's bathroom in hopes that I'll find a spare toothbrush, and luck is on my side because Aidan has multiple spare toothbrushes. Maybe for all the women who have slept in his bed? Women who have spent the night after having sex with the hottest actor on planet Earth? *Why does that bug me so much?* I've never cared about the various women Aidan has been with. Why do I care now? I spit the last bit of toothpaste out and rinse my mouth out. I look in the mirror and gasp at the egregious reflection. My hair is sticking up in all kinds of ways and I never washed off my minimal makeup from last night. It does look like I have sex hair. Not the best image to offer up to the mother of my fake boyfriend. But, again, why do I care?

Maybe because deep down, I want this to work out for Aidan. I want people to see him for the absolute gem of a person he is, and not judge him for a few bad decisions. He went through a devastating heartbreak, and I know what that feels like more than anyone.

15

Aidan

"Will you stop laughing? It's not funny."

I contort my face into what seems like a million different expressions, trying to stop my laugh from escaping my mouth. "It is funny."

Haley reaches over and punches my arm. I barely felt anything but she retracts her hand quickly and shakes it. "Ow. What about your mother meeting me for the first time, half-naked, in your t-shirt, with my hair sticking up on all ends is amusing to you?" She covers her face in her long-sleeved striped shirt. She took her sandals off about a half hour ago and her bare legs are propped up on the seat. I can't help but notice, her shorts are so short that it looks like she's wearing nothing. Again. God, those legs are going to kill me. "She probably thinks I'm some sort of loose woman just using you for one thing."

I belted out a loud laugh. I can't imagine anyone talking about Haley like that. Especially now that I know what her number is, that idea is even more comical. "Oh my God, Hales. She doesn't think that. Trust me."

I'm not lying. Haley went to quickly change into her dried clothes, I was able to talk to my mom. I didn't tell her about the deal Haley and I made. It was the first time that I've lied to my mom in my adult life. But I couldn't betray Haley's trust. Haley's trust means the world to me. My mom told me how happy she was that I found a down-to-earth girl who seems to be normal. She thought Haley was adorable, and she could tell she's a good person. Even though I have done very well in my career, I know the one thing my mom worries about more than anything is that I try to live a normal life. She never wants me to get caught up in the "toxic influence" of Hollywood. That's why I wanted to change the way I was living these past six months. I do not want to end up like my piece-of-shit dad, sleeping with woman after woman with no regard for their feelings, and I was sick of what the tabloids were saying about my love life (or lack thereof) even if their stories were, unfortunately, somewhat rooted in the truth. That wasn't the mirror I was afraid of looking into. My mom is my ultimate mirror, and I knew that she was disappointed in me, even if she didn't flat-out say so.

Now, I glance over at Haley and her knee is bobbing up and down. I've noticed she only does that when she is nervous. I reach my hand over and grab her thigh. A gasp escapes her lips, and she grows still. I was expecting her to move her thigh out from under my hand, but she doesn't budge. Maybe she is getting used to me touching her in this way, trying to not appear completely repulsed by my touch. Even though my eyes are on the road, I can sense that she is looking at me.

"Relax, Hales. Everything is going to be fine. My mom really liked you." *Loved you actually.* "Now remind me again what is happening tonight."

She groans. "Even though we've gone over the schedule ad nauseam? And I put it in our synced calendars?"

"Even though," I confirm. I know that running through the schedule again will help distract and calm her.

Sighing, she says, "Tonight is the welcome dinner. This is probably the most crucial night, Aidan. You are going to meet everyone–I mean EVERYONE–from my past."

We reach the rental house and park in the driveway. This house is huge. It has white siding all around, black shutters, and two black lanterns that frame a black door. The flower beds are filled with purple and white flowers. There are some clouds in the sky and the small breeze from the ocean makes the tree branches sway.

I am about to meet two of the most important people in Haley's life, and that makes me more nervous than pretending to date her for the tabloids. They've been her world for her whole life. For the first time, Haley is going to be the star of the show. The main character. My job is to be the supporting character. It's territory that I haven't occupied in a long time, but I am happy to do whatever I can to make Haley feel better.

Haley looks at me. "Are you ready for this, Stone? I need you to act like you are trying to win an Oscar. Got it?"

I grab her hand and kiss the top of it, throwing her a little off-guard. But instead of tensing up like she normally would, I sense her body ease. She's finally letting me touch her without flinching. That's the only way this thing between us is actually going to work this weekend. Capturing moments of us through photos is one thing. Being around family and friends for a long weekend is a whole other beast.

I squeeze her hand a little, hopefully assuring her that

everything will be okay. "Same goes for you, Swann. And to answer your question, this is going to be the easiest acting job I've ever done."

I don't know what reaction I expect from her, but it isn't this: she reaches over the console and wraps her arms around me so tight it takes my breath away. She whispers in my ear, "Thank you for doing this, Aidan."

I strengthen my hold on her. She smells like fresh cucumber and mint body wash and her hair smells like her pomegranate shampoo, which is unexpectedly comforting. They are scents that have been in my life for the past three years, and I never want them to go away. "You're welcome, Hales."

Unfortunately she breaks the hug and unbuckles her seat belt. "I know Anna is here since we share locations, but my mom texted me that she ran to the store for some groceries. She should be back soon. Let's do this." She opens the car door and gets out.

I take a deep breath, turn off the ignition and exit the car. I hear a loud scream and see a petite blonde run out from the front door and beeline it to my girl. Well, at least for the next five days, she is my girl. I immediately smile, watching Haley embrace her best friend. It's honestly the happiest I've ever seen her. I want her to smile like that forever. I want to *make* her smile like that.

That smile makes my heart want to jump out of my fricken chest.

Then a man, who I assume is Dan from the plethora of photos Haley made me study this past week, follows his fiancée out of the house. He embraces Haley for a split second, then Anna peels him off her best friend so she can resume hugging. It's nice to see Haley so loved; she deserves that. I pop the trunk and get all our luggage and clothing bags out. Haley told me that Anna has her Maid-of-Honor dress here, so I just needed to bring some dress clothes for the weekend.

I start making my way toward the trio and I hear, "Oh my God!" from Anna. She walks right around Haley and comes straight towards me.

I reach out my hand and start to say, "Hi. I'm Aidan. It's nice to mee–"

My introduction is interrupted by her lips landing on mine. *What the fuck?* Unfortunately, this has not been the first time a random girl has kissed me without warning. It's happened multiple times while getting bombarded by crazy fanatics at press events, or even on the street for that matter. I've learned the art of gently, gracefully pulling away.

"Um, Anna? What are you doing?" Haley frantically makes her way over to my side.

"Yeah, Anna. What the hell?!" Dan exclaims. "You realize that I am right here, right?"

Anna's eyes finally pop open. Her face turns beet red and her hand clasps over her mouth. A muffled "Oh my God" comes out through her fingers. She finally removes her hand and looks over at Haley, who appears horrified and confused and might I say, a little pissed.

"Hales, I am so sorry. I saw him walking toward us and totally thought I was dreaming and took a chance." She shrugs and we all start laughing. "I am completely mortified. I am so sorry. Hi. It's so nice to meet you. I'm Anna Morgan. I'm Haley's best friend." She formally shakes my hand, which was my original game plan anyway, and then turns to Haley and says, "You know this is Aidan Stone, right?"

Haley puts her hand to her face and lets out a laugh. "Yes, Anna. I am well aware of that fact. He's my date and..." Her eyes lock with mine and I nod slightly. "...and my boyfriend."

Anna's jaw drops to the floor. She mouths, "No way." She steps aside with Haley and I hear in faint whispers: *"What? How long have you been dating? How could you not tell me? This is huge news! You are dating Aidan fucking Stone, Haley! It is a big deal!"* and I am finally able to shake Dan's hand.

"Woah, bro, it's an honor to meet you. I love all your movies, man. You are really talented. Holy shit, everyone is going to flip out that you're here. Sorry about my fiancée. She doesn't know the definition of boundaries."

I laugh. "It's all right, man. Congratulations. Thank you for having me here. Haley has told me wonderful things about you both. I promise I will keep a low profile here. This weekend is about you and Anna, and I don't intend on casting a shadow over the most important weekend of your life." I pull Haley in for a side hug. "Haley and I made a stealthy getaway out of Manhattan, so I guarantee there won't be any paparazzi around. Pretend I'm not even here."

"Yeah, like that's possible, *Aidan Stone!*" Anna exclaims. "I want to hear all about how you two met, but let's go ahead and get inside. I'll show you all to your room." She turns toward Haley and raises her eyebrows mischievously. Haley blushes slightly and shakes her head, reaching down to grab her luggage.

"Don't even think about it, Swann," I mutter low so only she can hear, hoisting her bags along with mine.

She smiles. "Thanks."

"And this is y'all's room." Anna opens the door to one of the guest bedrooms. Correction. This is definitely the master bedroom. The large sliding glass door overlooks the ocean, with a private balcony just for us. The sheer curtains are blowing inward from the small breeze and the sound of the waves crashing against the shore fills the room. I roll the luggage into the small closet and hang up my clothing bags. There is a small sitting area off to the side next to the sliding door, and a large canopy bed in the middle of the room. *Shit, there's no couch.* I guess I'll be sleeping on the floor. I want to respect Haley's space.

"Why don't you two settle in and relax before tonight's dinner. Hales, I'll let you know when your mom gets here, okay?"

"Okay, thanks Anna," Haley says, plopping her bag down on the massive bed.

Anna gives me a little wink as she shuts the door.

"Oh my god, Aidan, I am so sorry about what happened outside! I cannot believe that she kissed you!"

I laugh. "It's okay Hales, really. Surprisingly enough, that is not the first time that's happened to me."

"Are you serious? So random women just come up and make out with you without your consent?"

It's cute she thinks that what happened earlier could be considered "making out." She doesn't know what making out looks like for me. I guess she never will; although the kiss we shared at the afterparty was a pretty good start. God, that kiss has kept me wanting more for days now. I want to show her what a real make-out session looks like. I'm sure I could shift her perspective of what that term means.

I shrug. "Yeah, it happens occasionally. It's always really jarring and I've never gotten used to all the hysteria. I mean, at the end of the day, I am just a person. I think people misconstrue who I really am with who I portray on screen. A lot of women love the idea of me rather than the reality. All they see is the guy on the movie posters and magazine covers. They just want fifteen minutes of fame. They just want one night—or if they do want a relationship, it's for the wrong reasons." I sit next to her on the bed, making her sink a little closer to me. "I want a woman who really loves me for *me,* and not because I make blockbuster movies or have more money than I ever thought possible."

"And not because you are the sexiest man alive," Haley adds. "I mean, according to People magazine. Not that I don't think you deserve the title. I mean, look at you. Not that I am checking you out or anything or have any merit to make that assessment. Oh my gosh, this is coming out wrong."

She is starting to spiral, so I save her from herself. "It's okay Hales, I know exactly what you mean." I look around the room. "So, I guess whenever we turn in for the night, I'll grab a couple of pillows and blankets for a nice little makeshift bed on the floor."

"Aidan, don't be ridiculous."

My heart thrums–I wasn't expecting *that* to come out of her mouth.

Haley must notice the surprise on my face, because she explains, "What if Anna decides to pop in unannounced? We can't have you sleeping on the floor. Then she will definitely be suspicious." Then she looks down at the king-sized bed we are sitting on, maybe regretting what she just said. "Um, maybe we could put pillows in between us."

"Whatever makes you feel comfortable." I can't imagine telling her that we actually slept next to each other last night. She would be mortified. Even though that was the best night's sleep I've gotten in a long time. If only she knew how much I want to scoop her up and wrap my arms around her right now in this bed. I can't let myself wander into those thoughts, though. She's made it perfectly clear how she feels about me in that regard. Damn contract.

"Knock, knock." I turn and see a woman who looks exactly like Haley. It's like I'm looking twenty-five years into the future. Haley's a dead ringer for her mom; the only difference is the eyes. Her mom has hazel eyes. I preferred Haley's dark caramel colored eyes.

"Mom!" Haley runs over to her doppelganger of a mother and nearly knocks her over. The smile illuminating Haley's face is unmatched. Forget the smile that I witnessed earlier. *This* is the smile I want to see on her face all the time.

"Oh Haley girl! I am so excited that you are here and you made it safely. Honey, you seem thin, are you sure you're eating enough out in L.A.?"

"Yes, Mom, I'm eating plenty, trust me."

I let out an involuntary laugh because in the three years I've known Haley, she's never been one to skip any meals. "I can personally vouch for that. This girl eats enough for an entire football team. There's no need to worry Mrs. Swann." I step forward and extend my hand to her. "I'm Aidan Stone. It's an honor to meet you, ma'am."

"It's a pleasure to finally meet you. And please, *ma'am* makes me sound so old. Call me LeAnn. I don't know why Haley kept you a secret from me. She usually tells me everything." She glances at Haley, who gives a little shrug.

"Well, Mom. We had to be discreet about our relationship, especially since Aidan is...was...sort of my boss."

LeAnn's eyes grow wide. "Wait, this is the actor you work for?" She covers her mouth in astonishment. *Here it comes.* "Oh my goodness. I didn't even process when you told me your name. You're Aidan Stone. I saw you on the cover of People Magazine. And in the tabloids with a bunch of random women, who dare I say, were not my daughter."

Shit. I revert back to when I was a child getting in trouble with my own mother for misbehaving. There is a sudden rush to beg for forgiveness from this woman. I don't want her to think the worst of me based on my most recent behavior. Before Haley can defend me, I have to man up and tell her the truth...well, the truth that Haley and I established with my own mother less than twelve hours ago.

"I know what you're thinking. Based on all the press that you have seen about me as of late, I'm not good enough for your daughter."

I look directly into LeAnn's eyes and notice a flicker of surprise. I don't think she was expecting me to say that, being who I am. I'm sure she has preconceived notions about me, just like the rest of the world does. That's the main flaw of being so famous–there is zero margin for error, for mistakes, for being human. If you make any misstep, it's hard to come back from. The world doesn't forget.

I lean toward Haley and take her hand in mine. Then I look back at her mother and continue, "LeAnn, your daughter is probably the best person that I've ever met in my life." Now for the little white lie. Actually, the big white lie–the same lie Haley told my mom this morning. We have to keep our story straight. "Those other women by my side these past six months were there to ward off the paparazzi and leave a trail of fake breadcrumbs, so to speak. I didn't want to jeopardize our relationship or Haley's privacy by having the world track our every move and infiltrate themselves where they frankly don't belong–in our love life." I feel Haley's hand flinch a little when I say the word *love*. It just slipped out. Maybe from all those scripts Chris has been sending me. The perfect words are spewing out of my mouth and I can't stop. I don't want to stop until LeAnn believes me.

I *need* her to believe me.

"Those women don't mean anything to me. They were pawns in a game of chess. All set up by my publicity team." I let go of Haley's hand, wrap my arm around her shoulders, and pull her in close. It's scary how much I like how she fits next to me. It seems natural and easy. I look down at Haley and her face is full of gratitude. She isn't tense in my embrace–finally, she is totally relaxed, which I hope will help sell this whole arrangement.

The crease in between LeAnn's eyebrows fades as she notices how relaxed her daughter is in my arms.

"Mom," Haley chimes in, "Aidan's right. Those other women were orchestrated to be in Aidan's life so our relationship could be protected. But since Anna's wedding was right around the corner, we decided it was time the world knew about our relationship. It may seem out of the blue, but–" Haley looks back into my eyes, searching for my permission to continue. It's as if we're talking in code. "–we couldn't keep it a secret anymore. Aidan's image was being tarnished and dragged through the mud, and plus I hated keeping this from you."

Guilt.

Instead of relief, I feel guilt. Guilt for making Haley lie to her mom about our "relationship." She is keeping a secret from her mom and it is all for me. If only LeAnn truly knew how much I wasn't lying when I said Haley is the best thing to ever happen to me. I don't deserve her–that much is true.

LeAnn smiles. "Well, in that case, welcome to the family, Aidan.

I look forward to getting to know you more. One thing you should know about my daughter is that she doesn't let people in easily. Her walls are usually impenetrable."

"Geez, Mom. Thanks a lot."

"That being said, you seem to have found a way to basically demolish those walls. Not many people have been able to accomplish that. You should consider yourself lucky."

Hugging Haley a little tighter, I respond, "Trust me, I do."

Haley

"Phew, I think we are in the clear." As soon as my mom closes the door behind her, I wriggle myself out of Aidan's embrace. I'm starting to feel too comfortable in his little nook. *No thank you.* I know that he was trying to convince my mom that our relationship is real, but what's really freaking me out is the fact that I was becoming just as convinced, even though I know what the truth is. Never in a million years would Aidan Stone actually date me or think those things about me.

Never.

Aidan clears his throat. "Yeah, I think we are." The energy shifts in the room, and I don't know why. There is tension rather than relief. And it is coming from Aidan's side of the room.

"Sorry about my mom. She can be a little intense, but that's because it's just been me and her for a while now. She worries about me. I think a little too much."

"She's a mom. That's their specialty." Aidan pulls his suitcase on top of the bed, unzips it and takes out some fresh clothes. The tension is starting to ease a little. I'm hoping it will dissipate completely before the welcome dinner in an hour. I look out the window—caterers have already shown up and are setting up their stations with silver buffet trays on the lawn. This is going to be an interesting night.

I take three deep breaths and look into the mirror. "You can do this." I decided to wear one of the dresses Rachel helped me pick out for this weekend. She took me shopping after she went through my closet and declared that I only own cardigans, which apparently is a problem. She had me try on this strapless light green dress with magnolia flowers that holds onto whatever curves I do have as if its life depends on it. I never wear dresses like this...ever.

To compensate for my lack of confidence, I chose shoes that are my favorite to wear with any dress: ballet flats. Not very glamorous, but I don't care; they are comfy and easy to walk in. Rachel isn't here to veto and I honestly don't want to plummet to my embarrassment in front of all my close family and friends, and oh yeah my stupid ex-fiancé, who will indubitably bring his new girlfriend with him to witness my downfall... literally and figuratively. Although I don't know if I could fall any further than the last time I saw Robert. I shake my head to clear that appalling memory from my brain.

I keep my makeup simple, natural, just like I always do it. I do put on a little lip liner and lip stain to step things up a little. But I want to look like myself. There's no point in trying extra hard; it's not like I'm trying to find a man. I already have one—well, kind of. And he doesn't care how I look one bit. Although I am pretty sure everyone else will notice how haggard I look compared to the Henry Cavill god of a man next to me.

A faint knock on the door helps ground me back to reality. "Hales, you ready?"

I take one last deep breath and unlock the bathroom door. Upon opening, I am grateful I took that breath a moment ago, since I am currently rendered breathless. Yes, Aidan looked amazing in a suit and tie, and honestly whatever else he wears. But tonight hits different. He is laid back and looks like he's belonged in the Hamptons all his life. An image flashes in my mind of what he might have looked like growing up here on the East Coast. It's a different type of beachy vibe than L.A. He's wearing perfectly pressed khakis and a light-blue button-down, with his sleeves rolled up to the middle of his forearms. Little tornadoes form in my stomach, demolishing anything sensical in their wake. The hue of his shirt also makes his eyes seem extra blue. And this is who I need to pretend to date for the next few days? How is anyone going to believe us? *I* wouldn't believe us.

Act normal, Haley. Act like it doesn't affect your body in ways you haven't felt in a long time. For goodness sakes, you've been around this man for the past three years. His presence shouldn't make you melt into an absolute puddle.

Then why oh why is that happening at this very moment?

I clear my throat and walk over to the bed to grab my phone. "You look...decent."

Behind me, I hear Aidan huff out a small laugh and walk over to me. He stops right behind me, so close that goosebumps sprout up my arms. A visceral reaction. Yet he never laid his hands on me. What the hell is going on with my body?

"Well you look *decent* too, Hales." The way he said "decent" should be illegal.

I turn around to face him.

His electric eyes pierce mine and he continues, "Every man, married or otherwise, is going to be kicking themselves in the ass for not locking it down with you once they see you walk out on that lawn." His eyes ferally survey my entire body, head all the way down to my toes, ending their journey back at my eyes. "Good thing you're taken."

Why does he keep talking to me like this? If it's to make me even more nervous than I already am, he's doing an excellent job.

I move around him and open the bedroom door. "Yeah, good thing. C'mon, I don't want to be late."

We walk onto the beautifully landscaped and decorated backyard. If I thought I had butterflies before, these new ones in my stomach are raging and not going away. I want to throw up. I seriously haven't seen the majority of these people since one of our friends from college got married. When I was still engaged.

A waiter comes around with tall flutes of champagne. I grab one and immediately down the entire glass. The bubbles harshly crawl down my throat. This is why I absolutely loathe champagne. A fact that I need to ignore tonight, especially if I want to survive the whispers, stares, and inevitable encounter with my ex and the woman who stole him from me. I grab another flute, and so does Aidan.

"Thanks, man," he says to the waiter, who finally recognizes Aidan in all of his glory. The waiter backs away, mesmerized, almost running into another waiter in the process.

I lean over to Aidan. "Geez, if that's how a male waiter reacts to you, I can't imagine what all the women are going to do." I take just a sip of the champagne this time. Chugging champagne was a dumb idea. Almost as dumb as fake-dating my boss.

"I think he was reacting that way because of you and that dress, Swann." Aidan takes a sip and winks at me.

I snorted. "Yeah right. You're sweet for saying so." Do I actually look that good for Aidan to keep mentioning it? I'm going to text Rachel in a little bit to thank her for pushing me to get a dress I wouldn't normally pick out. It's amazing how a piece of clothing can elicit reactions from people. I just wasn't expecting this dress to elicit any reaction from Aidan. He is a great actor because his compliments seem legitimately genuine.

We walk around and are greeted by a plethora of people from my past. All gawking at Aidan, while also saying how good it is to see me. One of my old classmates, Krystal, who has always been a little clueless and impervious to reading social situations, even has the gall to ask, "How are you doing? Have you seen Robert yet? I can't even imagine how you must be feeling, being here after everything that happened."

My mouth turns dry even though I've been drinking water after my second glass of champagne. I will get more later at dinner. I needed to take the edge off, but I don't want to be drunk for this event. This is about Anna, not about me. And that's what people don't understand when they ask me these types of questions. I mean, I don't mind talking about it behind closed doors with Anna, my mom or even Aidan, but I don't want what happened between me and Robert to be a topic of conversation at my best friend's wedding.

I purse my lips and I feel a little tug on my right hip from Aidan. He must've felt my body tense up at the mention of my own personal Voldemort.

Aidan pipes up, "You know what, I'm sorry–what was your name again, Krissa?"

"Krystal...with a K," she corrects Aidan, while also batting her fake eyelashes in his direction and standing up straighter to make her cleavage become even more prominent in her deep V-neck dress.

"Krystal, that's right. Would you mind terribly if I steal my girlfriend away for a little bit. There are a few more people that she wants to introduce me to– right, babe?"

I nod. "Yes...babe." Bleh that sounded weird for me to say to Aidan Stone. But here I am saying *babe.* "I'll talk to you later, Krystal."

Aidan grabs my hand tightly and leads me to the other end of the lawn, away from the inquirer. I knew people were going to ask, but I still wasn't ready for it.

"Thanks, Aidan."

"Well I could sense that you were uncomfortable with the topic, and I don't like seeing you uncomfortable."

I smile, even though on the inside I am screaming. Why did the universe send me the sweetest man on the planet as a boss? The more I get to know Aidan and spend time with him, the more I am finding that he is my comfort. And that terrifies me.

"Um, are you going to be okay on your own? I need to run to the ladies' room. All that champagne and water running through me." *Oh my god, Haley!! Did you really have to disclose that information? You could've just left it at "ladies' room." But nooooo, you have to be Awkward Haley.*

"I'll be fine," Aidan assures me. "Don't worry about me."

"But what if..."

Before I can finish my thought, he does something completely unexpected: he grabs the side of my cheek with one of his large hands and kisses my forehead. Then looks at me with those ridiculously precarious pools that are his eyes and says, "I'll be fine, Hales. I'm a big boy and I can handle myself." He grins. "Now go pee."

All I can muster up is, "Ha ha" and then I saunter over to the main house. For some reason, that casual cheek kiss seemed infinitely more intimate than the one I plastered on him at the premiere. We haven't kissed since then, but this kiss. This kiss was different. How can such a burly man be so delicate at the same time?

When I walk back out on the back porch, my eyes search for Aidan. I spot him by the pop-up bar, surrounded by almost every woman in attendance. I shake my head but also smile, because– at least for this weekend– he's mine.

Kind of.

"Hi, Haley."

Goosebumps immediately cover my body, but not because of

Aidan's presence. This voice has a completely different effect than Aidan's voice does. It is a voice I was hoping to never hear say my name again.

Robert inches closer to me, stopping when we're standing a foot away from each other. Damn, he looks amazing. I was hoping that he inherited male pattern baldness and it would've manifested in the past three years. I was hoping that he stopped going to the gym and developed a beer belly. But alas, none of that happened, much to my dismay. He looks as handsome as ever. Damn him. His sandy blonde hair is pomaded into a perfect bouffant and his hazel eyes stare down intimately at me as if he didn't completely shatter my entire being. He is a little taller than me; definitely not as tall as Aidan, whose stature I'm still getting used to. Robert now seems rather small, which is a new development because at one point he was my entire world. A man I stupidly put on a pedestal. A man I thought I was going to share my life with. A man who made me feel giddy and excited about life and about the future.

Why the hell did he say he loved me, and then completely rip the rug out from under me? After all, he was the one who proposed. Was that his master scheme–to get a girl to fall in love with him and then completely humiliate her to the point where she would move away from everything and everyone she knew just so she wouldn't have to endure the whispers and the stares that are ironically ensuing at this very moment?

"Hi," I barely croak out.

"Here," Robert calls over a waiter balancing yet another full tray of champagne, and grabs two flutes. He hands one to me, which I secretly am grateful for. I definitely need alcohol to get through whatever conversation is about to occur.

"Thanks."

"So, I haven't seen you in a while. What has it been– two, three years?" He takes a swig of his champagne, slightly smirking in the process. This jerk. He knows exactly how long it has been. I could break it down to the exact day. Exact hour. Exact fricken minute.

"Yup." I am starting to get hot on the inside. My ears are probably red right now and I am glad I wore my hair down to hide them. I want to cry but I can't in front of all these people. This is exactly what I didn't want. Becoming a damn spectacle when this event is about Anna. I hate being in the spotlight and being the center of attention, and I can feel the eyes of every person at this welcome dinner on Robert and me, waiting for a big fight. That's the thing about growing up in a small town. Everyone knows everyone's business and thinks it is their right to do so. I look back out to the crowd but can't find Aidan anywhere. I'm starting to panic.

"You look good, Hales."

"Don't call me Hales." Finally, the dam of one-word responses broke.

He looks confused. "Okay...but I've always called you Hales."

"Well you revoked the right to call me Hales three years ago. That name is reserved for close friends and family. You don't fit into those categories." I drink more of my champagne, wishing I could teleport back upstairs and lock myself in the bathroom and just cry. I want to be anywhere but here.

Suddenly I feel large, muscular arms wrap around my torso and waist. I relax into the best nook I could imagine. There is a part of me that doesn't want to ever leave this nook. I am safe and my panic immediately dissipates. I can breathe.

"There you are, Hales. Where did you run off to, babe?" Aidan's voice is music to my ears. Then I feel a quick brush of his lips on my cheek. If I thought that wrapping his arms around me and calling me "babe" was marking his territory, giving me an almost habitual kiss on the cheek is a clear sign to any onlookers that I am his. I mean he just engulfed my entire being and I don't mind one bit. Especially since Robert looks like steam is about to escape his ears like a character on the Looney Toons. He is trying to stand up straighter, almost going on his tiptoes to attempt to match Aidan's stature.

He is intimidated. Big time.

That's the thing about dating someone for a long period of time—you know what their body language is saying.

I expect Aidan to be staring down Robert, but when I look up at his face, he is just smiling down at me. His eyes search mine, trying to decipher if I am okay. A wave of shivers courses through my body for what seems like the millionth time since I started "dating" Aidan.

He is very good at creating chemistry. It's starting to get harder and harder to tell that he is acting.

At this point, not only is Robert staring at the Greek God of a man standing behind me, holding onto me like I am his, but I quickly scan the rest of the guests in attendance and they are all staring at us to see what will happen next. Is Hollywood's Golden Boy about to clobber his girlfriend's ex? Was the ex going to cause a scene and attempt to fight someone who trained like a fricken Navy Seal every time he was preparing for a role? I am a spectator too, wondering what either man's next move is going to be. Here I am—caught in the middle of the most bizarre situation I could have ever imagined.

Again, unexpectedly, Aidan is the first one to break the impasse and reach a hand out towards Robert. "You must be Robert. I'm Aidan. Haley's boyfriend."

Robert's cold, shocked eyes shoot to mine and I can't help but smirk a little. This is the moment those words matter the most. I *need* him to believe that I have moved on from him.

Robert finally stretches out his own hand and shakes Aidan's hand. His face winces as Aidan maintains a firm grip during the handshake. Despite Aidan's cool demeanor, I can sense his absolute disdain for the man standing across from us.

Robert manages to slip his hand away from the iron grip of Aidan. "Yeah. Robert Jameson the third." I roll my eyes. Robert only says his full name when he is trying to impress someone who doesn't know him, or maybe in court. He is starting a contest he is never going to win. Aidan already has him beat by a landslide in so many ways that I've lost track. "I've seen a lot of your movies, man. Not really my cup of tea." *Yeah right, he loves action and superhero movies.* "I've always been more of a book type of person. Um, Haley and I used to..."

"Be engaged. Yeah." Aidan shakes his head slightly. "I've heard a lot about you man." Aidan's tone is far from friendly and it almost seems like he wants to rip Robert's throat out. Aidan's hand makes its way back home to mine and he squeezes in such a caring, almost protective way, I want to melt on that porch right then and there. What is this hold he has on me now? It scares me that I want to see what more will come of it.

Just when I thought I made it out of this situation unscathed, I hear stiletto heels make their way onto the wooden porch. There she is. The other villain in my story. Julia Woods. The accomplice in my undoing.

"Hey honey. There you are! I was just chatting it up with the girls." She leans in to kiss Robert. Actually, no. Not kiss. A full on make-out session with my ex-fiancé ensues in front of me and my boss. This could not be more awkward. Flashbacks haunt my brain and I wince at the sight that is tattooed forever in my memory of these two making out. Except the last time I witnessed this, we were in a very different setting and they were wearing much less clothing.

Aidan clears his throat, seemingly bothered by the scene in front of him, but then he leans down and says the most earth-shattering thing in my ear: "We can definitely do better than that."

That's it. I am becoming undone in a completely different way. Shocked, I look up at him and he is smiling the biggest smile I've seen since we've been here. He knows he is making me flustered, and I am undoubtedly turning the deepest shade of pink. He isn't playing fair. His irresistible charisma is overflowing and I am drowning in it. Now I know why so many people are breathless in his presence. My breath hitches and he continues, "How 'bout it, Swann?"

Before I can answer, the clinking of glasses breaks the connection. My legs are jello and my body is on fire. Anna and Dan are calling everyone to come down to the lawn to eat. Thank god Julia didn't comment on Aidan being my date. She was too busy sucking face with Robert to notice.

We take one step down and I hear, "Oh my god! No way. You're Aidan Stone! Honey, did you see it's Aidan Stone?!"

Dammit. So close. We turn around and give half-hearted smiles to Julia. Robert, clearly annoyed, responds, "Uh, yeah. We just met. Aidan, this is my fiancée, Julia."

And just when I thought I glued the last piece of myself together, a crack rears its ugly head. *Fiancée? Since when? And why didn't Anna warn me?* My knees start to buckle, but Aidan's strong forearm holds me up. I start to see black spots in front of me and my breathing is becoming erratic. I don't know why my body is reacting this way. It's a tale as old as time and, in this particular tale, I am the fucking punchline. I am the fool who thought it would never work out between them. Hoping Robert would become just as heartbroken as I was. Maybe that was selfish, but I didn't care.

The screeching octave of Julia's voice isn't helping my current state. "Aidan Stone! I cannot believe it! I am such a big fan. I love all of your movies. What in the world are you doing here? It's so nice to meet you."

Is she serious? Is she so wrapped up in her own little world that she doesn't see me standing here? I guess she must really not be that observant. Since she had no regard for my presence in the past, why start now?

It is then that I see it on her outstretched left hand, waiting to shake Aidan's hand.

A ring.

And not just any ring.

My ring.

The ring that I threw at Robert three years ago when I discovered them.

Yet again, Robert gave Julia something that was mine. I shouldn't be surprised.

Then why does it hurt so damn much?

I am blinking back stupid, useless tears when Aidan squeezes my hand, again reading my energy and responding to it in the perfect way. He shakes Julia's hand. "Julia, it's nice to meet you. I am here because my beautiful girlfriend is the Maid of Honor in this wedding."

Julia's expression turns from excitement to absolute confusion, rendering her speechless. I don't blame her. I would be confused if I saw a couple like me and Aidan. It is truly unbelievable and yet, everyone is believing it.

"Now if you will excuse us," Aidan says, then turns to me: "I think the bride wanted to talk to you before dinner started, right babe?"

A lie, but I go along with it. Whatever gets me out of my head and back down to earth, I will gladly take it. "Um, yeah, you're right." I courageously look at the couple that ruined my happiness and say, "See you around."

Julia doesn't respond, clearly still dumbfounded by the situation. Maybe now she'll know what it feels like to question everything you thought was true. As we make our way over to where Anna and Dan are sitting, Aidan's fingers make their way into my hair and he kisses the top of my head. So endearing. So, dare I say it again, habitual. I am almost ready to call UConn's theater department and applaud them for training Aidan so well. "You did good, Hales. That must've been hard."

"Yeah, it was."

Robert and Julia follow close behind, and we all reach the happy couple. Anna's eyes shift between the two couples. Her eyes land on mine and she silently apologizes through her expression. She probably didn't want me to feel bad, and maybe she was scared that if she told me, I wouldn't have come out at all. I know deep down she was protecting me and my heart, but it still stings to be a part of this reality.

The silence lasts a little too long for my best friend's liking. "I see you guys have met, Aidan," Anna pipes up. She hates silence. I thrive in it. We are the epitome of yin and yang.

"Yes we have," Robert chimes in, with a hint of unwarranted contention. "I'm just really curious as to how you two met." He points toward Aidan and me. I totally freeze. Even though we reviewed the story what seemed like a thousand times, in this moment I can't get the words out of my mouth. The one time that I need my word vomit to make its ugly appearance, it isn't happening. My mouth is dry and my mind starts to feel hazy.

"Do you want me to tell them, babe?" Aidan, once again, swoops in and saves my day.

All I can do is nod. I don't trust myself right now. Not with all these new revelations and old memories colliding in my brain.

"Haley and I met on set about three years ago. She was carrying one of those flimsy trays full of coffee and we ran into each other." Okay, everything is ringing true so far. That is actually exactly how we met. "Coffee spilled everywhere. All over her. All over me. All over the carpet." Yup, still true. "We were both rushing to get to a table read for my next film and collided. My world hasn't been the same since. The moment I looked at her, I knew she was someone special." Okay, he did a pretty good job. Definitely embellished a little at the end, but still everything he said was legitimate. We agreed to just omit the massive elephant in the room–that we aren't really together. "So special, in fact, that I can still remember everything about her on that day." *What?*

"Care to enlighten us?" Robert inserts. Of course, he would be the one to ask leading questions. He is a lawyer, after all.

Aidan stands a little straighter, tightens his hold on me, and answers, "I remember seeing this woman, trying to swiftly clean up the coffee from my white shirt, repeatedly apologizing, who just looked..." *Ugly? A hot mess? Completely below his league?* Aidan smiles at me. "Effortlessly gorgeous." *What?* Talk about worlds not being the same. Mine just completely tilted on its axis. "She was wearing a light gray cardigan, a loose white scoop neck t-shirt, straight jeans and ballet flats. Her hair was up, twisted with a pen, holding up her bun. Tendrils were falling down, framing her face so perfectly." Okay, he is veering far away from the plan. He isn't bullshitting them, though. This is also the truth. I was wearing that exact outfit. With my hair exactly how he described. He really does remember how I looked the day we met. "Eventually, I couldn't keep my true feelings for Hales to myself. A few months ago, I finally asked her out and here we are. Best decision I've ever made."

Without hesitation, I respond, "I can't believe you remember that."

"I remember more than you think."

There we are, lost in our own little world. We lock eyes for what seems like forever. He is searching mine, trying to decipher if it was okay that he said those things. On the one hand, it is okay. He didn't tell them any lies about the facts of our first meeting. On the other, my gut is yelling at me, almost like a warning signal–things are about to get even more complicated.

17

Haley

I wake up the next morning with my arm draped over what I think is a pillow. Turns out, it is definitely not a pillow.

Aidan is fast asleep. One hand is laying on his chest, and the other is slightly resting on my own hand. I completely forgot that he fell asleep next to me. We stayed up late talking about the welcome dinner, my friendship with Anna, my childhood, and how writing my screenplay was going. I finally opened up to Aidan about the struggle I was having writing with the happily ever after for my characters. That was the block that was holding me back from submitting. Aidan nodded and said he understood and then he told me that the block will disappear eventually. I just had to keep writing. I was so grateful that he didn't press me for more details about my relationship with Robert. The last thing I remember before passing out was reading my novel that I've been trying to get through for the past month, while Aidan sat beside me reading through a script for a possible role. It was a romantic comedy, a genre of movie that he wants to do more of.

I don't want to wake Aidan. He literally looks perfect. Of course he does. My stomach is growling and making gurgling noises so loud that I'm sure it will wake him. I slide my arm from underneath Aidan's warm hand; luckily, he doesn't stir. Poor guy is probably exhausted from all the people he met yesterday and from keeping up pretenses. I successfully tiptoe out of bed, throw on some slippers and quietly open the door. I sneak out and gently close the door to the bedroom.

I find my mom in the kitchen, with a mug in hand as she scrambles eggs in a pan. There is a platter of cut-up fruit on the island.

"Morning, Mom. Did you sleep well?" I plop a strawberry in my mouth and head over to the cabinets, opening them blindly, trying to find the mugs.

"Morning, Haley Girl. Mugs are on the other side of me. Cabinet closest to the fridge. And yes, I slept great. It was nice having the window open and hearing the ocean throughout the night."

I find a mug of sufficient size–basically a soup bowl–and set it on the counter. I open the fridge and look for creamer. "On the door," my mom chimes in. I find it immediately. As I pour the creamer in my mug, she pours in coffee, causing it to mix perfectly.

"Thanks, Mom." I walk over the island and sit on one of the bar stools.

"How did *you* sleep?" she asks, leaning against the counter and sipping her coffee. A small grin on her face, the mug barely masking it.

"Really good. Why are you looking at me like that?"

"Like what?"

"Like you are thinking something you desperately want to say, but don't have the courage to say out loud. As memory recalls, you always had that look right before you were about to say something that would embarrass me."

"I was just wondering how you slept, that's all."

"You mean how did I sleep with an international movie star next to me? I slept fine, Mom." I suddenly get nervous about the fact that people are imagining us in bed together, but that's normal for people who are actually couples. The world doesn't know that we aren't a couple. More importantly, my mom doesn't know. *Play the part, Haley.* "Mom, we've been sleeping with each other for a while."

She raises her eyebrows and her smile broadens.

"I mean sleeping next to each other. Not that we don't sleep with each other....you know what? Please wipe everything that just came out of my mouth from your head, Mom. That was too much information."

"Haley, you are a grown woman. You don't have to pretend that you don't have sex with your boyfriend."

"Mom!"

"What?"

"Don't say that!"

"What? Sex? Really, Haley. I am not naive to think that you have never had sex with anyone in your life."

Is my mother really saying those words? Even though I am a grown woman, talking about my sexual encounters is *not* on the list of things I ever want to do with my mother.

"Okay, changing the subject please." I need to get food in my system immediately. Scooting past my mom, I turn off the burner, grab the spatula and scoop some eggs onto my plate, along with sliced avocado. When I return to my seat, I realize that I need to make sure my mother doesn't talk about me and Aidan's relationship to many people, *especially about the part...*

I clear my throat. "Oh, I was going to say. Can you not say anything about Aidan formerly being my boss? I don't know, I don't want anyone to judge or ask too many questions."

"People are going to find out, Haley Girl. You chose to be with someone who is always in the spotlight and people are going to have their opinions about it."

"And what's your opinion about it?"

"I have to admit, yesterday when you told me that he was your boss, I got a little scared."

"Why?"

My mom scoops herself some eggs on her own plate. "Because there is a power dynamic there that cannot be ignored, and it usually doesn't end well for the one in the subordinate position. I was scared that he was using you for one thing..."

"Oh my god Mom, you could not be more wrong!" I shuffle my food around with my fork, a feeble attempt to cover my nerves. I hate that my mom thinks badly of Aidan, but I guess with my track record with men and seeing him with those other women in the tabloids, I don't blame her for wanting to protect me.

I lift my coffee mug and bring it to my lips as she sits next to me.

"Can you blame me?" she says. "You are my daughter and as of late, it seemed like your boyfriend was gallivanting around L.A. with models and women who don't understand the concept of clothing."

I shake my head, trying to erase the plethora of photos I've had to witness these past several months. They never used to bother me, until recently. "Mom, those women were just..."

"Decoys. I know. I guess my main concern is, does he do the small things for you?"

I put my coffee down. "What do you mean?"

"Does he recognize when you are anxious? Does he rub your back when you are stressed? Does he open doors for you? Does he let you have the last bite from time to time?"

Time to pull out another white lie. But actually, come to think of it, in the span of two weeks, Aidan has done close to all of those things. So technically, I am not lying to my mother...again.

"Yes, Mom. He actually does." I don't even have to try and be convincing. I don't have to put on an act, because Aidan has already done all the grunt work by simply being a genuine guy.

"Good. I am asking these questions because, Haley, if he doesn't do those things, it's not worth it. He seems like a great guy. But I want you to be careful with your heart with this one. It crushed my own heart three years ago, seeing yours shatter. I want you to follow your heart, but I also want you to listen to your head. Things aren't always what they appear."

If only my mom knew how much my head is getting in the way of my heart, she probably wouldn't be saying this right now. My heart is encased in a locked steel box, and I threw away the key a long time ago. The only way someone is getting to my heart is by destroying the box completely.

I want to confess the truth so badly, but I can't jeopardize our cover. We've come too far already and we only have a couple of days left before everything resumes what it used to be. "Aidan's a great guy, Mom. You don't have to worry about him breaking my heart."

He's not getting to it in the first place.

Even if I want him to.

18

Haley

"Don't worry, it's going to be a friendly game," Anna tries to assure me.

I laugh. "Yeah, right! When has a game of volleyball ever been friendly when you are involved?" Anna was one of the best volleyball players in the history of our high school. Not only is she super talented, she is probably the most competitive person that's ever played the game. I remember how she used to be on that court—absolutely ruthless.

"True. I know my team is going to dominate Dan's team. I mean there's both of us, and of course your absolute hunk of a boyfriend. I'm sure he is super athletic, playing a superhero on screen. There's no way that body is going to waste. Plus, we can use his hot shirtless body to distract every woman on the other side of the net. You don't mind other women ogling your beau, do you?"

My cheeks get hot thinking about the fact that I'm about to see Aidan without a shirt for an extended period of time. I hope he decides to wear a tank-top or something. I am also extremely nervous about being in a bikini in front of him. I brought a one-piece, too, just in case an event like this popped up in the itinerary, but Anna snatched it from my hands and said absolutely not. I need to show off my rocking body in front of Robert, remind him of what he walked out on. Anna holds grudges close to her chest and won't ever let go, especially when it comes to the people closest to her. I really don't care about what Robert thought of my body. Granted, I'm in the best shape I've ever been in my life because of all the running and occasional barre class, but I did that for *me*–not to get revenge on Robert just in case we ran into each other again.

The teams are divided up between all of Anna's bridesmaids and their plus-ones, and all of Dan's groomsmen and their plus-ones. That is, if they want to play. When I told Aidan about the plan, he just grinned and said that he plays volleyball every once in a while on the beach with some of his closest friends, so it will not be a problem. "It's gonna be fun, Hales."

Yeah, that's a word for it...*fun*. It's one thing to play indoor volleyball with a jersey on and a solid court under your feet. It's a whole other thing to play in a bikini, on shifting sand...in front of your boss, who might be shirtless.

"Um, hello? Earth to Haley!" Anna interjects on my thoughts.

"Oh, sorry, I was spacing out. Um, to answer your question, I'm kind of used to women ogling at my bos–boyfriend! It kind of comes with the territory. It's fine." *Phew, that was close.* I grab the sunscreen out of my bag. "Do you mind helping me apply this on my back? Anna?"

My best friend has lowered her sunglasses down to the bridge of her nose, and her jaw is almost touching the sand.

Mimicking her earlier taunt, I say, "Hello, earth to Anna! What the heck are you staring at?"

"Girl, I don't know how you get anything done. Look at that fine specimen of a man. You are one lucky woman."

My pulse quickens as I follow her laser-focused eyes. Aidan is jogging toward us. Unfortunately, he is in fact shirtless. He looks like a fricken underwear model, perfectly tanned, every single ridge of his abs oscillating with every step, every slight twist of his body. To top it off, his skin glistens from the combination of the salty air and sweat. He is wearing a backwards hat and black Ray Bans. My stupid eyes cannot help but gaze upon his exposed taut abs again and notice that his swim trunks are hanging just low enough to showcase a perfect V. How is it fair that a human being can be this hot? The rest of us mere humans look inconsequential in comparison to this god of a man.

It's official. I don't want to take off my swim cover. I know what Natasha looks like in a bikini and I am nowhere near like her.

Yup, the cover up is staying on.

But apparently, Anna has other plans.

"Aidan, hi! I'm gonna start warming up out there. I think your girlfriend needs some help applying her sunscreen."

Instigator. Even though I feel super hot inside, I know that I probably look like a ghost right about now, as I feel the blood drain from my face. No way is Aidan Stone going to rub sunscreen all over my practically naked body. But what other choice do I have?

Act the part.

This is something a boyfriend would do.

As Aidan reaches his final destination, AKA the spot right next to me, I reluctantly hand over the SPF. Anna winks at me and starts running out to the court to greet the rest of the wedding party, including Robert who catches sight of me and Aidan sitting next to each other. His stare is interrupted by Julia, who throws her arms around Robert's neck and starts making out with him. Stupidly, my feelings revert back to three years ago. I thought the upset stomach wouldn't show up again, seeing them together. I thought last night was the last time I would feel my insides twisting in unbearable positions.

My intrusive thoughts come to a halt when the cool sensation of lotion hits my warm skin.

"Stop," Aidan whispers in my ear, causing goosebumps to travel along my entire body. I'll blame the cool sea breeze.

I furrow my brows. "Stop what?"

Aidan lets out a small laugh. "You think I need to see your face to know that you are closing in on yourself with your thoughts?" *Damn, he's good.* "Stop comparing yourself to Julia. She has nothing on you, Hales. Trust me."

I stay silent as he continues to rub lotion along the length of my back. Those intrusive past memories dissolve and I shudder a little when he slides his hands underneath the string of my bikini top and grazes the very top of my bikini bottom. This is uncharted territory, yet Aidan is quickly discovering it. And the scary thing is–I don't hate it. It is terrifying how comfortable I am becoming every time Aidan touches me. Quick! Call the Academy! He could definitely win an Oscar for this performance because right now, he is convincing *me* this is real. I am discovering that Aidan has the innate ability to ground me in a way that no one else does. He always brings me back to the present and magically, my worries scatter into oblivion, even if only for a moment.

I hear the click of the sunscreen cap and Aidan clears his throat. "Okay, Swann. Are you ready to kick some ass?"

He stands up and reaches his arms down, helping me up. I take his hands and he lifts me off the ground with great ease. I wipe excess sand sticking to the back of my sweaty thighs. "Ready."

The next thing I know, a squeal leaves my mouth as Aidan lifts me over his shoulder, my ass hanging in the air, my face in line with his butt. I try flailing my legs, and through a laugh, I plead, "Aidan, let me down."

"Not a chance, Hales. Besides, I'll do this all day if I could see that look on Robert's face stay there for the remainder of the weekend. Like he wants what I have."

I glance over. Robert's expression is pure jealousy. Even though that wasn't the intention, it is a little satisfying that the tables have turned. Now he is looking at me with someone else like that.

About an hour later, Aidan and I block the last spike from the opposing team. Icing on the cake? Robert was the one who attempted the spike.

"Dammit!" Robert yells out of frustration. Aidan has been shutting him down all game. It was seriously a sight to see two grown men volley back and forth as intensely as they did. Only once did Robert have a one-up on Aidan and his victory dance lasted for maybe a second before Aidan served the ball and it landed right in front of Robert's dumbfounded face.

I could tell how defeated Robert was progressively getting during the game. It was always a tell that his nostrils started to flare. For a moment, I thought the sun was getting to him, but then I realized his face was turning red out of pure anger. That's another thing about Robert. He hates to lose.

I turn to Aidan and high-five him. "You were absolutely ruthless! Robert doesn't know what to do with himself. It's almost unfair how good you are at volleyball."

"Well, you know what they say, 'All's fair in love and war.'"

Before I can process what he just said, Aidan playfully scoops me up from behind and twirls me around, holding me so tight that he inadvertently tickles my sides. Did I mention that I am extremely ticklish? I squeal like a fricken teenager and start laughing so hard.

"Oh my god, put me down Aidan!" I plead between laughs. "You're tickling me! Stop! I seriously can't catch my breath!"

He lowers me to the ground and turns me around so I didn't have the choice but to look directly at his Captain America (post super soldier serum) body. If I thought I was out of breath before, I was wrong. He lifts my chin up slightly and brushes the slightest kiss along my lips. Just enough to make my entire body liquify. How could the slightest brush of his lips cause my body to react this way? Scientific studies should be conducted on the phenomenon that is Aidan Stone.

"Out of necessity," he says. It's hard to read him with his sunglasses on, but I could've sworn he said that with a sarcastic tone.

"Right." I can't help but feel slightly disappointed. All of a sudden, I don't want it to be out of necessity. I want it to be just because. "Out of necessity," I repeat.

I look across the net. A pissed-off Robert glares at me and Aidan. Julia is at his side, attempting to console him, but it seems to have no effect on him whatsoever.

"I like your tattoo, by the way," Aidan whispers in my ear. "A rainbow suits you."

I quickly cover the side of my torso. I forgot I was wearing a bikini that almost bares all. Usually my tattoo is covered by my bra strap. Not that I'm ashamed of it or anything, I just don't really want people to ask questions about it.

"Thanks," I respond evenly, trying not to reveal that I'm a little taken aback.

"You are just full of surprises, Haley Swann." It is ridiculous how perfect he still looks after playing an hour of intense beach volleyball. His backwards hat is still in place on top of his head. The sweat that glistens off of his skin makes him look like a vampire from *Twilight*. While my hair probably looks like I just rolled out of bed and my skin is probably crimson – not from sunburn, but the heat alone is enough to make my fair skin turn a deep shade of red, especially after working out.

Before I can respond, Anna crashes into me, knocking us both down onto the sand. "We won, Hales!! Ha ha, suck it Dan!" she yells back to the groom.

Dan shakes his head and smiles at the woman he is about to marry. Even though Anna is acting like a crazed woman, all I see is love in Dan's eyes. He knows exactly who he is marrying and he wants it all, and that is such a beautiful thing to witness.

She pulls me up from the ground and my ass and most of my upper thighs are covered in sand.

Great.

"Drinks tonight are completely on Dan. That was the consequence of losing this game. The loser has to buy all the drinks for the opposing party's entire team. Now do you see why I wanted to win so badly?"

I honestly don't think Anna needed an excuse for her competitiveness, but that would have sucked to pay for all the drinks the bachelor party is going to consume, which I assume will be an exorbitant amount. Anna's party will be no different.

"Hey McHottie, why don't you help your damsel in distress here get the sand off her body?" Anna says to Aidan.

"No, no I got it!" I start brushing the back and side of my legs frantically. *Hell no, is Aidan Stone going to touch my legs or ass for that matter.*

"Nonsense! You'll help our girl out, right handsome?" Anna devilishly winks at me and prances away toward her man.

Aidan smiles, inches closer to me and responds, "Yes, ma'am. I've got it covered."

Now I am turning bright red for an entirely different reason. I am melting with the thought of Aidan's hands all over me, attempting to get the smallest speck of sand off my body.

Once Anna's attention is completely on her own man, mine leans down and says, "Relax, Swann. I'm not going to touch you." At some point during my mortification and getting into my own head yet again, Aidan must have gone over to where I placed my belongings and grabbed my cover-up. "Lift your arms, Hales." I do as I am told, completely shell-shocked that a man didn't capitalize on an opportunity to touch a practically naked woman. This is the second time in the past few days that Aidan has seen most of my body, especially my legs, and he seems completely unphased. He is either the world's sweetest gentleman, or he is completely repulsed by me.

I am convinced that it must be the latter.

19

Haley

"I still cannot believe you are here."

Anna gives me a side-hug as we walk up the porch steps of the Hamptons house. We went into town to get some much-needed coffee before our wild bachelorette night.

"I wouldn't have missed this, Anna, you know that." I take a sip of my coffee as we sit down on the lounge chairs facing the gorgeous ocean. "No matter the circumstances." Robert's stupid smug face flashes into my mind.

"I was also honestly surprised that you brought someone. I still don't understand why you didn't Facetime me immediately when you first went on a date with that hunk."

"No one says hunk anymore, Anna."

"Well, I do. It's gonna come back, you'll see."

I roll my eyes and smile.

"Speaking of," Anna continues, "where is Prince Charming?"

"Um, he had to go run an errand or something. He got a call and said that he needed to run into town to go take care of some business." I'm kind of worried about him, actually. He had that serious look on his face that I know all too well as his assistant. His eyebrows would furrow a little and his jaw hardened slightly as if he was holding back what he really wanted to say about whatever situation he was dealing with. I hope everything is okay, but I didn't ask because I don't want to pry. Just because we are fake dating doesn't give me the automatic right to become privy to what is going on in Aidan's brain. Even though I desperately want to know what he is thinking about me and my family and friends. He probably left because he wanted to escape this crazy circus, he was just too polite to say so.

"Ooooh, so mysterious. Maybe he is going to stop at a jewelry store and, you know, *browse*." Anna raises her eyebrows twice like she is up to something mischievous– and, let's face it, with Anna, she probably is.

I couldn't help but maniacally laugh at the insane notion that Aidan would even think about looking at engagement rings for me. He did buy me jewelry the other day, but that was different–it was to help make me look like I belonged on the red carpet next to him. "I highly doubt that."

"Why would you highly doubt that? It's not so out there to assume that this man would buy you jewelry. Or maybe he is going to shop for some lingerie for you. Gosh, I can only imagine how that man is in the bedroom. With that body and those massive hands..."

I choke so hard on my coffee that some spills out of my nose.

Anna set her coffee down on the side table. "Okay, girl. Spill it."

I cough. "I think I just did."

"Don't be quippy with me and don't try to evade the subject. I've known you all of my life, Haley Swann. I know when you are lying. Spill it!"

Damn, she knows. I knew I couldn't lie to Anna. She's like a fricken bloodhound when it comes to detecting lies. She should have gone into detective work so she could interrogate people. She's a natural at it.

"Okay fine."

So I tell Anna the entire story. Everything from the meeting in Samantha's office, the diner, the premiere, and even the night in Aidan's apartment. It feels so good for someone other than Aidan, Rachel, Samantha and Chris to know. I need someone in my inner circle to know what is going on. I am just too embarrassed to tell my mom and God knows what my dad would have thought about all of this.

"I swear I won't tell a soul...not even Dan." Anna takes my hand in hers. "I promise." That's the thing about Anna. She is sincerely genuine and she has never judged me for anything in my life. We have a bond that's truly unbreakable. We support each other no matter what.

"Anna, you can tell Dan if you want. He's your person. I don't expect you to keep anything from him. He's about to be your husband in, like, 48 hours."

She shakes her head. "Nope, not even Dan. I am taking this one to the grave. You were my person first, babe. You'll always be my person. Dan just comes in as a very close second."

"Thanks for understanding and listening...and not judging." I graze my finger on the black lid of my coffee cup.

"I would never judge you, Haley and of course. This is what best friends are for." She reaches an arm around me and pulls me in for a hug.

I take a deep breath of relief as I sip on what is left of my coffee.

"But," Anna says, "I have to be honest with you, Hales, it doesn't seem like Aidan is faking anything."

I almost spit out my coffee yet again and laugh. "Yeah, okay."

"Why do you say it like that?"

"Like what?"

"All sarcastic. You are seriously telling me you don't feel ANYTHING when you are around him, and that he doesn't look and act like he is totally head-over-heels for you? I am pretty good at reading body language, as you well know, and what I am reading is definitely attraction."

I do not want to admit that of course I feel something, but nothing can really happen between us. Aidan and I have a deal.

I sigh. "Okay, maybe just a tiny teensy bit, but..."

"Ha! I knew it!"

"But...nothing can happen, Anna. We are already scratching the surface of unprofessionalism and I really cannot jeopardize my connections at the studio. I need to get my work seen and be taken seriously. I don't want to be a personal assistant forever."

Anna shakes her head.

"What?"

"Are you sure that's all it's about? The work?"

"Yes, what else would it be?"

"Are you sure you aren't putting up too much of a wall with Aidan?"

I know where this is going and I don't want to go further. "I don't want to talk about this."

"C'mon, Haley. All I am saying is I know how much Robert hurt you. And ever since then, you've been afraid of opening up your heart again. I get that. What Robert did is unforgivable. There is no denying that."

Tears are welling up at the memory of what Robert and Julia did...in our shower. In our home.

Anna squeezes my hand. "I sense a real spark between you and Aidan and I don't want you to diminish it because you're scared of letting someone else in again. You deserve to be happy, Haley. And I think he legitimately makes you happy. He could be your person."

"I guess if you believe that, he really is a good actor."

20

Aidan

My hands clench the steering wheel. My jaw hurts from locking it the whole drive to Connecticut.

You don't have to go in. He doesn't deserve your fucking time.

But at the same time, I can't help but think: *but he's your father.* He may be a bastard, but he's my father. No matter how hard I try to get away from him and his bullshit, I can't escape the fact that the same blood runs through our veins. He has that hold on me for life and it's a hold that I wish I could sever forever. Especially for my mom's sake.

It's kind of hard to lie about your whereabouts when it's plastered on every website and E! News. I got the call a couple hours ago. Luckily, there are no more events until this evening with the last-minute bachelor and bachelorette parties, and Haley already had plans to hang out with Anna this afternoon.

Let's just get this over with.

I turn off the ignition and head inside the diner. My dad said he would meet me here at three. It is 3:01 when I walk in and hear the door chime above me. I spot the back of my dad's head right away. My dad is never late. I pull down my hat a little so that hopefully no one will recognize me. I can already feel my nostrils flaring out of annoyance and anger. I sit down in the booth, still not giving my father the satisfaction of looking him in the eyes. That is one trait that I'm glad I didn't get from my father: his eyes. I have my mother's eyes and I am infinitely more grateful since they are kind–directly reflecting who she is as a person. My dad doesn't have a flicker of kindness. Never has and never will.

"Hello, son."

I finally look up at my dad. He looks like a haunted man. His eyes are sunken in, his skin looks weathered and dry–a side effect of years of drinking. I expect to feel happy about that, but instead it makes me even more sad. He ruined a perfectly good life the moment he drank his first drop of alcohol.

"Well, this should be interesting. I haven't heard from you in almost ten years and now you reach out to me. What do you want?"

"What? I can't have lunch with my son?"

"No, Dad, unfortunately you can't."

The waitress comes over and asks, "What can I get you?"

"I'll have water, thank you."

She nods. "Anything to eat, hun?"

"Just the water," I respond, probably a little too curtly.

"Got it. Another for you, sir?"

It's then I realize that my father is drinking a beer yet again. I wonder what number that is today.

My father clears his throat, picking up on my obvious disappointment. "I'll switch to water. No food for me either." He runs his hand through his graying hair. He's let it grow long. If this was a couple of weeks ago, the only way people would be able to tell us apart from a distance would be the color of our hair, since mine was practically the same length. Even though he is still sitting tall, I can tell he is shriveling inside. *I don't care.*

"Look Aidan, I just wanted to see you to tell you how sorry I am for everything. If I hurt you when you were young..."

I scoff. "If? You got a lot of nerve using that word, Dad."

"You're right. It's not an *if.* I did hurt you...and your mother... and I am truly sorry for that."

This again? I adjust in my seat, pull the bill of my cap down a little further. "Are you in rehab again? Is this what all of this is about? Well, I can save us both a lot of time and energy and tell you that there is nothing you can say to me right now that will change how I feel about you."

My dad's eyes shift toward the window. "And your mom? How is she...?"

"Don't ask about Mom. You don't deserve to know. You lost that right a long-ass time ago. The moment you laid your fucking hands on her, you lost that right to know anything about her."

My dad starts fiddling with his thumbs, a nervous habit I first detected when I was young. His eyes keep shifting back and forth, from outside to me. *What the hell is he looking at?* I glance out the window myself and notice some cameras sticking out of bushes. *Paparazzi. I fucking knew it. Unbelievable.*

"What's your cut?" I ask.

"What?"

"Your cut, Dad. How much are you getting from the paparazzi for photos of me?"

My dad doesn't answer.

I get up from the table. "Some things never change."

The poor waitress is on her way with our waters in hand, but she stops cold in her tracks.

"Jesus, Dad. I know you lost your practice, but come on. To capitalize on the infringement of privacy on your own son. You always find a way to use people." I throw money on the table. More than enough for a couple of waters. I want to give our waitress some extra compensation for dealing with my drunk father and the uncomfortable conversation she had to somewhat overhear. "I am not going to give you the satisfaction of accepting you back in my life. You can go to hell, Dad."

I am almost out of the vicinity of the booth when I hear, "I need a new liver."

I should've left before he had a chance to say anything. Now my damn conscience won't allow my body to walk out the restaurant doors. I retrace my steps and find my seat across from the hollow man who used to be my father. The man I share a likeness with. I can't escape him. Even in a damn mirror.

"It's bad, Aidan. The doctors say I need a new liver as soon as possible. I was wondering if you would consider..."

"Let me guess, you want to see if I'm a match?" My jaw clenches and I take a deep breath. *I owe him nothing. He made his own bed, he can lie in it.* From being disbarred and closing his law firm, to dealing with copious amounts of sexual harassment allegations from former paralegals, some of which were during the time when my parents were still married. And now to his liver failing because of all his drinking.

"Dad, you got yourself into this, you can figure out how to get yourself out of it. I owe you nothing. You were not a father to me. If anything, you were an example of what *not* to be. How *not* to treat the people you love." I feel tears well up from the past thirty-five years. Thirty-five years of being scared to tell my dad the unfiltered truth. "You know, these past six months, I started to become you—and I hated myself for it. I started sleeping around with so many women. I would get drunk by noon and have crippling hangovers the next day. I was running away from the hurt of getting my heartbroken by Natasha. I thought she was the endgame. But I was wrong. I promised myself a long time ago that I would never become you. The only person who has pulled me out of that dark space has been my assistant, Haley. I owe everything to her. She has saved my career. She has saved my life. I won't let my hurt ruin my life and hurt the people I love."

I get up from the table for the final time. "Look, I have to get back to New York." Against my better judgment, I place my hand on my dad's shoulder. "I hope for your sake that you find a match." Remembering the paparazzi that are awaiting my departure from the restaurant, I lean down and whisper, "I hope you get your money's worth with those men out there, because you aren't going to have the opportunity to profit off me again. Goodbye, Dad."

21

———

Haley

There is still some time before I have to get ready for the bachelorette party. I decide to go down to the beach and sit and read a book that has been burning a hole in my TBR pile for way too long. I am completely immersed in my psychological thriller when I hear a disgruntled, "Hey."

My body dramatically convulses. "Oh my God, you scared me. When did you get back?"

When I look at Aidan, his hands are in his pockets and he is gazing out into the ocean, avoiding eye contact. He kicks some sand with his flip-flop before he sits next to me. "Just a few minutes ago. And sorry, I didn't mean to scare you." His voice is flat. Deflecting, he asks, "What are you reading?"

"Um, nothing important." I close my book quickly and set it

aside. I am kind of scared to ask the next question, but I can tell Aidan was affected by something that just happened to him. He is off-center like I've never seen him before. It's a different kind of shift than what I witnessed with the Natasha fiasco. He looks like a little boy, struggling to find the words to something that legitimately bothers him. Needing validation from an adult that his feelings are real. I have a sudden urge to fix anything that is wrong with Aidan at this moment, just to spare my eyes from seeing this wonderful man in such distress. "Aidan, what's wrong? What errand did you have to go do?"

"My dad contacted me and wanted to meet me for lunch. Down in Connecticut."

His dad? From what I gathered from our conversation in his apartment, he despised his dad. Why would he go and meet him?

"Okay," I say trepidatiously. "What did he want?"

Aidan shakes his head and lets out a laugh. "That is the question, isn't it?" He stands up and puts his hands back in his pockets, still not looking at me. He looks out into the ocean again as if it holds the answer he needs. Like it is housing a secret key to a locked box that he is considering opening. But the way he's acting makes me think he's going to unleash the contents of his own personal Pandora's box.

"Aidan, what happened?"

"Oh you know, same old Steven Stone. Just when I thought I escaped him forever, he weasels back into my life."

I still don't understand, and it pains me to see Aidan in this kind of affliction. I stand up and join him where the water meets the sand, allowing the ocean to wash up to our feet, with a childlike hope that it will cleanse us of our ailments. I just stand there, silent, letting Aidan take the lead of this conversation. From what I've gathered about his father, I have a feeling that Aidan never really had control until he was an adult and could literally get himself out of a toxic situation.

Aidan takes a deep breath. "He wanted to apologize for everything he's done to me. To my mom. He is on some sort of redemption tour and I was one of the stops. And the sucky thing about all of this, Hales, is that he was still fucking drinking as he was saying how sorry he was for the pathetic, drunk person he was to me and my mom." He is starting to pace along the shoreline, each step getting erased by the water, hopefully washing away all this hurt. "He was working with some paparazzi to get pictures of him and me together. He's in such dire circumstances that he conspired with the very people who try to expose everything about me just to make some money. He doesn't fucking care about me or my mom. And you want to know what the cherry on top of this fucked-up sundae is?"

"What?" I swallow hard, knowing that what Aidan is about to say next is the real reason he is so upset and conflicted.

"My dad is dying, Hales."

A rush of memories floods my mind. It is like I am stuck in the undercurrent of the wave and getting tossed and turned in every direction, unable to find my way out. The sound of the flatline replaces the soothing waves crashing at our feet. My mother's voice replaces the flatline. *Dad's dying, Hales.* I want to throw up again. Just like I did when I got the life-altering news. Just like I did when he died.

"Aidan, I..."

"His liver is failing and he asked me if I could see if I am a match and it sucks because no matter how much I fucking hate him..."

"He's still your dad."

"Yeah." Aidan looks into my eyes for the first time since he met me on this beach. We stand there, looking at each other, searching for what to say next. I honestly don't know what to say to him. And then he asks me the question I am dreading the most: "What should I do?"

"Aidan, I can't answer that or make this decision for you." I need to be honest with him because that is how our working relationship always operated. I am never afraid or intimidated by Aidan. I always have felt I could share my thoughts about what was going on in his career or the roles that he has decided to take. But when it comes to the personal stuff, I don't know what to say. I don't think I had a right to say anything.

But the thing about that logic is that everything has changed for us. And he is asking me for my advice.

"I know what I would do if it was *my* dad. I would do anything to save his life."

Aidan rubs his forehead, clearly conflicted by my answer.

"But," I continue, "I had a very different relationship with my dad than you have with yours. I know that this is a complicated situation for you. I can't imagine being in your shoes." I suddenly feel an overwhelming need to go over to Aidan and give him a hug. Two weeks ago, my body wouldn't allow me to step near Aidan in that capacity.

But like I said before, everything has changed.

I inch closer to Aidan and wrap my arms around him, tightening my grasp as hard as I can. He returns the hug and holds me just as tight. This hug feels different than all the other physical interactions we've had of late. It isn't fueled by inexplicable tension. It is purely platonic. Friendly. Comforting.

I open my eyes toward the horizon and see a faint rainbow making its timely appearance. "Do you want to know why I have a tattoo of a rainbow on the side of my torso?"

"I do. Ever since I saw it earlier, I wanted to know."

"Whenever I was having a bad day, or my anxiety was getting the best of me, my dad would tell me, *Look for the rainbows*. He told me that rainbows are a sign of hope and promise. They are the beautiful prize that awaits us after the storm of life. They are there to assure us that there will always be beauty and clarity following times of doubt. Times of tribulations and trials. He told me that whenever I felt uneasy or felt like I couldn't escape what was bothering me, to look for rainbows. Search for the rainbows in life because they are always going to pull you through the dark times. Growing up, I thought that was so corny of my dad to say." I smile as I see my dad's face when I close my eyes. Small droplets of tears escape my blinking eyes. "Now, it's the advice that I hold closest to my heart. Right before he died, he told me to look for him in the rainbows, Haley Girl."

Aidan pulls away just enough so he can see my face fully. I finally am brave enough to look at him after this confession. I expect him to look at me with pity in his eyes. But it isn't a look of pity that I see. It almost looks like admiration and wonder.

"I guess I wanted a permanent reminder of him. Even though I knew my dad would always be with me in moments of happiness, sadness, all of the above – I needed physical proof that he is always with me. Hence the tattoo. And whenever I see rainbows like that one over there," I gestured my head toward the faint rainbow, "I know that my dad is watching over me and everything that I was worrying about vanishes."

"Thank you for sharing that with me, Hales."

"Of course. I just figured that since you had a tough day, you needed to see the hope at the end of it. It's not going to stay terrible forever." I place my hand on his chest and continue, "And back to your question: I don't have a clear answer for you and honestly, it's not my place, Aidan. You know your dad better than anyone and you are under no obligation to give any part of yourself – organs or otherwise – to a person who always sees you as 'less than' and has already taken pieces of you that you can never get back. I understand that. That being said, if you decide that you do want to help him, then I don't think anyone will judge you for that."

"My mom will. And I have to protect my mom, Hales. I don't want this to open the door to any line of future communication with him or involvement in my life because my mom is so important to me. She is the one who raised me into the man I am today. My dad's lifestyle choices led him to this very moment. The choice to drink. The choice to beat my mom. The choice to beat me. All behind closed doors. All the while he was pretending to be an upstanding lawyer in court and prosecuting people who were doing the exact same things he was doing. He was such a hypocrite. *Is* such a hypocrite." He pauses, "He is the face of all the demons I have inside of me. Demons that I hope will never come out. They started to rear their ugly heads after Natasha. I was turning into him and it was a hell I don't want to enter again. I didn't recognize myself and I realized that my biggest fear in life was emulating my father. I don't want to be him."

"You won't, Aidan. You are leaps and bounds from being like your father. Yeah, maybe you lost yourself for a while, but you have the strength to pull yourself out of it. I've seen it with my own eyes." He halfway smirks and I tug a little at the back of his shirt. "Remind me if I ever see your mom again, to thank her for raising such an incredible man. A man who puts her well-being first more than his. She would be proud of you. But I will say that your mom is stronger than you might be giving her credit for, and I don't think she would allow your dad back into her life in any way. You get your strength from her, Aidan. Not your dad. Don't underestimate your mom. So I am going to say it again: if you do decide to get tested to see if you are a match for your father, that will be okay. She will be okay. Either way you choose, that will be the right choice for you." I lace my fingers through Aidan's hands. "Find the rainbow."

The wind is starting to pick up a little and my hair keeps getting stuck on my lips and getting into my eyes. Aidan looks at me intently, brushes my wild hair out of my face, tucks the strands behind my ear, and says, "I'm beginning to think that you are my–"

"Haley!!! Get your sexy ass in this house so we can get ready for tonight, girlie!" Anna yells from the balcony directly outside the bedroom Aidan and I are sharing. "Hi, Charming."

I roll my eyes. "Oh Anna. Always with the perfect timing." Both Aidan and I seem to sigh at the same time. I point my thumb back toward the house and say, "Um, sorry. I better go. I have been summoned by the bride. Are you going to be okay?"

"Yes. I'm going to be fine. I just have a lot to think about. It's okay, go be with Anna. You girls have fun. Don't get in too much trouble."

"I won't, I promise. It's Anna who we have to worry about getting into trouble. You know how impulsive she can be, from personal experience," I say, referencing her initial introduction to him. I feel a tinge of possessiveness in my gut, like I never want to see Aidan kiss another girl ever again. Even if it is a part of his job. Maybe we can negotiate that in my contract when we return to L.A.

I reluctantly leave Aidan's side, jog back to where I was reading and pick up my book and blanket.

In the midst of the wind, I hear Aidan yell, "Hey Hales!"

I quickly turn to face Aidan. I know it's unfair to leave him like this, especially with him looking the way he does, but I have a feeling he's telling me the truth. He really is okay for the time being. I know he is going to make the right decision for him. "Yeah?"

As if he is superhuman – a thought that has certainly crossed my mind over the past two weeks – he is at my side in .02 milliseconds. That scared little boy is now replaced by an enlightened man. He kisses the top of my forehead and says, "Thank you for being you."

22

Haley

"Okay, last bar of the night!" Anna exclaims.

"That's what you said at the last one, Anna." I laugh. Anna certainly hasn't changed. She has always been the life of the party and tonight has been no different. She has a quality about her that makes anyone feel like they can join in on the fun, even if said person was content reading in a corner like I was in college. She was the one who influenced me to let go, relax, and partake in some sort of social interaction.

"I know, but I promise *this* is the last one," she says as she enthusiastically texts someone, a smile permanently stuck to her face.

We make our way into the small dive bar off the coast. It has been nice to finally let loose with my best friend. It has been a long time coming, and tonight has been a blast. As Maid of Honor, I feel it is my duty to get the bride as drunk as possible without getting sick, and I am definitely succeeding... and I am getting just as drunk in the process.

"Okay, Anna, I love you but I think I only have one more shot in me. After that, if I have any more, I'm going into blackout mode."

"Okay, fine. Let's get that shot in you!"

We make our way over to the bar with the posse of bridesmaids and some of Anna's other friends behind us. The bartender is tipped off that we are a part of a bachelorette party due to Anna's veil headband and large sash that reads "Bride to Be."

"This round is on the house, ladies."

"Thanks, handsome." Anna winks at the bartender and throws back the shot.

"Down girl, you know that you're the one getting married, right?" I say to Anna, downing my own shot.

"Oh calm down, this is seriously the last time I am ever going to get to flirt with another guy in my life. I love Dan more than life itself. Don't get your panties in a wad."

I roll my eyes. "I know you do. You're lucky, Anna. And I am so happy for you and Dan. Not many people's relationships last as long as yours. I wish I had that."

"Oh, I bet you are going to have that, Hales. I've seen the way Charming treats you."

My pulse quickens. I try to rid my mind of thoughts about Aidan. His smile. His eyes. His body. He texted me earlier to make sure I was okay and said to text if I need him at all tonight.

"He worships the ground you walk on," Anna continues. "Believe me. A man doesn't look at a woman like he looks at you for no reason."

"You're just saying that to make me feel better," I say, trying to convince myself of those exact words. *He is just acting. That's his job.*

"No, I am saying that because it's the truth." Anna purses her lips and taps me lightly on the arm. She turns toward the bartender. "Hey handsome, can we have two more shots?"

"Coming right up," the bartender responds, grabbing two shot glasses and the bottle of Patron.

"Actually I'll just have water, please," I yell at the bartender. I whip my head back to Anna, "Seriously, I need to stop drinking. I am way past my threshold and besides, it is my duty to watch after you as your Maid of Honor."

"Ugh, fine. I'll just take the shot for you."

"Have at it." I laugh at my best friend as she takes two shots in a row. Her threshold is most definitely higher than mine. *Mental note: make sure that she starts drinking water ASAP.*

The next thing I know, Anna is squealing with excitement as she bolts toward the middle of the dancefloor. I follow her to her final destination: the arms of her groom. Dan looks just as inebriated in his own right, but I watch them as they smile at each other–those aren't drunken smiles. It is as if they sober up in each other's presence.

I slowly sip my water. My mind is getting cloudy. I am entering a kind of haze. A haze that hasn't been present in three years. I close my eyes, trying to lift the haze with my positive thoughts of being sober. As much as I love letting loose, I hate feeling out of control.

"Hey man, can I have a double shot of Jameson?"

A chill runs up my spine. There is only one person I know who orders that drink, and he is the last person I want to see tonight. "And a shot of tequila for the lady here."

"No thanks," I say without even looking in Robert's direction.

"C'mon, Haley. We're celebrating. Our best friends are getting married."

"I said no." My eyes shoot daggers at him. *Sense my tone, Robert.* "What are you even doing here, anyway?"

"Dan has been texting Anna all night, and she texted him your ladies' location. Figured we would stop by after the last bar we went to." Of course Anna and Dan have been texting all night. They couldn't stand not talking to each other for a night, let alone a few hours. The other groomsmen and bridesmaids are out on the dance floor, looking like college kids at a house party, completely uninhibited with no worries in the world. And here I am, just as drunk, but sadly I can't escape one thing that has been my constant worry this entire weekend. Unfortunately, he isn't leaving my side. My breathing becomes erratic when I don't see Aidan right away. I'm not going to give Robert the satisfaction of knowing that he is annoyingly getting under my skin.

"Nice dress, by the way." I feel Robert's eyes glide the length of my body. I squirm a little, immediately hating myself for putting on this dress—or rather, Anna picking out this dress and me going along with it. I can hear her words ringing in my ears over the loud music: *"Trust me, Hales, this black, short, strapless one is the dress to wear tonight. You are my hot friend. You need to dress the part, little missy. You are dating the hottest man in the universe, right?"* I suddenly wish I had one of my cardigans to cover up. Why the hell is Robert scanning my body, anyway? I know Julia couldn't come out tonight with us, news that was music to my ears. At least the universe was on my side on that front. With Robert, not so much.

"Thanks." I cross my arms over my chest, hoping to hide some of my cleavage.

Robert inches closer to me and nurses his drink. Even when he doesn't say anything to me, his mere presence is suffocating. "You never wore those kinds of outfits while we were together. I guess being out in L.A. has changed you."

I finally make eye contact with the man I once thought I was going to love forever. Right now, all I feel is hate. And despite what some might say, I can assure you, love and hate are *not* the same thing. "Let's not start this, okay?"

"Start what? I'm just making conversation." He finishes his drink and gestures to the bartender for another one. *How many has that been tonight?*

"A conversation I don't want to have." I shift my weight to my other foot and prop my hand on my hip. My feet are killing me. I am half-ready to take these heels off right now. I am just scared that without the physical pain distracting me, I would have to face the emotional pain on its own.

"What? I can't even compliment you anymore?" Robert scoots even closer, closing the necessary space between us. It is amazing that at one point, I didn't want there to be any space between us. Oh, how times have changed.

"Not when the compliment is laced with an insult."

"A little close, aren't you?" I could listen to that deep, dare I say it, possessive voice all day and night. The suffocating air lifts as Aidan stands right next to me. His arm slides around my waist and his hand squeezes my side as he stares down my ex. I thought *my* eyes were daggers. I was clearly wrong– that was nothing compared to Aidan's piercing blue eyes, which turn dark as he glares straight at Robert.

Robert instinctually backs off a little. "Just keeping Haley company since you weren't around."

"Hmmm." Aidan's jaw clenches, clearly annoyed with Robert. His hand doesn't move. Not an inch. "Well, I'm here now." Aidan squeezes me closer into his side, making it undoubtedly explicit that I am here with him.

Robert scoffs, finishing his second drink. "Thank you for gracing us with your presence. Where were you, anyway? Girls swarming you at the door?"

"Thankfully, no. I had to find the restroom. Not that it's any of your business." I've never felt so much tension in my life between two men, and it has only gotten worse as the weekend has progressed. "But, I knew my girl could take care of herself."

Robert flinches slightly when Aidan utters the words *my girl*. I know it's a power play. He is marking his fake territory and it is working. So much so that Robert taps the bar counter twice, awaiting his next escape from reality. I am so confused about why he is acting like this. He was the one who ruined everything in the first place. Now he's acting like I am still his. But I'm not his anymore. I am Aidan's...well, sort of.

Then the Tazmanian devil known as Anna swoops in and grabs

my hands. "Excuse me, Charming, but I need to steal my best friend. Our song just started and I really need her to come shake her fine ass on the dance floor. You don't mind, do you, handsome?" Anna bats her drunken eyes at Aidan and smiles.

"Not at all." Aidan finally releases his hand from my waist. My body suddenly aches for his hand to return back to that exact spot. *Must be the drinks talking.*

Anna leads me out to the middle of the dance floor. Our favorite song from our college days is on and we start doing our own little dance routine. It's like we went into a time machine and we're celebrating the end of midterms. The only exception? The guy who used to be behind me, holding onto my waist and dancing, is standing over at the bar, drinking yet another double-shot of whiskey, next to this dreamboat actor that I get to call mine for the weekend. If someone were to imagine something surreal, this situation would pop up in their mind. The haze of the alcohol is settling in and I feel my body fully relax, with no regard of how I look, who I am dating, or what is going on in my life. I was fully out of my own head and in the moment. Anxiety gone. It is like a curse has been lifted.

I am convinced that when I look over at the bar, I'll see Aidan looking down at his phone or looking completely bored out of his mind. He is seriously a trooper for going through this whole charade with me. I wouldn't blame him if he wanted to skip out on this whole ordeal, go home and sleep. He has to hang out with people he's never met before and pretend to be in love with me. That's a lot to ask of him.

But to my surprise, Aidan's eyes are only fixed on one thing–me. I immediately get flushed when I see that perfect smile and realize that I'm the reason for it. The heat in my body isn't going away. I'm blaming it on all the dancing.

"He's so into you!" Anna yells in my ear over the music blaring out of the speakers.

"Yeah, okay!" I respond sarcastically, trying to act unphased.

"*Yeah, okay* nothing, Hales." Her eyes move from me to where the bar is located. Where the man of my fricken dreams is located. "Tell me something, if he isn't into you, why is he making his way over here right now with his eyes fixed on you the entire time? Did I mention that his eyes look dangerously hungry?"

I am too chicken to look. "You're crazy." My heart is racing with hope that what she's saying is true. Even though it has only been five minutes, my body is craving his touch. Craving everything about him.

I am in trouble. It is a tangled web we were weaving, but for some reason, I want to get caught in it. I want the web to swallow us whole.

Hands that I am becoming way too familiar with wrap around my body and now Aidan is the one behind me, protectively encasing me in his arms. I let my body sink into his, knowing that no matter what situation we are in, I am safe when I'm near him. He has been my savior since the day I met him. When I had no job, he took a chance on me. When I needed him to pretend to be my boyfriend, he did so without hesitation. Despite my protests about Anna's claims, deep down, I want them to be true.

I turn my body and bravely move my hands up Aidan's chest until they clasp behind his neck. It scares me that this feels so natural. Like we've been doing this for years. Is it possible to have this type of connection with someone in such a short period of time? It's like the roots have been there since the day we met. And now this monster of a tree has taken form, trying to withstand any storm—any doubt of our relationship.

Aidan leans down and whispers, "God, I wish I could read your mind right now, Hales."

"Why?" I suddenly become self-conscious because I'm afraid that he could actually read my thoughts.

"Because you are looking up at me like I've never seen you look at me before." He smirks that devilish smirk of his. Like he knows a secret I'm not privy to.

"Oh, yeah, and how's that?" *Uh oh.* It's like he was Sherlock

Holmes and he cracked the case. It's like he can read my mind, and he is just putting up a pretense that he can't.

"Like you want to…"

"Kiss! Kiss! Kiss!" Anna chants loudly. The bridal party, with the exception of Robert, starts following suit. She's the bride and leader of the pack, after all. Now they are all chanting at Aidan and me.

Meanwhile, I desperately want to know the ending to Aidan's sentence. *Like you want to…* My heart is throbbing with anticipation and wonder of all the possibilities that could end that statement. Because if I am being honest with myself, there is a running list of words or phrases in contention for those endless possibilities. It's like a fun game of Mad Libs that I am yearning to play with Aidan. I don't know if that's the alcohol talking or if those are my honest feelings on the subject. Everything is starting to get blurred.

"Kiss! Kiss! Kiss!" Anna keeps chanting.

My eyes widen at Anna and I mouth, *What are you doing?* Although on the inside, I am secretly hoping that Aidan will actually kiss me because he wants to, and not because it's out of necessity.

Aidan most definitely is a mind reader because the next thing I know, he is cradling my face in his hands and kissing me. My mind flies back to the kiss we shared at the premiere afterparty. It starts off soft and slow and innocent. Anna is cheering, as is the rest of the crowd. *Another mental note: kill Anna later.* After a sufficient amount of time elapses, I start to pull away, but Aidan just pulls me closer. If I thought my heart was throbbing before, I wasn't nearly prepared for what my pulse is doing now. Shivers course through my body as Aidan's tongue comes in contact with mine. This kiss is no longer slow and innocent. It is explorative and uninhibited. It is morphing into a kiss that weakens my knees and makes my thoughts even more cloudy than before.

When he finally pulls back, I whisper, trying to ground myself in reality, "Necessity?"

Aidan pulls his eyebrows together, then smiles and whispers in my ear, "Absolutely not, Hales. I *wanted* to kiss you."

My heart leaps, but I can't admit that to Aidan. I don't want to scare him with the fact that I am, despite my best efforts, falling for him.

23

Aidan

Call me biased, but Haley is the cutest drunk person I've ever been around. It's refreshing to be around someone who is a happy drunk. I grew up around an angry and violent drunk. After we kissed at the bar, she said that she wanted to go home, and I didn't hesitate to grant her request. She's already too far gone for my liking. Not because she's not her own woman and can't take care of herself or do whatever she wants to do. But because, even though she is a happy drunk, she isn't really the Haley that I've grown to know. Yeah her inhibitions are temporarily gone, but I think I know Haley well enough to know that she doesn't like to feel out of control.

I call an Uber as soon as she tells me she wants to go back to the beach house. The whole drive home, she rests her head on my shoulder and closes her eyes. At some point, she kicks off her shoes, which she claims are killing her feet and she's going to murder Anna for making her wear them tonight.

"I didn't want to say no to my best friend. She's the bride and I just wanted to make her happy. I was going to be a bride once. Did I tell you that? I feel like I've told you that." She nestles her nose into my neck, causing my body to vibrate from the sudden, foreign touch. And I don't mind it. I graze her bare shoulder and feel goosebumps appear.

"Yes you did, Hales," I respond.

The brakes of the Uber squeak slightly as we come to a stop in front of the beach house. It's completely dark except for the porch light that was left on–Haley's mom must've turned it on before she went upstairs for the night.

"Thanks man," I say to the driver as I pull Haley out of the car with me.

Once I shut the door, I scoop her up into my arms and carry her like she is a real damsel in distress–which to me, she is tonight–and who I have no problem rescuing. I can't imagine being in such close proximity to Natasha and Isaac for an extended weekend, watching them kiss and be all up on each other. I may have played a superhero in the movies, but Haley is truly the one with superpowers to withstand that type of company.

"Okay, beautiful, I have to put you down for a second so I can open the door." I carefully place Haley down next to me. But once I do, she starts to sway to one side and I immediately strap an arm around her torso to prevent her from face-planting into the ground. I pull out the key from my pocket, unlock the door, and find a light switch so I don't trip over something and fall with precious cargo in my hands. I lift Haley into my arms again and she lets out a little squeal.

"Shhh, Hales, we're going to wake up your mom," I say, half-laughing.

"Oh my God, it's like I'm back in high school, trying to sneak back into the house after going out with Anna to a party. Do you think we'll get grounded if we get caught?"

I let out another laugh and whisper, "We just might, that's why you have to be quiet."

"Okay." She lets out a goofy smile and puts a finger to her lips in a shushing manner.

We make it up to our room and I shut the door quietly. I place Haley on the bed and instead of the overhead light, I find the small black switch of the bedside lamp. Much more forgiving to someone who is intoxicated. Haley throws her shoes toward her suitcase and they plop right into the open compartment.

Then, she does the thing I am dreading the most. And it's not because I won't like what I am going to see. It's because I know that I'll like it so much that I will never, ever see Haley the same again.

She unzips her little black dress, a dress that is dangerously sexy. So sexy, in fact, that I noticed every straight man in that damn bar had his eyes transfixed on Haley. Even that prick, Robert, had his eyes glued to his ex-fiancée. This whole night has been torture not being able to throw an afghan blanket over this total babe of a woman and tell the rest of the world to back off–she is all mine. No one else should look at her like I am looking at her, even though she deserves every single one of those stares. She deserves to be unmistakingly wanted.

Against my carnal instinct, I rummage through her suitcase to find her matching pajamas as quickly as I can. Even though I've seen her in a bathing suit and I already knew that she has a rocking body, this just seems more intimate somehow. I don't want her to feel disrespected or awkward around me. I want her to feel the opposite. She kicks her dress playfully toward me and I catch it as it hits me square in my chest. I suddenly am very aware that Haley is in fact almost naked again in front of me and for some reason, this time it has much more weight than the other times. I place her dress in her suitcase as Haley clumsily falls onto the bed, groaning as if she is in pain.

I rush over to her. "Hales, are you okay? What's wrong?"

"Is the bed on one of those thingies–you know like at a playground and they go around and around?"

Like I said, the cutest. "Um, you mean a merry-go-round? No, Hales the bed is not on a merry-go-round. I think you might have the spins. Let's go to the bathroom just in case." I lift her up from the bed so that she is level with my eyes. I brush her tousled hair away from her face. Even in her drunk state, she is still Haley. She has the same kind eyes I have come to know these past three years.

"Aidan don't be silly, I don't need..." There it is, that dreadful pause that occurs every time a drunk person realizes that, in fact, they are not as okay as they thought.

"Okay, bathroom. Let's go babe."

We barely make it to the toilet before Haley starts throwing up. I grab her hair just in time and hold it up for her and rub her back. I can feel her body convulse each time she lets out all the alcohol she consumed tonight. I was worried this was going to happen, but I also didn't want to tell Haley what to do. She was finally letting loose and I wanted that for her. I felt comfortable with her doing it tonight because she had me looking after her, and I sure as hell was going to make sure she got home safe and that she was taken care of. And now I don't care if my night is going to consist of me holding a beautiful woman's hair back as she expels half her body weight in fluids – I would do it a thousand times over for Hales. I spot a black hair-tie on the counter, grab it, and put Haley's hair in a ponytail to free up my other hand for anything else she needs.

"I think I'm okay," Haley says as she flushes the toilet. She grabs some toilet paper from the roll next to her and wipes her mouth. "I need to brush my teeth. Ugh, Aidan, go away." She unsuccessfully starts pushing me out of the bathroom. I can tell she is putting in all the strength she has left. "My god are you legitimately Iron Man? Or Captain Underpants? Or whatever your character's name is. How much do you have to work out to get this body?" Now she starts to caress my abs and I tighten up and not because I don't like it–I definitely do. She is just tickling me and her hands are like ice.

She makes a face. "Ugh, seriously though, get out. You are probably super grossed-out. I seriously can't talk with you until I brush my teeth."

"Fine. I'll be right out here if you need me."

She shuts the door in my face and I start taking off my own shirt. I throw on another old UConn shirt from college and pull on some sweatpants. I am in for a long night. I need to get comfortable.

"Aidan." Haley dreadfully calls from the bathroom.

I zip up my suitcase and run over to the bathroom door. "Yeah? Is everything okay? Do you need to throw up again?"

"No...I um, I just need my pajamas. They are in my suitcase, I think."

I grab them from the bed and gently knock on the door. The door cracks and all I see is Haley's arm sticking out and her hand open, awaiting the pajamas. I laugh and say, "Hales, you know that I just saw you in your bra and panties, right? That was me in there with you."

"I know, but now I am very aware of how almost-naked I am and I just got really self-conscious. I mean, have you seen yourself?" Now I am full-on laughing, clasping my hand to my mouth, trying to stifle it so as to not wake Haley's mom. How could this woman become even sexier through what she thought were insecurities? It will never cease to baffle me.

"Aidan M. Stone. Give. Me. My. Pajamas."

Contemplating pulling a George Bailey in *It's A Wonderful Life*, and not giving her clothes back, I decide against it and hand her the pajamas. This is a "very interesting situation" indeed. She closes the door again. Even though I can't see her face, I know that her nose is scrunched-up out of anger and her eyebrows are pulled together. Her brown eyes possibly ablaze with both fury and drunkenness. I know that she is clouded, but I certainly have never been more clear. I know it is an unfair advantage, but I don't care. Haley is always putting walls up and I feel like I am finally chipping away, slowly but surely, with every conversation, every glance, every touch, every kiss. She isn't timid around me anymore. The nerdy assistant with the glasses is no more. She has been replaced with this talented, confident woman who intimidates me to no end.

In this moment, it becomes abundantly clear to me that I want to be like George Bailey in an entirely different sentiment–I want to give Haley the moon.

She finally emerges from the bathroom in all her pajama-set glory. She placed her hair in a messy top bun while she was in the bathroom and I can tell she washed the makeup off. Color has returned to her face. She looks like Haley again and that makes me all bubbly inside. She no longer smells like tequila and champagne, but rather mint and the clean scent of her moisturizer. She tentatively takes a step and runs into the bedside table, clearly still very drunk. I get up quickly and grab her arm to steady her.

"Are you also The Flash, too?"

"Your superhero name-dropping game is on point tonight, Hales. Especially the Captain Underpants one," I chuckle. I lead her to the bed and help her lie down. I pull the comforter over her legs and stop mid-torso.

"I've seen the movies. I know what I am talking about. You know all your *Avenger* buddies, including Captain Underpants. Oooo, Chris Evans. Would you mind introducing me? He is so hot."

Even though Haley is drunk, I still feel a little deflated and my ego takes a hit. Luckily the odds are ever in my favor. "Um, hate to break it to you Hales, but Chris is now married."

"Ugh, why is life so unfair??" She puts a pillow over her face, muffling her cry. "I wouldn't have a chance anyway. I am sure his wife is nauseatingly stunning."

"Not as stunning as you."

Something clicks in Haley's brain because I feel the energy shift between us. *Shit, was that too much?* I am just telling her the truth. She's going to kick me out of this bedroom in 2.5 seconds.

"Aidan, can I ask you a question?" She sits up and gets dangerously close to my face. She looks serious.

My stomach drops. She is definitely going to ask me to leave. She is going to ask me to get lost. Good riddance, Aidan Stone.

"What's that?"

She sheepishly looks down and her voice shakes slightly, "What is *your* number? You never told me the other night."

Has she really been thinking of that since the other night? I guess I can't blame her. I've been thinking about the fact that she has only slept with one person in her life. Jealousy courses through my veins as I think about her in bed with Robert. He is the only person in this world who has seen Haley in her most vulnerable state and he fucking ruined it. The only positive is that he is never going to sleep with Haley ever again. I kneel down next to the bed, rest my forearms on the mattress and exhale. "You really want to know?"

She returns my gaze. "Yes...and no. I don't know." Haley takes a pillow and covers her face with it. A muffled, "Never mind, just forget it" comes through the blockade.

I snicker and lower the pillow. Haley is biting her lip and her knee is bobbing. She's nervous. I need to be honest with her. That's how our relationship has always been. My heart races and there is a pit in my stomach. Now I'm suddenly nervous. I don't want Haley to judge me or think less of me because more than half of my number is from the past six months. I have always been a monogamist. I need to reassure her that I'm not that guy she is imagining. I am not a rake or a play boy. My hand instinctively lands on her knee, hoping to calm her. "Seven. I had a high school girlfriend, a college girlfriend, Natasha, and then four other flings I guess you can call them."

Her mouth parts and looks surprised. "Seven? That's it?"

"That's it."

"Wow. That's a lot lower than I expected." A hint of a smile graces her face.

"So...you didn't sleep with all the women in the pictures then?"

The nervous pit in my stomach turns into full-blown flutters. She has been keeping count. She cares about who I am with. About who I have slept with.

She cares.

I lift her chin up a little so I can look at her in her hazy, tired eyes and say, "No."

She looks into my eyes and I can tell that she is relieved that I did not turn into the person that the media thought I turned into. The real me never went anywhere. They just didn't bother to look beneath the surface.

Haley's chin escapes my grasps as she sits back up. "Aidan, can I ask you another question?"

"Shoot." I lower my hand and wait for the next question in her drunken interrogation.

"You have my birthday as your security code at your apartment. Why?"

"Because it's easy for me to remember, but it's also a detail not a lot of people would know about because it's not directly related to me... And it's a reminder of you when I am in New York and you're back in L.A." If she's going to be vulnerable, so can I.

Haley puts her fist under her chin and looks at me, seemingly contemplating what I just revealed. Her brown eyes seem to focus for the first time since we got back tonight, and I can't stop staring at them. I never want to stop staring at them. "Can I kiss you?"

I am floored by the intimacy of the question. We have been kissing each other for several days now without each other's permission right beforehand. I've never had someone ask to kiss me before. It is refreshing. I quickly realize that I would do just about anything that Haley asked me to do. Even if that means kissing her over and over again.

Especially kissing her over and over again.

I smile. "Of course you can kiss me, Hales."

Haley slowly closes the gap between us and gives me the softest, most innocent kiss imaginable. It is clear this isn't out of lust by any means. It is PG-13 at most. I haven't been kissed like this since my very first kiss. Only this time, I know what I am doing. And so does Haley. That much is true.

Unfortunately, she leans away and her lips depart from mine. I fight back all the urges to bring those lips back to mine and up the rating, because I never take advantage of a woman. Especially a woman who is drunk and not fully herself. No, I am going to reserve those kisses for lucid Haley. I want her to remember those kisses on those sweet, soft, pink lips.

She looks up at me doe-eyed and says, "Thank you."

"For what?"

"Always saving me."

What does she mean? "Hales, you are the last person who needs saving. If anything, you have saved me. How have I saved you?"

"Are you kidding me, Aidan? You've saved me from making a mockery of myself at this wedding like everyone was expecting me to. You've saved me from my own fears. You've saved me from dealing with Robert this entire weekend." She looks down and grazes my hand with her finger, sending shockwaves through my body. Who knew that such a small gesture could have such an impact? "Most importantly, you are saving me from myself."

I can tell she's opening up to me in a way that she hasn't done before in all the years I've known her. But I also know her well enough to know that the moment she exposes her vulnerability, that's when she'll put those damn walls back up. Never again with me. I am always going to be armed with dynamite around Haley.

"Well, if that's how you feel, Hales, then you're welcome. And I would gladly save you every single day if that meant I could see you happy." I want to bring her back to my lips so badly. I want to hold her in my arms and tell her that I feel so much more than I ever thought I could. Things are starting to change for me. The terms are not as cut-and-dry anymore. We are well past the point of no return. I want to renegotiate. Immediately.

I need to tell her the truth about how I feel. I don't think I can wait any longer. I swallow so hard, I know my Adam's apple clearly bobs up and down. "Hales..."

"Captain America!!" she shouts, hitting my pectoral muscle so hard, I wince slightly.

"What?" I ask, legitimately confused, pressing my hand to my now-stinging chest.

"I said Captain Underpants earlier. I meant Captain America!" She starts laughing at her own mistake and snorts in the process, which makes her laugh even more. I can't help but laugh too. I didn't think snorts could be sexy but apparently I am learning that just about anything that has to do with Haley turns out to be mind-bogglingly sexy.

"All right you goof, I think it's time for bed." I reach beside Haley and tap the pillow twice. "We have a busy day tomorrow, babe."

"Ugh, fine."

I tuck her in, then go into the bathroom and get the small trash can. I place it right next to the bed–just in case. I reach over her head to snag an extra pillow so I can fashion together my makeshift bed. Haley grabs my forearm and says, "Do you want to know a secret?"

"Always."

"I have a dream date."

"Is that so?" This is so random, but I'm curious about what is in the recesses of Haley's brain. I want to get to know every piece of her. Especially her hopes and dreams, since I intend to make them all come true.

"Yes. It is on the beach. At sunset. With my favorite pizza and wine. With blankets and pillows. And the guy has a laptop where we can watch one of my favorite movies. And watch the sun go down. And on my dream date, my date would kiss me, unreservedly, passionately, with no regard for the world around us because we would be each other's world."

She is starting to doze off. I finally grab the pillow from behind her. I very much want to be that guy in her dreams. Hopefully she feels the same way.

"That sounds perfect, Hales." I give her a small kiss on her forehead and place my pillow down on the ground.

"Do you want to hear another secret?" She turns to her side and clutches the pillow as a way to almost anchor herself. "Well, technically it's two more secrets."

"Go on." I could listen to her talk all night.

"I love the way you look at me."

Maybe I haven't been so guarded with my own emotions. I don't want to be guarded with Haley and part of me is glad that she has noticed my genuine reaction to her presence.

"And?" I egg on.

"And what?" She is barely holding on, nestling her head in the pillow. I want her to get rest, but selfishly, I want her to tell me her other secret.

"You said there were two secrets. What was the second?"

"I love that you call me babe. It makes this whole thing seem real." She finally drifts off to sleep, creating a soothing cadence with her breathing.

It is a bittersweet confession. No actually, I feel dejected in every possible way. It brings me back to the reality of the situation. Our deal. She clearly doesn't know how I *really* feel. Even after the kiss we shared at the bar, she still doesn't believe that this is starting to become real for me. In her defense, we did start this whole relationship based on the pretense that all of this is fake, any romantic notion we display is for the sake of appearances, and we are doing this to fulfill some other agenda.

The thing about plans and deals? They sometimes change.

And that is definitely the case with our deal. I just hope I can convince her that everything has changed—at least for me.

Aidan

The waves crash against the shoreline. Haley is getting ready for the rehearsal dinner. She's been recovering after her wild bachelorette party night for most of the day, so she finally wanted to take a shower and slowly get ready since she's still a little hungover. (I'm being nice. She is *extremely* hungover.) I told her I needed to check some emails and look at a script Chris sent over to me a couple hours ago. I'm sitting in one of the wooden chairs on the deck, overlooking the ocean.

"Is this seat taken?"

I look up. Surprisingly, Anna is standing next to the empty chair. She's holding two small disposable cups of coffee.

I click the side button on my phone and give her my full attention. I gesture to the chair. "Nope, all yours."

"Thanks." I notice her hair is curled and it seems like her makeup is done. She is already ready for her own rehearsal dinner. Minus the outfit. I doubt that Anna is going to show up to her rehearsal in cut-off jean shorts and a white tank top. Or maybe she would. What do I know?

She extends one of the cups to me. "Coffee?"

That's probably a good idea. I have a feeling I am in for a long night.

I accept the cup from her. "Thank you, that's very kind."

She finally takes a seat next to me.

"So how are you feeling, bride-to-be?"

"Oh me? I am just dandy." She smiles and sips her coffee.

"No nerves yet?" If I were getting married in 24 hours, I would be a nervous wreck. Not that I don't want to get married. I actually do. I want the whole gamut. A wife, kids, a house, a huge yard for Ginny and any future pups. The nerves would stem more from my fear of fucking everything up. My schedule as an actor is insane, yet I would want to be there for every moment with my family. I really need to find the right woman to share this crazy life with. That's probably the first and most important step.

Anna squints out at the water. "I don't know if I would call it nerves. I think it's more excitement than nervousness. I've been waiting to marry this man for almost fifteen years, that's probably why. Anyway, I am here on official best friend business."

Oh god, where is she going with this?

She looks me dead in the eye, and in an oddly flirtatious but accusatory tone she says, "Aidan Stone, I know your dirty little secret."

Shit.

"And I am telling you right now: if you hurt my girl, I am going to hunt you down and have Dan kick your perfect little ass, okay?" She smiles after her threat.

I try to hide my amusement, but am unsuccessful. Through my laugh, I say, "Got it."

"I promise not to say anything. Your secret is safe with me. I haven't even told Dan." She drinks her coffee. "And I tell him everything."

I press my eyebrows together. "Why haven't you?"

"Because I know my best friend and how important this is to her. How important for this whole relationship to be believable for everyone else. I wouldn't betray her like that. Apart from Dan, she is the most important person in my life." She inhales. "Aidan, she is like my sister. I've seen her get hurt badly before and I am not interested in seeing my best friend crumble to pieces again." She looks down at the styrofoam cup and grazes a finger along the black plastic lid.

"You mean crumbled by Robert?"

She nods in confirmation.

"What exactly happened between them?" I ask.

"She didn't tell you?" Anna says incredulously.

"All she said was that they were engaged and he broke things off. That's it. She never told me what actually happened."

Anna shakes her head and sighs. "Well that asshole never truly treated her like the absolute queen that she is." *I couldn't agree more.* "One night, Haley came home a little early from one of our epic hangouts because she had a headache. Robert was supposed to be working late on a deposition, but she found him AND his colleague – now fiancée – Julia, having sex in the shower."

A rush of pure anger courses throughout his body. My jaw clenches. God I could destroy that son of a bitch.

"Yeah, I wanted to kill him too."

I relax my jaw and hand, but inwardly I am still fuming. It takes everything inside of me to remain sitting here next to Anna rather than track Robert down and beat the hell out of him. My eyebrows furrow. "I take it that wasn't the first time between those two?"

"Haley learned that Robert was cheating on her ever since Julia started at the law firm. He said it was an 'instant attraction.'" *I instantly want to pummel him.* "I mean, he and Haley were together since their freshman year in college. I thought they were endgame. I have never seen her so devastated. The wedding was only a month away." Anna exhales, shaking her head a little as if to clear the memory of that time. "Robert is the reason that my best friend since kindergarten moved 3,000 miles away. And I honestly don't blame her. She's had her heart closed off for a while now. That's why when she brought you here, I knew there was something about you that had to be different."

"Well, if you know the truth about me and Haley, then you know that we have an expiration date. She is just playing along." I look away from Anna into the ocean. "And so am I."

"Sure, you are, Casanova."

My stomach drops, but I chuckle to mask my nervousness. "What do you mean?"

"I see the way you look at her. It's the way Dan looks at me." *Dang, she's good.* "It's real for you, isn't it, Aidan?"

"You really are her best friend."

"You didn't answer my question. Your good looks and status don't distract me, Aidan Stone. I am madly in love with someone else. Sorry to disappoint."

I smirk at her. "As I told Dan last night at the bachelor party, he is a lucky man. And Hales is a lucky woman to have a friend like you."

Anna tips her cup of coffee towards me and winks. "Damn straight they are."

I shake my head slightly and smile. The seagulls are calling out, confiding their own deep dark secrets to each other. The tide slides up and down the shore line, erasing the past and providing a blank space for the future. "Yes."

"Yes what?"

I looked over at Anna and gulp, "Yes, it's real for me."

25

Haley

The rehearsal goes on without a hitch. Well, I guess a small hitch is the ring bearer gets scared, starts crying, and runs to his mom, Dan's sister. She assures Dan and Anna that he will be ready for the wedding tomorrow. I keep a straight face and truly try to focus on what is going on in the ceremony.

Flashbacks of last night slowly make their way into my current consciousness. Most of what I remember is Aidan's perfect face, his perfect smile, his perfect everything. I remember him holding back my hair while pretty much all of the alcohol I consumed exited my body. I do remember him admitting what his number is (*Seven!!*) and that he uses my birthday as the code to his apartment. Two admissions that made my stupid, drunk heart pound so hard I thought it was going to literally burst out of my chest. The problem is:

I don't remember exactly what *I* said, but I do remember not shutting up. I become very chatty when I drink and when I am nervous. And that's what scares me. I probably humiliated myself and Aidan is probably going to fire me once we get back to L.A.

I haven't had that much to drink since the night I found out about Robert and Julia. I vowed to myself that I would never drink that much again. How ironic that I broke that vow as my best friend is about to make the biggest vow of her life tomorrow. I've purposely avoided Aidan all day. Partly because I am embarrassed that my boss saw me absolutely hammered due to the fact that I was stuck in ex-fiancé hell. Last night, I just needed to escape mentally since I couldn't escape physically, and I used the bachelorette party as the perfect excuse to drink.

Oh, and I am also avoiding him because of that kiss at the bar. I vividly remember that kiss. That kiss felt like a *real* kiss. That kiss rocked my entire world. But I can't admit that to Aidan, because he most certainly doesn't feel the same way.

When we return to the house, I decide to distract myself and help set up the folding tables and chairs outside on the backyard lawn. Anna and Dan decided to get food trucks for the rehearsal dinner, since tomorrow is a more formal dinner at the reception. They wanted to keep tonight as low-key as possible. I place tiny purple and white flowers in small clear vases and make sure that every table has one in the center of it. I pretty much do everything under the sun to avoid the inevitable conversation I am going to have with my fake boyfriend at some point in the evening. I wince as one more memory of me snorting while laughing infiltrates my mind. The haze has lifted and everything has become clearer.

I am on my third glass of wine for the night. Anna is busy talking with her future in-laws, and my mind can't stop replaying what happened last night at the bachelorette party. Also, I need to get away from the groomsmen, especially Robert, who is getting egregiously drunk. I think I am safe until I feel muscular arms wrap around me from behind. I feel flutters in my stomach, which I need to cease. But that is impossible when he nestles his face in the crook of my neck and says, "Hey, gorgeous."

Too real. I shrug my way out of his enormous arms. "Stop."

"Stop what?"

"Stop calling me that."

"I'm not going to call you things that you aren't, Hales. It's not in my nature. I call it as I see it. You *are* gorgeous."

"We need to talk about that kiss." I need to stop his antics now if we're going to make it out of this deal with no feelings attached. I need to guard my heart.

"Okay, to what kiss are you referring?" He looks down at me with that annoyingly perfect smirk. He really needs to stop doing that.

"You know what kiss I am referring to." I finally look into his eyes. They are gleaming in a way that I've never seen before. This is exactly the problem. "It's starting to feel too real, Aidan. I don't know if I can do this anymore. Maybe it would be better if you go back to L.A. without me. And not come to the wedding tomorrow."

His face falls. "And why would you think that? I am in this, Hales."

"I know. That is my point, Aidan. We have a contract and we have come dangerously close to..."

His eyebrows furrow. "To what?"

I sigh. "The lines are starting to feel blurred and that scares me."

"Why does that scare you? Isn't this a good thing, that we might have something real here?" He reaches down to grab my hands, but I quickly escape his quite literal hold on me.

"Why doesn't it scare *you*? I don't understand why you even agreed to this in the first place. It doesn't make any sense. You could literally date or fake-date anyone in the entire universe and you chose me."

"Because...it's always been real for me, Hales. Our connection. From the moment we met, I knew you would genuinely have my back and be there for me. I knew you were the nicest person on this fucking planet. I knew there was something special about you. I was so intrigued to find out what made you so special. Why I was so drawn to you. Did you ever consider that all this time, you've been it for me?"

I am utterly speechless. My heart rate is going a million miles a minute. Is he seriously saying that he has liked me from the day I stumbled into that conference room and spilled scalding coffee all over his pristine white shirt and nearly gave him third-degree burns?

"I just...I can't do this." This would never work in the long run. He is a movie star and I am his assistant. *Remember your place in this world, Haley.* What if he gets bored of me and drops me like Robert did? What if I let him in and he utterly rips my heart to shreds? What if I let myself fall for him completely, so much that I can't breathe without him near me? What if that has already happened and I am terrified that I will lose him someday? The only way to lose someone is to have them to begin with. I am not about to lose him. No way.

I start to speed-walk toward the house, hopefully not generating any attention. I desperately want to get back to the room upstairs and pack all of my things and try to find another place to stay. Maybe Anna will let me bunk with her tonight – after all, she and Dan are staying in separate rooms so that they don't see each other until the altar. I run into the house, door slamming behind me, and make my way upstairs. Maybe Aidan realizes it was a stupid idea to sign that contract in the first place. I am hoping his feet magically got superglued to the ground outside so he can't follow me.

I reach the bedroom and grab the door to close it. Like it was perfectly scripted in a screenplay, right as the door is about to shut, a hand presses against it to stop it. I could recognize that hand anywhere. It's the hand that has cradled my face, has held my hand in the worst moments of this weekend, has run through my hair, has playfully grabbed the back of my thighs during a friendly game of volleyball. A hand that I never want to let go of, ever. And that scares the hell out of me.

Aidan steps inside the room, closes the door and locks it to ensure no one will follow us in.

And here he goes again, weaving his perfect fingers through my hair and cradling my jawline, raising my face so that I have no other choice but to look into his hungry, sultry blue eyes. "Promise me something, Haley Swann."

How is this really happening to me right now? "What?"

"Never run away from me again. Seeing you run away from me gutted me. I never want to be the thing you run away from. I want to be what you are running to." He presses his forehead to mine, reaches his arms underneath my thighs, lifts me up and pins me against the bedroom door. I wrap my legs around his torso for security, but I have a feeling that he could hold me forever and never tire.

"Aidan."

"Promise me." Now his hard body is pressing me up against the door, which leaves his hands free to wander and deliciously graze parts of me that for the past three years I forgot existed. I knew in the right hands they would be awakened again.

"What about our contract?" I whisper shakily. Even though these words are coming out of my mouth, the rest of my body is yearning and confidently holding onto this magnetic man pinned to me.

Aidan's thumb brushes my bottom lip and he bites his own bottom lip, as if he is trying to restrain himself.

But I don't want him to.

Not anymore.

He looks down at me. "You still haven't promised me, Swann."

Breathless, I say, "I promise."

He smiles so big that those delicious dimples appear. I've honestly never seen him smile like this entire time I've known him. I contest back, "You still haven't answered *me*, Stone. What about our contract?"

His eyes are on fire. "Fuck the contract, Hales. Actually, I would like to make an amendment to our little contract."

I breathe unevenly. I've never seen this side of Aidan before. Feverish. Uninhibited. Almost devilish. And I want to know more. "And what amendment would that be?"

"You're about to find out." He presses his lips to mine, returning to the kiss we shared last night. Only this time, it isn't for show and it isn't because people are chanting for us to do so.

"Wait, stop!" I break our kiss and Aidan groans.

"I mean, don't stop, but stop." I can't find my words in this whirlwind scenario. A scenario that never in a million years did I imagine I would ever find myself in. I have to lay all my fears out on the table. "Once we do this, we can't go back."

"I don't want to go back. I want to keep moving forward and discover all the facets of you, Haley Swann."

"But, what if..."

"Just let me love you, Haley." Aidan looks fiercely at me, with a naughty grin on his face, like he's up to no good–a look that is rendering me utterly defenseless. I want to find out what it means for Aidan Stone to love me. "I promise you won't be disappointed."

"Whose being presumptuous now?"

His smile widens even more as he looks down at my lips. "You take that back."

"Prove me wrong then."

26

Haley

Aidan's mouth collides with mine so vigorously that it takes me by surprise, so much so that I can't help but giggle against his lips.

"What are you laughing at, you goof?"

"You just seem very eager to kiss me."

"Well, maybe that's because I've been wanting to kiss you for a while now Hales, I mean *really* kiss you, and I am not wasting any more time not kissing you. I never want to waste time again." He looks intently at me with his teal eyes.

My feet finally reach the ground after what felt like an eternity propped up in Aidan's arms, which I've decided is my preferred method of transport from now on.

When I finally get my bearings on solid ground, I bend down and slide off my shoes. I am about to unzip my dress. Aidan's hand stops me.

"Don't you dare."

"What? You don't want me to take off my clothes?" I ask, lifting one eyebrow quizzically.

"No."

For a moment I am deflated, self-conscious that I'm really not what Aidan wants. Then he wraps his hands around my back and finds my zipper. His hands clench tight around the fabric and he pulls outward, causing it to rip and hang off my shoulders, exposing my bra underneath. "*I* wanted to."

I stand there, breathless, as the sexiest man in the universe slides what is left of my dress all the way down my body, keeping one of his hands glued to me, tracing my figure slowly and intentionally, pausing only to feel my lace panties and tracing the hem dangerously with his fingertip. How is it possible to feel so exposed and so secure at the same time? That's the magic that Aidan brings to the table, and I am here to revel in it.

"It's my turn," I say playfully. I stare at Aidan's white button-down shirt and decide to take the opposite method that he used with my dress a second ago. I slowly start unbuttoning his shirt, ogling him in the process. I want to take my sweet time with him. These past two weeks have been a whirlwind, decoding what was real and what was for show. And then tonight I discover there has been this invisible string tying me to Aidan since the very first day we met. After every small translucent button, I touch his skin, which is on fire beneath my cool fingertips. With every touch, his abs tighten, showcasing each ridge, taut and cut to perfection. I want to tease him a little. I want to take in the sight of him shamelessly and freely, something I haven't been able to do since I've met him. Now it's just him and me, and I can finally enjoy Aidan in all of his glory.

Aidan growls in frustration. "You're killing me, Swann. I'll rip my own shirt off if that means I can continue kissing you."

I reach the last button, satisfied that I evoked any sense of urgency in Aidan. I trace my hands along his unbuttoned shirt, reaching the top of his broad shoulders and sliding his shirt all the way down his arms, stopping momentarily at each curvature, each muscle. When his shirt falls, Aidan takes control and feverishly kisses me, like he is making up for lost time. One hand is completely entangled in my hair and the other presses my back, causing our bodies to mold together. I swallow hard as I feel how much I am really affecting his body. There is definitely no mistaking my affect on him. Chills make their way all up and down my skin, which is in direct contrast to what's happening internally–everything is on fire. Sparks fly with every touch.

Aidan lowers me to the bed, carrying my entire body weight with one arm, his other arm busy holding the back of my head so that our lips won't part. I'm not planning on unlocking my lips from his anytime soon. My pulse rings in my ears, as I suddenly become acutely aware of who I am making out with and who, undoubtedly, I am about to have sex with. My body tenses with that thought.

Aidan is the first one to break our kiss. "Don't."

"What?"

"I feel you holding back, Hales." He kisses me again, moving my body toward the headboard. Then he whispers in my ear, sending shockwaves through me: "I don't want you to hold back with me. Not now. Never again." His massive hands move deliciously down my body, slowly, firmly, as if he is memorizing a path that is vital to remember.

Our lips and bodies move in sync, like we were always meant to do this. Like we were meant to be here, in this moment, forgetting about the world outside these four bedroom walls, forgetting about what awaits us when we return home.

Aidan presses kisses onto my collarbone, his tongue slightly coming into contact with my delicate skin. My breath hitches and I gasp at the sensation coursing through my veins.

"Can we add *this* to the contract?" he asks, knowing full well what my response is going to be.

"Yes," I exhale.

"Good." His hands are busy making their way down my body, going further south, without any detours. His thumb brushes against my lace panties. My body instinctively gives into his touch and I groan. "What about this?" Aidan presses his lips hard against mine, gliding his fingers inside my panties and then into me, making me gasp. The sheer size of his fingers alone inside of me makes my skin flush. I could feel him smile against our locked lips, clearly satisfied with how wet he is making me.

"It's more than okay, Aidan. Do whatever you want with me," I say, finally admitting to myself and Aidan how much I want this to happen. How much I want those sparks to turn into a fire. How much I never want him to stop touching me like he is right now.

Aidan gives me yet another devilish grin as he pins my hands above my head. "As you wish, Hales."

In one swift motion, he reaches a free hand behind my back and unhooks my balconette bra. I try to move my hands, but Aidan only strengthens his hold on me. "I have your hands up here for a reason, Swann." It's dangerous what one hand is capable of doing. In what seems like no time at all, my bra is suddenly stripped from my body and strewn onto the floor. Aidan's lips traverse along the curves of my body. Kissing. Sucking. Licking. All so delicious and ravenous. My back arches as he nears south of my belly button. He is no longer treating me delicately. And I don't mind it one bit.

He pauses, lets go of my wrists, and props himself up to where he is still hovering over me, but just enough that the weight and warmth of his body has departed from mine. I need it back immediately. My mouth lets out a guttural reaction. "What are you doing, Aidan? Why did you stop?"

His eyes journey across my entire body – it is his turn to ogle me, apparently. I get flushed all over again. Talk about ravenous. Aidan's eyes are turning dark, like he doesn't want to hold anything back anymore.

"I am taking you all in, Hales. You don't realize how fucking gorgeous you really are."

Feeling brave, I sit up completely, so my chest is flush with his. I grab his belt buckle and loosen it, sliding the entirety of the belt out of the loops, throwing it on the floor next to the rest of the scattered clothes. It is my turn to wrap my hands around his waist. The elastic band of his underwear peeks above the top of his dress pants. Suddenly my bravery flies out the window and I retract my hands.

"Wait, why did *you* stop?" Aidan asks.

"I'm nervous," I admit. I want to be truthful to Aidan, especially in a situation like this. A situation that can never be reversed and will live forever in my brain.

Aidan kisses me, leaving me breathless again. It is a kiss of reassurance. In between kisses, Aidan says, "Everything is going to be okay, Hales. I promise."

I press my forehead to his and exhale out of relief. He knows how to calm me, even when he is the one making my heart race.

As if my hands are independent of my own hindering thoughts, they find their way to the button of his pants and unbutton them. "I want you, Aidan."

Aidan helps me with what I didn't finish and his pants slide down the rest of his perfect body. It's a shame that he can't walk around like this all the time, but I guess seeing this man in his underwear 24/7 wouldn't help the hysteria since he looks like a model for Calvin Klein. He should be their fricken ambassador. I'm sure sales would skyrocket. *Step aside, Jeremy Allen White.*

"I want you too, Haley." He leans down to where his pants are and reaches into one of his pockets, pulling out a condom. I prop myself up on my forearms and watch as Aidan rips the condom wrapper with his teeth and rolls it on in one fluid motion. Then he leans down and his teeth grab onto the hem of my panties. He slides them all the way down my legs, causing them to tear slightly from his aggressive pull.

Nervously laughing, I tease, "At this rate, you're going to have to buy me a brand new wardrobe, Stone."

Aidan slowly crawls back on top of me, clearly gloating because he knows that he has me. He has set my soul on fire and obliterated any semblance of walls I had left. He brushes the hair out my face, looking at me with such tenderness it makes my heart explode. Although his actions are tender, his words are laced entirely with sensuality. "Gladly." He eases into me and my need for him overtakes my body in such a way that I no longer have control. Normally I would hate to feel this way. Not now. This is a lack of control I am happy to give into.

So much has built up to this moment and the spark has now fully ignited between us–it is near combustible. I wrap my legs around his sculpted back, exploring every muscle with my heels. I kiss him, gliding my tongue in his mouth, and he returns the gesture. My fingers dig into his back and he lets out a groan. A groan that fuels my need for him even more. Every movement he makes against my body electrifies me. I can't live without feeling this sensation. I can't live my life without Aidan. Every touch, every kiss, every move this man performs makes an impression in my soul, and there is no way those will ever be erased.

"You're so damn gorgeous and I love that you're all mine," Aidan whispers in my ear, almost like it is a secret and I've sworn to keep it all to myself. He thrusts deeper into me, and I can't help but indulge in every movement. He must sense I am close because luckily, he doesn't stop moving. My toes curl and my muscles tense, finally releasing tingles throughout my entire body. He quickly comes right after and continues to hover over me, arms sexily flexing on either side of my body. How is his body not quivering like mine is? Maybe he is, but his outer armor isn't revealing that whatsoever.

Before I can fully catch my breath, Aidan steals yet another kiss from me. This man is pure magic and he's proved that over and over again. Now, I know Aidan on a whole other level, an otherworldly level.

"Did I prove you wrong?" he asks, dimples making their appearance on his handsome face, his fingers tracing my swollen lips. I'm in so much trouble.

"So wrong." My fingers trace Aidan's lips, which are just as swollen. He softly kisses my fingertips. He is so beautiful and sexy and insert whatever word to describe your fantasy man, because Aidan is certainly mine. He makes his way down to my neck and presses his lips against my insanely sensitive flesh. I gasp as if his touch is brand new to me, which at this point it's safe to say that nothing about Aidan is foreign to me anymore. Not after tonight.

"Be right back." Aidan walks into the bathroom and shuts the door. I pull the duvet over me and drape an arm over my face, processing what just happened. There has been a seismic shift in our relationship, and there is no turning back. This is definitely something I will never forget.

I reach down to the floor and find what is left of my panties and bra. I am putting them on when I hear the bathroom door open and see the light shut off. Aidan stops short of joining me in bed and says, "What do you think you're doing?"

After securing the last clasp, I say, "Um, I thought I would put my bra and what's left of my panties back on, and then go to bed?" I question my own actions based on the almost unlawful look Aidan is giving me right now. No one should be allowed to look at anyone like that—like he wants to devour every inch of me. Actually, scratch that—I would allow Aidan to look at me like that every day for the rest of my life.

He chuckles and confidently walks over to the side of the bed where I am sitting, anxiously awaiting what he is going to say, or do, next. Did I mention he is completely naked? And completely made of pure marble, apparently? My eyes can't stop staring at what is below his navel and I become very hot again. He finds the clasps of my bra and undoes my handiwork again. My lips part as I became aware of how much my body already aches for Aidan.

"You're cute if you think that was all I'm going to do to you tonight."

27

Aidan

I walk over to Haley, locking in the image before me. Long, sculpted legs that I want to grab and shamelessly caress for the rest of my life. Ever since she walked out of my bedroom in my t-shirt a couple nights ago, I have been wanting to glue my hands to her. She is fucking perfect, and I want more.

She is staring intensely at me, and I can see how hard she swallows when she takes me in. I wasn't lying when I told her that I'm not done with her. Not even close.

I am inches from Haley when I notice her staggered breathing.

"Ask me what's going on in my head," I tell her as I grab the back of her neck and kiss the side of it. Her pulse is racing and it makes me want her that much more.

"What's going on in your head?" she says almost breathlessly.

"How much I want to hear my name come out of that beautiful mouth of yours while I make you come again." I pause and kiss her neck again. "And again." One more kiss. "And again."

Haley lets out a breathy laugh. "That's it? Only three more times? Why Mr. Stone, I expected more from you." Her sultry eyes pierce into mine and she has no idea how much her teasing fuels me even more. My dick is getting hard again. I need her. Now.

I drop down to my knees, wrap my arms around her beautiful ass and pull her towards the edge of the bed. I slide my hands up and down her legs, which start quivering underneath my touch. I love the effect I have on her. I love seeing goosebumps follow wherever I touch her. The crazy thing is, I don't think Haley knows just how sexy she really is and how much men want her. I lightly press my lips to her ankle and leave a trail of kisses all the way up her leg. Haley's fingers grab my hair in response. I know what she wants and I am so willing to give it to her.

I look at her already-torn panties and smirk. I grab what is left of that flimsy fabric with one hand and rip the rest of them off. "Now you have no choice but to keep them off."

Haley's breath hitches and her eyes look extremely dark. She is so incredibly turned on. Even though she doesn't say a word and I can't read her fucking mind, her body is telling me everything I need to know.

I move my hands to her upper thighs and press down slightly to keep them in place. She scoots toward me and tugs my hair even harder, wanting this and wanting me. I tease her by licking both her inner thighs.

"Aidan...please..." she pleads.

I place her legs on top of my shoulders so she can't go anywhere if she wants to. My tongue enters her sweet, wet pussy and her groans fill the white noise that surrounds us. Her fingers clutch my hair tighter and tighter with every movement my tongue makes against her. My tongue makes its way to her clit and I stick my fingers inside her, resulting in a gasp and Haley begging me, "Don't stop."

I'm not planning on it. I love how fucking amazing she tastes and feels. Her pussy is tightening around my fingers and I know she is close. Her body tenses once more, causing her to dig her heels into my shoulders as she comes. My dick is throbbing from wanting to release, but I'm still not finished yet. I never back down from a challenge. Haley breathes heavily, grabs the sides of my face and kisses me hard. She is the eager one now and I don't mind it one bit.

"That was one," I whisper against her lips.

Haley bites her bottom lip as she regains her breath. Her long brown hair is a mess and her pale skin is flushed, but it is the most beautiful, messy sight I've ever seen. She isn't her usual neat-as-a-pin, always-put-together-in-some-form Haley. She is fully exposing herself to me. All her vulnerabilities. All her insecurities. All of what makes her her. She is allowing me to see a side of herself that she doesn't reveal to the world and for that, I consider myself lucky. I am pulling back the layers.

I grab her ass once more and lift her up as I get onto my feet. As I move toward a wall near the bedroom window, I reach into my toiletry bag on the dresser and pull out another condom.

"Do you need to put me down while you put that on? I'm sure you're tired from holding me," Haley interjects.

We hit the wall as I bite the condom wrapper open and proceed to put it on as I hold her up with my other arm. She wraps her gorgeous legs and arms around me tighter. Once I'm done, I encase her jaw with my now free hand and say, "Babe, you have no idea how much I actually lift at the gym, do you? I guarantee you, I will never get tired of holding you in my arms." Her body quivers as my dick presses against her, and her legs spread a little more apart. The party is still going on down in the backyard, but we are stuck in our own universe, totally abandoning all notions of the outside world.

I bring Haley's lips to mine as I pin her harder into the wall, trying to brace her for what I am about to do. I thrust into her and don't hold back. There is now going to be a clear before and after with Haley. I am going to memorize every way that she responds to my touch. Because I want to recreate this feeling with her again and again. I want to recreate this moment, because this moment is fucking life-changing. The way her hands hold onto my shoulder blades, the way her thighs clench the sides of my torso, the way her head falls slightly back and to the side with every unsteady breath, exposing her neck so that I can kiss her sensitive skin. Her pussy tightens around me. I grunt from the sensation it sends throughout my entire body, but I'm not going to come yet–this night is about Haley. All about her. She is never going to doubt how much I want her after tonight. Tonight is going to cement how much she means to me. How much I want to be with her. No deals. No conditions.

I bite her bottom lip and brush it with my tongue. "Come for me again."

I press my body closer to hers. I can feel her heart pounding as I pound into her. Her groans become louder, and I love that I am the one making her groan. Making her feel like she is the sexiest woman on this planet–which she is. She is so tight and wet and amazing. I drive into her so rough that one of the paintings on the wall crashes down and hits the floor, contributing to the intensity of the moment. "Oh my god, Aidan," is all Haley says as her legs shudder around me as she comes again.

"That's two," I say smugly.

Her dark brown eyes search mine and then there is a flicker of understanding. "Are you keeping count of how many times I...?"

"Come? Yes. By my count, I need to make you come at least one more time, right Swann?"

Her fingers get tangled in my own tousled hair as she kisses me, opening my mouth with her tongue. Her walls are finally fully demolished. I want to infiltrate all of her boundaries and never retreat. My hands caress her back and I grab the back of her head. I want her lips to be glued to mine forever. I never want to come up for air if this is the alternative. I walk over to the bed and lay her back down on the rumpled sheets.

I reluctantly break our kiss and whisper, "Hold onto the

headboard," into her ear, causing her back to arch up from my demand. I'm not holding back anymore and neither is Haley and for that, I'm fucking grateful. Her hands find the dark iron rods and clasp onto them tightly. She is already so ready for me that I ease into her for the third time tonight. The base of my spine tingles out of sheer need to release into this fucking perfect woman, but I made a promise and I fully intend to carry that promise through. I want to memorize every curve, every sensitive spot, every inch of Haley.

As if possessed by my need for her, my hands travel all around her body, savoring her. She is mine and like hell if I'm not going to fulfill her every fucking need in this life. Our bodies crash into each other with every oscillating movement. I want to drown in the scent of her skin, a faint hint of coconut and the invigorating pomegranate wafting off her long, curled, brown hair. She is the only woman in my life who has made me literally weak in the knees with her pure essence. I can tell that she is close again, and I reach underneath the base of her back and lift her up toward my body. She lets out a groan and my name escapes her lips once more, charging me with a fucking electric current that travels throughout my body. We come at the same time.

If every time is going to feel like this with Haley, I never want to leave this damn bed.

28

Haley

I am itching to see Aidan again. After last night, I can't stop thinking about him. I woke up this morning wrapped in his arms, but unfortunately my bliss was interrupted by a call from Anna already freaking out. I had been wondering when the dam was going to break– she has been remarkably calm this whole time. Luckily my phone's vibration didn't wake up Aidan, who looked so peaceful in the morning light. I didn't want to leave the bed, but I am the Maid of Honor and the bride needs me today.

I wrote a note saying that I would see him at the wedding.

I'll be one of the ones in light yellow. ;)

I left the note on my pillow, gathered my things, and headed out to see Anna.

If you were to look up "bridezilla" in the dictionary, I'm pretty sure you would find a picture of Anna's face in place of the definition. The girl has been majorly stressed since I arrived at Bridgehampton Tennis and Surf Club at 9 o'clock this morning. First, her hair isn't cooperating with the hairstylist. Then her dress has wrinkles toward the bottom and one of the many buttons up her back comes off. She gets a phone call from the caterer saying they are running a bit behind, but they promise everything will be ready by this evening. Even though her soon-to-be sister-in-law assured her that the ring bearer would be ready for today, he is being very difficult putting on his little tux, throwing tantrums left and right. Luckily, the makeup artist is on time and thankfully all of our makeup looks natural and elegant, in no way overdone, which is what Anna wants. She doesn't want us to look like clowns. I am in charge of last-minute steaming of all of the bridesmaid's dresses, while Anna takes bridal photos in her white robe.

Once we are all ready, Anna finally breathes. I smile at her. "Wow, you are one beautiful bride. Dan isn't going to know what hit him after all these years. He better cry or else I am disowning him forever." I hug her, careful not to wrinkle her dress or possibly have our makeup rub off on it. "I'm so happy for you, Anna. Are you ready, best friend?"

Anna smooths out her stunning, mermaid-style gown. Her blonde hair is pinned up on one side with a large, floral hair clip. She grabs her bouquet of yellow, purple and white flowers and beams back at me. "Ready."

I hear the processional music and let go of Anna's hand, hold onto my bouquet, and start walking down the aisle. White rose petals are scattered along the sides of the walkway and I do my best to look up and smile for the camera. A practice I surely perfected after attending a blockbuster premiere. At least this time, there is only one flash.

The ceremony is perfect. The weather cooperates and it isn't too windy on the beach. I love that they decided to get married in the evening. The photos will be beautiful and twilight is probably the most romantic time of day. I definitely shed a few tears during the vows and laugh at Dan trying to sing for Anna. He's a horrible singer but the sentiment is sweet. I do my very best to not look out into the crowd because if I were to lock eyes with Aidan, my knees would completely buckle. Even though the majority of the attendees are looking at the bride and groom professing their love to each other, I can sense a pair of eyes staring directly at me. Goosebumps cover my skin and it isn't because of the ocean breeze. The memories of last night are infiltrating my mind. I do my very best to pay attention to every detail of this wedding, but I can't stop thinking about Aidan's hands all over my body, how he lifted me effortlessly off of the ground and kissed me like it was the last time. How when I thought it couldn't get any better, he proved me wrong. He proved me so wrong.

"With the power vested in me by the State of New York, I now pronounce you man and wife. Dan, you can kiss your bride," the officiant proclaims.

Cheers erupt from the crowd. The tears that were building up finally escape down my face, and I applaud with the rest of the crowd while Dan dips Anna into a fairytale kiss. And the funny thing is, in this moment, I am so thankful that I didn't go through with my own wedding to Robert. I mean, he kind of made that choice for me– but regardless, in the end, I wasn't meant to marry him.

Unfortunately, I have to walk back down the aisle back toward the reception with my ex-fiancé. When I link arms with him, I can already smell the tequila permeating from his pores. I force a smile as I look out into the crowd of people clapping for the newlyweds, who are happily striding away in front of us.

"You look gorgeous, Hales," Robert whispers in my ear. The strong smell of tequila only confirms how drunk he is, which catapults me into a flood of memories of Robert coming home late from work, completely smashed, saying how tired he was and what a hard day he had and he didn't have the energy to deal with the day I had, even if it was terrible.

I whisper through my teeth, "I don't think that is an appropriate thing to say given that your fiancée is sitting right here in the audience. And let me remind you, I wasn't the one who screwed our relationship over...you are."

We finally reach the reception space and I weasel my arm out of Robert's overtly strong grip.

Luckily, Anna doesn't want to take a bunch of pictures, especially since the photographer is trying to beat the clock of the sun. The lighting has to be perfect. Right before sunset, but not quite twilight. Anna is very organized and particular about the exact photos she wants, which I am grateful for because unfortunately, many of the photos consist of me next to Robert.

I am craving to see Aidan. I have been so busy with all things wedding that I completely abandoned my date. I know he is a big boy and can take care of himself–his words–but my body actually aches for him. For his presence. I just have to get through one stupid dance with Robert in a few minutes, after Dan and Anna have their first dance. They want all their wedding party to join them for the song immediately after to kickstart the party. Unlike other weddings I've attended, they want the dancing to start immediately, and then have dinner served a little later. They've always been about the party, ever since college. They threw the best parties back in the day.

I finally catch sight of Aidan out in the crowd. He is smiling and talking with my mom. I wish I had an invisibility cloak so I could waltz over and listen in on their conversation. My mom is also genuinely smiling, and that warms my heart. I haven't seen her smile like that since my dad was alive. Aidan is truly a special human being.

He finally catches my eye and gives me one of his heartthrob winks, yeah the one that makes women's knees go weak and the blood race through their veins, livening up anything that was once dormant. He is a guy who makes you want to abandon the outside world and live completely in the wonderful new reality he creates when you are near him. And it isn't because he is a movie star. It isn't because he is the most dangerously good-looking man on the face of this planet. It is because he has a heart of gold and he isn't afraid to show it to the world. I know many women think that men who hide their emotions are sexy. I think the opposite. Aidan baring all of his emotions and laying them flat on the table – that is sexy. Vulnerability is sexy.

"Introducing for the first time as husband and wife, Mr. & Mrs. Dan Buckley."

My heart leaps as I watch my best friend take the dance floor hand-in-hand with her now-husband. I can't help but cry in this moment of pure happiness. I hope that they remember this moment for the rest of their lives. The moment when everything is perfect. The moment when you marry the person you are meant to be with. I know deep down that relationships are far from perfect, but these two people understand each other like no one else does. They know each other's demons and love each other anyway. They make each other better.

"How Long Will I Love You" by Ellie Golding starts to play, and the bride and groom dance as if they have shut the world out around them and it is just the two of them. How it's supposed to be.

I grab a white cloth napkin and dab my eyes. All the craziness and stress from the morning washes away, and what is left is the perfect image of two people who love each other unconditionally. Oh lord, if I am crying this much now, I am going to be a blubbering mess when it comes to my Maid of Honor toast. I am glad I wrote it down because I can't imagine trying to recite it in front of a crowd of people. I'm already nervous as it is. Even though I am a writer, the actual presentation of my work has always been a problem; hence why I am usually in the background or out of the spotlight.

The song finally reaches its coda and Dan elegantly dips his wife and gives her a sweet kiss. The photographer's camera is flashing like crazy to capture this flawless moment. Everyone claps, and then the DJ's voice belts through the speaker: "Now the bride and groom would like their wedding party to join them on the dance floor to get the party started."

I reluctantly make my way toward the dance floor. Robert makes his way over from the bar–of course. He is walking a little off-center already and he slightly bumps into me as I get ready for him to take my hands. Okay, he is way drunker than I initially thought. He must've been drinking from the flask that Dan gave all of his groomsmen as their gifts. He smells horridly like tequila. It is practically seeping out of his pores, like I've been thrown in the deep end of Bourbon Street.

It's just one song, I repeat over and over in my head.

The photographer comes by and says, "Smile, you two!"

Robert pulls me in a little too close and presses the side of his face to mine. I force what probably resembles more of a grimace than a smile. I tried. I really did.

"So Hales," Robert slurs. I shoot him a death stare. "Oh right, I am not supposed to call you that anymore," he states in a mocking tone. God he's being a dick, alcohol just exacerbates that fact.

"What?" I say, a little too snippity. One second thought, it was the perfect amount of snippity that I wanted to exude.

"I know your little secret," he whispers into my ear.

Ice runs through my veins and my stomach drops.

"I know that Aidan Stone is your boss and you are his measly little assistant and that you two are just faking being together. I thought you moved out to L.A. to become a writer. What a fucking joke. I knew you weren't dating him." *How the hell did he find out?* "And I gotta be honest: I don't trust him at all, Hales. He is clearly using you to be his little distraction and to make himself look better after months of him going around and sleeping with every little hot thing that walked in his path. And what's worse is that you are too stupid and naive to realize he is just using you."

I finally look up into his cold hazy eyes, glossed over from the booze."I don't understand...how did you...?"

"How did I find out? I have connections, honey, and money. I know a private investigator. I have been using him for years to find dirt on the opposing party's clients and even the opposing party themselves. I called in a favor right after the welcome dinner and he did some digging out in L.A. The timeline just didn't make any sense and honestly the entire fucking concept of you getting a famous actor to date you. I mean, *you*. Look at you and look at him." He gestures over to where Aidan is sitting.

My eyes are definitely puffy from the tears that are involuntarily streaming down my face, and Aidan notices immediately. His jaw clenches and his own eyes narrow in on the man who has me in his arms. Aidan loosens his tie a little and crosses his arms. He stands up, looking dangerously pissed-off. I can tell it is taking everything inside him not to stomp over here like the Incredible Hulk and cause havoc on Robert in every way.

Robert leans in again. "And honey, what makes you think that you are good enough for him if you weren't good enough for me?"

My gut clenches and my eyebrows furrow together. "You are such an asshole." I push him away. I know this song well, and it's about to end anyway.

But Robert doesn't ease off his grasp on me. It actually seems like he is pulling me in closer.

"Robert, the song is over. Let me go, please."

"Why? So you can go back to him? Not a chance, babe."

"Don't call me that!"

"Why, because your fake boyfriend calls you that?"

"No, because you *shouldn't* call me that. You have a fiancée, remember? Or are you so drunk that you forgot that you had a fiancée *again*? You certainly must've forgotten you had a fiancée when you were cheating on me." I push against his chest and without avail, try to escape from this nightmare.

"I never forgot about you. Even when you left me. Look, you're back in town and since you really aren't dating that pretty boy over there, let's just hook up for old times' sake."

Robert leans in to kiss me and I finally find the strength to push him off me. He almost runs into Dan's mom and dad dancing.

I wipe tears off of my face and say, "I'm so sorry. He's always been a clumsy dancer." They go back to dancing and I seize my means of escape. "Stay away from me," I hiss to Robert.

I try my very best to be as inconspicuous as possible as I hurriedly walk off the dance floor and head toward the wrap-around deck of the venue. I want to find the perfect hideaway from this incubus of a situation. I have to be back in like twenty minutes for the toasts, but I need that time to get my bearings again. I need to prepare to talk about love in front of a crowd of people and try to convince them that it won't ultimately lead to fucking heartbreak.

29

Aidan

I follow Haley out onto the deck. I wanted to break up her dance with that asshole of an ex the minute I started to see her close in on herself, but I didn't want to cause a scene. I could tell he was saying some bullshit to purposefully hurt her, and that set my teeth on edge.

There she is. My angel looks absolutely defeated, wings clipped, alone underneath strings of Edison bulb lights hanging from the eave. I never want her to cry like that again. I want to be her protector. Her comfort. It kills me to see her like this.

When I reach her, I pull her close into my chest. She doesn't flinch when I touch her. That's a total one-eighty from last week, when the thought of me touching her freaked her out. I stroke the back of her head, letting her soft hair run through my fingers. "Are you okay, Hales?" I feel her head shake side-to-side and my stomach sinks. "What happened? What did he say to you?"

She finally reveals her face. It is red and splotchy and wet. She uses the back of her hand to wipe the tears on her cheeks and she inhales sporadically, attempting to stop herself from crying again. Even in this vulnerable state, she is still the most beautiful woman I've ever seen.

She sniffles and explains, "Robert somehow found out that you are my boss and that this whole relationship is fake and he thinks you are just taking advantage of me. As if I couldn't take care of myself." *How the fuck did he find out?* "And he said that you will hurt me because of how you've acted in the past and because of who you are. He said..." Her words cut off and she looks down and starts to cry again.

"What did he say?" I lift her chin with my hand. "Hales?"

"He said that if I wasn't good enough for him, what makes me think that I am good enough for you?" Now the tears come down in waves. I'm going to kill him. I swear he better not cross my path for the rest of the weekend. To make someone as sweet as Haley cry like this infuriates me. I can't imagine how much she cried when he cheated on her and effectively ended their engagement. She continues through her tears, "And you know, he's right. I am not go–"

I place a finger against her lips. "Don't you dare say that you are not good enough for me. If anything, Hales, it's the opposite." I pull her into my chest again. "I promise you that everything will be okay. Robert knows nothing about our relationship. He has no right to say anything."

Speak of the devil. Robert stumbles his way through the doors onto the deck. I have had my fair share of experience dealing with drunk, angry men in my lifetime, and I am already pissed that I have to deal with this again. It triggers my defenses right away.

Disoriented, Robert slurs, "There you are, Haley. Why the fuck did you leave me out there alone on the dance floor? Typical Haley, always running away from her fucking problems. You know you made me look like an asshole in front of all our friends, right?"

When he is inches away from grabbing Haley's arm, I step in between them. He has no right to lay his skeezy hands on my girl. "I think you are doing that all by yourself, Robert. Good for you for realizing that you are a problem. Admission is alway the first step." I have a solid three inches on him and I know I could lay him flat in two seconds if needed. It takes everything inside of me to not make that a reality. He is pushing it, though. He's been on my shit list since before I even met him. "I think you need to head back to the reception, man."

Robert starts to laugh and he stupidly advances on me. The asshole decides to shove me. Hales steps back, scared of what's about to happen next. And I don't blame her. "And what are you going to do if I don't?"

"Trust me, man, you don't want to know," I say, rolling up my sleeves. "And it would be highly inappropriate, since we are at your best friend's wedding. I wouldn't want to embarrass you more than you are already embarrassing yourself right now."

"Ha!" Robert lets out a taunting laugh. "You think that you're better than me, you pretentious asshole? Just because you're a famous movie star? What are you going to do to me, pretty boy?" He shoves me again.

"Don't push me, Robert." I instinctively guide Haley to go behind me. I want to shield her from this jackass in every way. If she had to deal with this version of Robert at any point in their relationship, I feel terrible for her. I wish I could magically erase those memories from her mind.

"Or what? We both know you're just going to drop her, just like all your other little girlfriends in the past."

This prick. I'm done being cordial.

"At least I didn't cheat on her, you dick. At least I have some fucking dignity and realize that Hales is the best thing that could happen in anyone's life. Don't take it out on us that you fucked it all up."

"Well if Haley would have put out once in a while, maybe I wouldn't have…"

I swing as hard as I can and hit Robert square in the face. He falls to the floor. Yup, he is definitely going to have a busted lip. But I don't fucking care. That bastard deserved it.

Jesus, I haven't punched someone for real in a long time. The last person I punched was my dad, years ago, in defense of my mom. I always have a stunt double or I fake-punch my castmate. I shake my right hand, then flex my fingers out and curl them back in. Even though I haven't done that in years, it felt good to release all my frustrations out on this asshole.

"Oh my god!" Haley rushes to my side, grabs my bicep, then my hand. "Are you okay? Did you hurt your hand? Is it broken?"

"If you properly know how to punch someone, you won't break anything. Nah, it just hurts a little." I nod down to Robert, who is attempting to stop the blood from making its way down his chin but to no avail–some drips onto his white collar. "I think he got the worse end of the deal."

Haley places her hand on the side of my face and forces my gaze to leave Robert and arrive at her gorgeous brown eyes. "I don't care about him. I care about you."

I immediately want to swoop her back up into my arms, take her to our bedroom and show her how much I care for her.

Robert finally finds the strength to stand up. Wiping blood from his lip, he points to me and says, "What the fuck, man? This conversation doesn't fucking concern you. You're not even her real boyfriend. You don't fucking love her."

"And you did? Well you have a hell of a way of showing it to the people you love. And for the record, my love for Haley is none of your goddamn business. You come near her again, and I promise you, you won't get up off the ground once I'm through with you."

"Is that a fucking threat, pretty boy?"

"It's a fucking guarantee. You're lucky that all I did was bust your lip. That was a courtesy to the bride and your fiancée." I step toward Robert until his forehead is almost touching my chin. He isn't brave enough to hit me, I can see the cowardice in his eyes. He's all talk. "Don't come near my girl again," I growl.

The only thing that breaks the tension is the clearing of a throat. "Um, they are ready for the Maid of Honor and Best Man to do their toasts now." It is Haley's mom. *Shit.* I hope she didn't see me punch that son of a bitch. Or I hope that if she did see it, she knew I was defending her daughter. But I know better than anyone that often glimpses of other people's lives isn't the entire story.

Haley lets go of my arm and starts walking toward her mom. LeAnn gives Haley a small smile and as Robert passes, she hands him a napkin. "Maybe you should stop by the bathroom real quick to clean up before you stand in front of a crowd and talk about what it means to *love* someone."

Damn. I may have beat him up physically, but LeAnn just clobbered him with her words. She glares Robert in the eyes before he walks away, hunched over in multilayered defeat.

Now it is my turn to face the possible wrath of LeAnn Swann. These Swann women have no idea how intimidating they are when they are standing stoically. They say a lot when they don't say anything at all.

She breaks the silence first. "So..."

Geez, it feels like I am about to get scolded. I revert back to my seventeen-year-old self trying to explain to my mom that it wasn't my fault that I was late for curfew. It was my buddy Lucas' fault, his car broke down because he didn't get gas. I rub the back of my neck as I hesitantly look her in the eyes. "So...look, I was just trying to..."

"You love my daughter."

That isn't a question. That is a flat-out statement. I was so sure that she was going to take me down with her words like she just did with my arch nemesis. Relieved, I allow my arm to fall to my side. "Yes, ma'am, I do."

She points a finger at me and gets into a lecturing stance. I thought I was scot-free, but she can't help it–she's a mom. My mom would've done the same thing. "Don't make me look at you with disdain as I just did with Robert, do you understand me? My daughter is everything to me. She's my world. I just want her to be happy and to be treated right in her relationship. Can you do that?"

"Yes, ma'am."

"Okay then. Thank you for defending my daughter. Robert had it coming." She lowers her guard. She has the same look in her eyes that Haley does when she lets someone in. "And again, call me LeAnn, Aidan, please."

"Okay, LeAnn." I offer my arm so we can walk back to the reception together. She slides her hand through my arm and rests hers on my forearm. It means the world that I have LeAnn's blessing to date her daughter. I just want to make sure she has no doubt about how I feel about Haley. "And just for the record, I wouldn't dare hurt her like he did. Not under any condition. She's too important to me. She's my world, too."

We make it back to the reception and take a seat. Robert is finishing up his slurred speech about a topic he knows nothing about. He does manage to convince the people around him, though, as I look at the crowd. Some people are tearing up. He might be a good lawyer, but he sucks as a person.

He hands the microphone off to Haley as she stands up, removing my jacket I gave her in the process. She has a piece of paper in one hand and the microphone in the other. I can tell that she is nervous to be speaking in front of a large crowd of people, but I know she can do it. This woman is strong enough to accomplish anything she wants to in life.

"Hi everyone. My name is Haley. I'm the Maid of Honor and Anna's best friend. Um, I could be up here all night talking about how much Anna means to me and even tell you embarrassing stories about the bride, but I know it would be a moot point since Anna doesn't get embarrassed by anything."

The crowd laughs as Haley smiles that beautiful smile of hers and looks back at Anna, who nods at the statement and mouths, "It's true."

"I know the word 'honor' is a part of my title, but to tell you all the truth, it's an honor to know Anna and to have her as my sister. You know, when she and Dan met, I was a little worried that our relationship was going to change. That the world we created for ourselves would change. The world full of Barbie dolls, jamming out to Britney Spears and N*Sync, making friendship bracelets, talking about the boys we liked, talking about our first kisses. That our sacred bond would be broken, even though we swore to each other that no boy could come between us."

My heart jumps a little at that image. I desperately wish that I was Haley's first kiss and now my stomach is twisting, aching that I will hopefully be her last.

"I was worried that our perfect sisterhood bubble would pop and my person would be taken from me forever. What a relief it was that Dan just fit into our world and didn't completely upend it. If anything, he added to it. He loves Anna so immensely and completely that what Anna and I had established was never threatened, but rather nourished and nurtured. I thought everything would change. And I guess it did, but in a way that made our relationship stronger and through this process, I felt that I gained a brother. Our time with each other became more intentional. Instead of dreaming of who our prince charming would be or what they were going to be like, we were actually discussing the real ones in our lives."

This is when Haley starts to break. Just a little.

She looks at Anna and says, "You two were made for each other. And Dan, there is no one else in the world I could imagine loving our

Anna the way you do. Or who can handle Anna's crazy antics like you do."

Laughter ensues again, but people are now sniffling in the midst of the laughter.

"Now, I am not saying that your marriage is going to be perfect or that every day is going to be sunshine and rainbows. Just remember that on the best days and the worst days, love is always going to be a part of the equation. It is the foundation to any secure and lasting relationship. It is the common thread that binds all of us together and that thread is going to fray at times, but it's also going to mend in others. Love never fails us. It finds a way into our lives when we least expect it."

Haley glances over to me, eyes glittering from the twinkling lights and tears. *That's it. I'm done for.* It is then I notice that all eyes are on Haley and only on Haley. For once, I'm not warding off stares from people in the distance. Finally nobody cares that I am in their vicinity. It feels so liberating. I haven't felt this freedom since before my first blockbuster film took off. I am glad that Haley is finally the center of attention. She sure as hell is mine.

"Find the beauty in every moment with each other and never allow the world to tell you that your love is too good to be true, because real love is never too good to be true. It just is." Haley puts down her paper and grabs her glass of champagne. I grab my own, along with the entirety of the guests, and raise it up.

"Here's to the bride and groom and to a love that will withstand any storm that comes your way. Congratulations. Love you guys."

There is not a dry eye in the house. Everyone starts clapping. With the exception of the stone-cold face of Robert, who isn't even looking anyone in the eye and is now drinking from his flask again. Julia is trying to console him and I see her mouthing, "What happened to your face?"

Haley makes her way to Anna and they embrace with tears streaming down both their faces. It is a beautiful sight to see. The love between them is so apparent and so strong. There is no storm that is going to break their love, either. After Haley hugs Dan, the DJ starts playing more music. "All right now! Let's really get this party started! Get out on the dance floor!"

I need Haley in my arms immediately. It is no longer a want anymore. I need Haley like I need air to breathe.

"Will you excuse me, LeAnn?"

LeAnn nods and starts talking to the guest sitting on her other side. I roll up my sleeves again and adjust my tie. As I approach Haley and Anna, they are laughing about some sort of inside joke. I reach out a hand toward Dan. "Congratulations, Dan. You're one lucky man."

"Thanks, man. Don't I know it."

"That's right," Anna chimes in, winking and plastering a kiss on Dan's lips.

"Anna, would you mind if I steal the Maid of Honor away for a dance? I haven't had that pleasure yet."

"Steal away. Just make sure she's back by midnight, Charming."

"Oh my god, that is the cheesiest thing you have ever said, Anna." Haley grabs my hand and makes her way around the bride and groom's small table.

"I can't guarantee that," I respond to Anna. "Sorry to disappoint, but I have a feeling that I am going to be keeping her way past midnight." I like bantering with Anna because I have a feeling that is Anna's way of approval and acceptance into their sisterhood bubble. I am for sure in, and that is important to me. Almost as important as being in with LeAnn.

Anna's jaw drops, as does Dan's, as does Haley's. But I don't care. I never want to spend a night without this woman. Especially after last night.

"Well...she's all yours. Don't be too rough with our girl." Anna playfully winks at me.

"Oh my god, Anna!!" Haley exclaims out of complete embarrassment.

"Can't make any promises." If I thought Haley's jaw dropped

before, it is completely on the floor now. Her face turns the brightest shade of pink I've ever seen and it is also the cutest sight I've ever seen. I love making her flustered, especially since she now has a point of reference of what to expect from me.

"Thatta boy. Have fun, you two." Anna waves at us, then turns her attention to some older guests who want to say their congratulations before their departure.

Out on the dance floor, I place Haley's arms around my neck and my own hands on her waist. I make a mental note of where the zipper is located. Hell, I didn't need to know that information, as long as it is material that can easily rip, I'll be fine. She will never wear this dress again, even though she looks like a total knockout. She is rocking this light yellow dress and here I thought lavender was her color. Who am I kidding? Haley could be wearing a fucking potato sack and she would be the most stunning woman in the world.

Haley is looking everywhere but up at me. Her face is still flushed.

"Where's your head at Hales?"

"Oh my little old head, maybe it completely exploded back there where Anna and Dan are sitting after you told them that you were going to be 'rough' with me."

"Those were Anna's words, not mine." I laugh. "And did you want me to lie to your best friend?"

Haley finally shoots me a look and her nose crinkles up like it does when she is upset. I can't take her seriously when she looks like that. It's the cutest face I've ever seen.

I return her look with a big smile. "That's what I thought."

"Why are you smiling like a goofball?"

"Because you're cute when you crinkle up your nose when you're mad."

Haley purses her lips together, trying not to smile from my

comment. I hold her tighter to me and feel every curve of her body meld into mine. I want to get in that head of hers. I know she is overthinking. "Seriously, what are you thinking about?"

"You."

"What about me?"

"How you didn't hesitate in defending me with Robert. How you actually punched him."

"Are you mad at me for that?"

"Not mad. Just confused. I mean, you are so concerned about your image in Hollywood. That was the whole point in us dating, right? For you to return to your Golden Boy status? I'm just scared that if we continue this relationship back in L.A. and someone even looks at me the wrong way – which, let's face it, would probably happen because not to be a broken record, but look at you and look at me – that you are going to fight every person who talks ill of me. People are going to talk and criticize and doubt this. I don't want you to have a reputation you don't want, especially when I know the real you – or at least, I think I do." She looks down. She is starting to doubt it, which is so insane given everything we've been through these past three years – and more importantly, all that we've been through and discovered about each other these past couple of weeks.

"You're right. I will take down anyone who talks bad about you because you're my girl. And let them talk, Hales. People love to talk about things they know nothing about. They just want the attention. We know what we have and that's all that matters. I will punch a million Roberts if they ever talked to you or touched you like he did. All I care about is what you think of me. No one else matters."

I can tell by her small smile that she isn't convinced. I have an idea that will hopefully bring her out of her own head.

"Stay right here. Don't move." I run over to the DJ and ask him to play a song that I know is one of her favorites. It's one of my favorites too.

I jog back to Hales and resume our position.

"What song did you request?" she asks.

"You'll find out in about five seconds."

Jazz music blasts on the speakers and Harry Connick Jr's voice takes over the night air. Haley recognizes the song immediately and she flashes me her immaculate smile. "*It Had To Be You?* Really?"

"I know it's your favorite. And I have it on good authority that it's this version specifically that you love the most."

"Oh do you now?"

"Yup. Rob Reiner has good taste. I'm going to have to tell him that the next time I see him."

Haley's shoulders are at ease and she peruses my face, really looking at me for *me* and not just what I look like on the outside. She is looking into my soul. "Oh you're good, Aidan Stone."

"You're better, Haley Swann." I kiss her forehead and her hands grab my neck a little tighter, welcoming the gesture. I lower my head to meet her eyes and say in the most serious tone I can possibly muster up, "And I want to make something abundantly clear: there is no *if* with us, Hales. I'm not going anywhere."

She finally relaxes and nestles her head on my shoulder. For the first time in a long time, I feel like I am safe. I feel like I am at home. Haley is quickly becoming my home.

30

Haley

"Have a safe trip back, Mom." I close the trunk of the taxi after placing my mom's suitcase in it.

"Thanks, Haley girl, you too." My mom encases me in a hug and squeezes me extra tight. I know that she is going to miss me beyond words, because I miss her in equal measure. "When are you both heading back to L.A.?"

"Tomorrow. I actually have to go back inside and finish packing. Dan told us that we can stay an extra night so we don't have to head back to the city right away."

"That's sweet of Dan. Plus, it will be nice for you both to get the privacy you need. This weekend was very eventful and it will be nice to decompress before heading back to reality."

My stomach drops like it used to when I was a kid on winter break, dreading that my vacation was about to end and I had to go back to school where my only saving grace was Anna and my English class. That inevitable fear of reality is not something I want to face just yet. It's like Sunday evening and I am ten years old again, wishing tomorrow was Saturday.

The taxi driver looks back at us, clearly getting impatient.

"Well, Mom, you better be on your way. I don't know where Aidan is. I know he wanted to say goodbye to you."

"Oh he found me earlier and already said his goodbyes. He had to go run some errands." My mom's eyebrows raise like she is up to no good.

"Okay," I say skeptically. "Mom, why are you looking at me like that?"

"Like what?"

"Like you know something that I don't. I am very aware of that look because I inherited the same one."

"No such thing."

I know she is lying but I don't want to push further. I just laugh and open the back door to the cab.

When I shut the door, my mom rolls down her window. "You know, I was scared that the fire inside you got completely extinguished after Robert. But now I see that Aidan isn't going to let it extinguish and more importantly, *you* aren't going to let it extinguish. You are stronger than you think you are, my sweet girl. I have this instinct that you are going to break free and your work is going to be seen and made into a movie or show or something. The world deserves to see your greatness." My mom gives me one more hug through the small window and a kiss on both cheeks. *One from me and one from your father,* she started saying after Dad died. "I'm going to miss you, Haley girl. But something tells me that you are going to be well taken care of. Your mother can breathe now. Take care of him, too. I can tell he's one of the good ones."

My heart skips a beat. That was a glowing review from LeAnn

Swann. She doesn't just give out "one of the good ones" willy-nilly. She never said that with Robert. Come to think of it, neither of my parents did. I give her a wave. "I love you, Mom. You take care, too. And remember if you ever need me to come out, I will."

"I love you too, my amazing daughter. I promise I will visit you out in L.A. more this year. Talk to you soon?"

"Text me when you land. Bye, Mom."

The worst thing about travel is packing, especially packing to return back home. I groan when I see the messy state of my open suitcase. Aidan's suitcase is already packed, zipped and ready to go. That's another thing about Aidan: he is extremely neat and organized, which honestly always made my job easier. He loves schedules as much as I do. He loves a clean trailer and home as much as I do. Instead of tackling my suitcase, I plop onto the bed and close my eyes. My body fully relaxes for the first time since we drove onto this property. The only thing I can hear are the waves and seagulls outside.

Even though I am in a complete state of relaxation, my stomach aches. I haven't eaten since brunch this morning. I think it's also aching because of Aidan's absence. I wasn't aware of how much I yearn for him when he isn't near me. Maybe that is the hunger talking. Where did he go? Maybe he just abandoned me and his suitcase and left for the city. Maybe he realized how boring I really am and he needs someone who gives him a life of adventure. Someone who belongs on his arm on that red carpet. Someone who no one would question. I wince at the thought and sit up, rub my face and open my eyes.

It is then that I see it. A note taped to the vanity mirror on the dresser across from the bed. I slowly get up and walk over to the mirror. It is addressed to me. I carefully pull the note off and open it:

Hales, I think it's time for us to relax and have a real date night. Meet me on the beach at 7:30.

Take a nap and change into something comfy. See you then, beautiful. —A

I smile and hold the note to my chest like it is my most treasured possession. I yawn, also realizing we really didn't get a whole lot of sleep last night. I pack really fast, leaving an outfit for later to change into after I nap. I set an alarm on my phone so I won't miss my first real date with Aidan. I definitely wouldn't miss that for the world.

The cool ocean breeze makes my hair flop about, probably making me look like fricken Bellatrix Lestrange. *Sexy, Haley.* Aidan won't know what hit him. I decided to wear some linen shorts, a white tank top and a cardigan. I have to take off my flip-flops once I reach the sand, since they keep getting stuck. I wrap the cardigan around my torso, looking left and right as I walk, trying to find Aidan. I walk a little further left, head around a large rock, and there he is. Standing with his hands in his pockets next to a blanket that has a bottle of wine in an ice bucket, two wine glasses, two pizza boxes and a laptop.

I make my way toward him with an astonished smile spread across my face. When I finally get within a foot of Aidan, I say, "What is all this?" I gesture to the set up. Glancing at the open laptop, I see that *You've Got Mail* is at the ready.

"*You've Got Mail?*"

"Since we didn't have a chance to finish it at my apartment."

My eyes survey the scene in front of me. "How did you know that this...?"

"Is your dream date?" Aidan finishes my exact thought.

"Yeah."

"A little drunk birdie might've told me a few nights ago. Figured I'd take a shot."

"Nice shooting." Suddenly I'm not so cold anymore. My body is all warm and fuzzy and I so desperately want it to stay that way. I smile and approach Aidan's little picnic set-up. There are pillows and blankets. And there is something that I probably didn't mention as a part of my dream date because I didn't think any guy would plan ahead of time to acquire them.

Flowers. And not just any flowers.

Lavender roses.

I lean down and touch the soft petals. "I haven't seen lavender roses since before my dad passed. Every date night, my dad would have a bouquet of lavender roses waiting for my mom on the kitchen table. He said that he liked lavender because they represented enchantment and wonder. Everything that my mom reminded him of." Tears well up. Damn, why does Aidan have to reach deep into my soul and awaken the emotional beast inside of me? Deflecting, I say, "I thought you were a red roses type of guy based on what you left me the other day."

"Lavender has become one of my favorite colors lately."

"Oh yeah, since when?" I sit down on the massive blanket on the sand.

"Since I saw you in that lavender dress for the premiere. My heart did a somersault the moment I saw you, Hales and it's never fully recovered." He joins me on the ground, never taking his eyes off me. He presses the spacebar on the laptop and pours wine into glasses. He looks effortlessly breathtaking in his khaki cargo shorts and long-sleeved, slate-blue Henley. His sleeves are rolled up, revealing every large vein in his forearms, causing my heart rate to quicken. I've never been around such a paradoxical man. Someone who is so masculine yet soft. Brawny yet delicate. This hard exterior definitely protects the teddy bear of a man inside.

My heart does more than somersaults, more like full-on back flips and back handsprings. It's as if Simone Biles is doing a whole floor routine in there.

"The roses remind me of you." He hands me a glass of my

favorite white wine. We clink glasses and I slowly drink, trying to convince my brain that what my body is feeling is real. I clear my throat and tuck some hair behind my ear, turning beet red. We are definitely in an unfamiliar place now. If someone would have told me a month ago that I would be falling madly in love with my boss, I would've laughed like a maniacal hyena in their face.

There have been moments where all of this has felt like a dream. A dream that I am terrified to wake up from. I feel this cosmic shift with me and Aidan, and I know that no matter what happens, things are never going to be the same. *How the heck are things supposed to "go back to normal" like we discussed in the diner?*

"This is all really sweet of you, Aidan. Thank you." Before I spontaneously combust from all the excitement racing through my veins, I point to the pizza boxes, "What kind did you get?"

Before he could answer, I open the lid to one of the boxes. Hawaiian. Disgusting. I must've put a mental block on the fact that Aidan loves pineapple on his pizza, so much so that he always asked for extra whenever I ordered for him.

Aidan must've noticed my slightly scrunched-up nose because he laughs and says, "That one's not for you. Check the box underneath." Damn, he knows how to read me like an open book. "I know how much you hate pineapple."

"It's not that I hate pineapple. I love pineapple. Just not on my pizza, you weirdo."

He scoffs. "Did you just call me a weirdo?"

"Yes, I did. I know that you don't hear that often, Aidan Stone. I know you are used to people constantly telling you how amazing you are, which they aren't wrong by the way, but yeah you liking pineapple on your pizza makes you a certified weirdo."

I close the lid to the pizza box and slide it over to Aidan with my tongue sticking out in disgust. I hear Aidan's deep chuckle, the one that makes shivers run all up and down my body. It is a sound I want to put on repeat on a Spotify playlist.

I open what I assume is my own pizza box, which gloriously has just one topping on it–the ultimate topping, in my opinion–pepperoni. "Now this! This is a pizza." I grab a slice and take a huge bite. And it isn't a sexy bite, either. It is a bite that results in cheese and sauce all over my chin. *Perfect.* I'm sure Aidan doesn't want to be with someone who eats like a toddler.

But instead of looking disgusted by my obvious lack of grace, his signature smile appears. He grabs a napkin and wipes my chin and the sides of my mouth. Then he did something I wasn't expecting him to do. He kisses me. And not in, like, an *I need you now* kind of way, but in a gentle, habitual way.

Which for some reason, I find so much hotter.

"Is it weird that I love you calling me a weirdo?"

"No...it's not at all weird." Suddenly I feel myself closing in, becoming the version of myself that I hate. The Haley who starts to overthink everything because her anxiety gets the best of her. Yeah, that one.

"What's in that beautiful head of yours, Haley Swann?"

"Just thinking." Yeah, thinking about the inevitable downfall of this entire relationship.

"About?"

"Going back to L.A. Leaving this nirvana that we've been in for the past week. I don't want all this..."

I gesture to the scene around me. The sun has definitely set now and the sky is a beautiful medley of pinks and oranges and purples. I never want to forget this sight. I want to lock it in a safe and throw away the key. And then my heart sinks when I come back to reality. Who knew how long this thing was going to last? I am too scared to let someone in, knowing it will most likely turn out to be temporary. Tears begin to well up.

"...to end. I can see it slipping away when we get back to our regular lives in L.A. When all the pretense is over. When all the questions start bombarding us from all different angles. And not just from the paparazzi. From our co-workers, from the press, from our families. People are going to find holes in our story and then it's all going to blow up in our faces. Just like it did with Robert. We can't hop on a plane and escape to the Hamptons all the time. You have to work, hell I have to work. We've both worked too hard for everything to crumble down. I mean, isn't that the reason we made this agreement in the first place? To help your career, and in some sort of twisted way, my own?" My knee starts bobbing and my fingers grab on for dear life to the softest blanket on planet earth that is beneath us. My knuckles are literally turning white. Then I say quietly, in almost a whisper, "I definitely don't want this all to end."

"But that's just it, Hales." Aidan grabs my hand that is clutching the blanket and kisses my palm. "I don't want all of this to end either. I told you that the other night and I meant it." He laces his fingers between mine. "And if people find out the truth about how we started, who cares?" He grabs my outer thigh and pulls me on top of him, so I am now straddling his lap. Now I have no choice but to look straight into his eyes. Poor little writer girl. What torture. "Besides, that's Samantha's problem." He smiles that smile that makes the sides of his eyes wrinkle. My favorite smile.

"Oh god help us with that woman. She seriously scares me." I cradle Aidan's face in my hands and now take in the sight right in front of me. Forget the sunset. This man is magic. Aidan runs one of his hands through my hair and grabs the back of my head, securing his hold on me quite literally. If only he knew the hold he has on me already. He turns me into a puddle whenever I'm near him, and I don't think that is ever going to change.

"Don't worry about Samantha, her bark is worse than her bite. Plus, she's damn good at her job. She keeps me accountable and I need that in my career. I never want to make others look bad because of my stupid actions. That's what I love about you, too. You have never coddled me or treated me differently because of who I am in Hollywood. You have always been so professional and sweet and...

just everything to me. I really can't imagine my world without you in it. You make it harder to breathe when I'm around you, Hales."

I release a side of his face as I blush and tuck some hair behind my ear. Thank god the sun already set so that my cheeks don't give me away too much. "Aidan, no one's ever said those things to me before...not even Robert, and I was with him for years." How could someone so painstakingly gorgeous utter those words about me? Me– the girl whose hair looks like a psychopathic witch, with red sauce all over her face?

"Well I think it's safe to say that Robert is a first-class jackass and he doesn't deserve to walk the ground that you walk on. No one does. Not even me."

Tom Hanks and Meg Ryan are bantering about something in the background. I laugh. "Are we ever going to actually watch this movie together?"

Aidan bites his bottom lip. "Actually, beautiful girl, I was hoping that I could kiss those soft lips of yours and make all of those worries bouncing around in your head disappear. The movie was kind of a prop."

"Aidan! We can't make out on the beach! There are people around and what if they see?"

"Haley, I don't care if there's one person or millions of people who see us–I am going to kiss my girl. Like I've said before, let people talk. They are going to anyway. Might as well live our lives on our terms. Plus, you kind of have to get used to me kissing you because I am going to do it every chance I get. I hope you don't mind."

In the sassiest voice I can muster, I playfully retort, "Well, what if I..." Then Aidan's full lips land on mine before I can finish my answer. I could get used to him interrupting me with the best kisses I've ever had. I am tempted to protest his every statement just to get his lips on mine. Although, I have a feeling that Aidan doesn't need any provocation. He is going to kiss me because he genuinely wants to and because he craves my lips on his. I know that because that is my truth and it terrifies me. But I refuse to let my fear ruin this moment on this perfect beach with this perfect man on this perfect date.

I am going to take a page out of Aidan Stone's guide to fearlessness and allow myself, for the first time in a long time, to be incandescently happy.

31

Aidan

I light a candle and have coffee already brewing, knowing that will make Haley feel like she is home. Ever since we got back from New York, I can't stop thinking about her. I know it has only been a couple days, but her absence by my side is so noticeable that I can't concentrate on anything.

On the plane ride home, I held her hand the whole time, knowing this hand-hold is different from all the other times I've held her hand before. I invited her with me to my European tour. There is no way I'm going to be without her for that long. It was hard enough being away from her when she was just my assistant. Now that we are officially together, I know I am going to suffer every second we are apart.

I invited her to stay over that night we got back to L.A., but she stubbornly insisted that she go home. "I promise that I'll come by in a few days. I need to desperately do laundry and decompress from the weekend. Too much socialization for this introvert."

Reluctantly, I let her go.

Even though it's only been a couple days, I miss Haley's presence so much. I can't wait to see her flushed cheeks when I flirt with her or even come near her.

There's a knock at my door. That's weird. I told her to text me when she was in the driveway so I could come open the door for her. Maybe she forgot.

I open the door with excitement, ready to hold her in my arms and not let her go for the foreseeable future. But as the door swings open, my excitement is stifled immediately. Because the person waiting there on my doorstep isn't Haley. The image of Haley is replaced by someone I never want to see again. Her caramel skin is barely covered by the nude dress she is wearing. It clings to her body in a way that leaves nothing to the imagination.

"Natasha, what are you doing here? I'm expecting..."

Natasha lunges forward, grabs the back of my neck and pulls me down to her lips. It is forced and messy and it feels so *wrong*. It's amazing that six months ago, I thought there was nothing in the world that could compare to Natasha's lips on mine. That kissing her would be the best part of my day. I was gravely mistaken, and I am so glad that I was.

I release her hand from my neck and break our kiss. I step back all the way to the edge of one of my couches. I lean against it and cross my arms. I watch Natasha close the door behind her, slowly walk over to the kitchen island, and put her Birkin bag on the counter. "Why did you stop kissing me? I thought you would be happy to see me."

"Well you thought wrong. Look, I am expecting someone and you need to leave. Now."

I head toward the door but before I could reach the handle, Natasha's hand presses against my chest. "Wait. Aidan."

This should be interesting. I cease walking and put my hands in my pockets. "What? Why the hell did you kiss me, Nat? What are you even doing here at my house?"

She looks down at her hands and starts playing with her nails. "I don't know. I am just really confused right now. I don't like seeing you with that little assistant of yours. I miss you, Aidan."

I huff. "Well, I'm sorry you feel that way. I didn't really like seeing you with Isaac either, but you had no regard for my feelings six months ago, or rather, what was it, more like nine months ago, right? How is your new boyfriend by the way? Does he know that you're here, telling me you miss me and kissing me, no less?"

Natasha looks down at her feet. "He's fine. He's on location filming a movie on his days off from the show. I don't know. I don't really have butterflies anymore in my stomach. It's not exciting anymore for me." Is that what happened between us? She didn't feel the butterflies so she decided to search for them in someone else? "I didn't mean to hurt you, Aidan."

"But it happened anyway, didn't it." I plaster my hand to my face and drag it down. "Look, it's not my problem that you don't feel butterflies anymore. You made it that way the moment you broke up with me, Nat." I finally make my way around Natasha's barricade and open the door, hoping Haley isn't right behind that door. Luckily, she isn't.

"Haley's on her way here. I really need you to leave. Our relationship is in the past, Natasha, and I have no interest in going back."

Natasha scoffs as she grabs her purse and starts walking out the door. She finally turns around in the hallway and says, "I don't understand what you see in her. She's a fucking nobody, Aidan."

Unfuckingbelievable.

"She's sure as hell a somebody to me. As a matter of fact, she might just be my everything. Goodbye Natasha." I close the door on her shocked face.

I know that I will have to see Natasha in the upcoming months with all the premieres, and we'll potentially be cast alongside each other in movies or TV shows in the future. Our paths will surely cross, but for the first time since Natasha walked out on me, that reality does not hold much weight. The only person who matters right now in my life is the woman I am waiting on right now.

I hear my phone ding and head over to the couch to look at my screen. My heart drops slightly when I read the text from Haley.

> Sorry. Something came up. My stomach started bothering me. Probably should stay away. I'll see you in a couple days on set.

32

Aidan

My stomach is in knots. And not the good kind. I haven't seen Haley in four days and it's making me anxious. Ever since she texted me that she wasn't feeling well, I have been in a constant state of worry. She caught a "bug or something and don't want to spread it to anyone" as she put it. I even offered to bring over some soup, but she said Rachel was taking care of her. I sent some anyway.

When I walk into the studio, I'm not expecting to see her back at work. She's by craft services, getting a croissant and a banana, with a couple of coffees next to her on the table. I thought she would've let me know she was coming in.

"Good morning, Hales."

"Morning." Without looking at me, she hands over my coffee. What the hell is going on?

"Here is your call sheet. You have a lunch meeting with Samantha again today. You have a night shoot tonight and tomorrow night. I have a few calls to confirm some things in Europe for your press tour..." She starts walking fast in the direction of my trailer.

I have to jog a bit to catch up with her. "Wait, Hales, slow down. You're talking a mile a minute."

"Do you need me to send this information to you in an email or voice memo? Because I can." Her tone is short. Clipped. Professional. She hasn't looked at me once, which is unfortunate because she is looking extra beautiful today. Her look is effortless. Her hair is in a ballerina bun with a pen through it and a light gray cardigan. Classic Haley. Her soft look does not match her hard demeanor towards me. It's killing me that she isn't looking at me.

When we finally reach my trailer, I grab her hand and pull her inside. I shut the door behind us a little more forcibly than I should.

"Okay, what's going on?" I press.

"What do you mean?" Haley continues to type on her phone and avoid eye contact. She is wearing her blue-light glasses, obstructing her beautiful brown eyes. Damn those glasses. I want to rip them off and break them in half.

I put my hand over her phone screen and lower her phone down. Haley sighs and finally looks up into my eyes. Her eyes are really puffy and red, confirming that something is definitely off. She has, in fact, been crying. "Hales, what's wrong?"

"Nothing. I just didn't sleep well last night. I've been sick, remember?" she sniffles.

"Bullshit. I don't think that's what it is."

"Then why did you ask me?" she retorts, her tone clipped.

Okay, she is definitely pissed and hurt. What the hell happened between a few days ago and today? I need to tread lightly here. "I'm sorry...it just looks like you've been crying and I want to know what's wrong."

Haley sniffles and her voice is a little shaky when she says, "Maybe you should ask Natasha."

I shake my head out of disbelief and confusion. *What does Natasha have anything to do with this?* "Wait, what?"

Tears start rolling down Haley's face, but she is still as stoic as ever. All of her walls are up again. All the walls I have been trying so desperately to take down. "When I was pulling into your driveway, I saw Natasha and you...kissing. Then she went into your house, still kissing you, and I just..."

My heart plummets. "You assumed something happened between us?"

"Didn't it?"

"Do you really think that low of me, that I would cheat on you with an ex-girlfriend?"

Haley averts her eyes again, confirming that she does in fact think that.

I scoff, "Wow."

"Oh don't 'wow' me, Aidan. It's not completely out there for me to think you hooked back up with her. You were *in love* with Natasha. I witnessed it. All of it. The only reason you started '*dating*' me in the first place was so that you could get out of your own way after your break-up. What am I supposed to think? And you know, it doesn't surprise me. You both make sense together. I think it's easier if we go back to the way things used to be. The deal is over anyway."

I put my hands on my hips and I clenched my jaw. I can only imagine how it looked to her. Natasha was barely dressed, and Haley is right. I was in love with her. *Was* being the most important word. "It's not what you think... I had no idea that Natasha was going to come over. I swear. I didn't invite her over. Nothing happened. Haley, you have to believe me."

"But something *did* happen...you were kissing her, Aidan."

"*She* kissed *me*. Not the other way around. And I pushed her off immediately. The kiss meant nothing, Hales. "

"A kiss always means something." Then Haley holds her hands to her face, attempting to block the inevitable tears coming out. I don't know what to say to her. It is clear she doesn't believe me. I am losing her. She is closing in again. Building that impenetrable wall of hers that I worked so hard to break down.

"It's fine, Aidan. We agreed this whole relationship, or fake relationship rather, was going to end. We had an expiration date, remember?" Haley's phone starts ringing. "I need to take this, excuse me," and she starts stepping out of the trailer.

"Haley."

She looks back at me.

"Can we please talk later?"

Her phone keeps buzzing. "I gotta take this...Hello, this is Haley." She steps out of the trailer and the door slams shut.

This explains so much. Natasha ruined everything good happening in my life. Again. But I was an idiot in the first place for ever letting her step into my house at all. The moment I saw it was her, I should've closed the door in her face.

I can't let Haley go like this. I push open my trailer door and run after her. I catch up quickly and take the phone from her hand.

"Aidan, what the hell?" she fumes.

I put the phone to my ear. "Hey, she's gonna have to call you back." I press the red "end call" button.

Haley crosses her arms. *Damn, why does she have to look so cute when she's mad?*

The little crease between her eyebrows is very prominent now. She places her hand out. "Give me back my phone, Aidan. I have a lot of work to do. Especially since..." She looks down at her feet and bites her bottom lip. "...I'm giving my two weeks."

What? No. "Are you serious? You're quitting?"

She snatches her phone out of my defenseless hand. She looks down again and says, "I don't see any other way. I'll make sure that all of your appointments for the next few months are finalized and confirmed. I'll make sure everything is taken care of before I go. I just...can't be around you anymore. Everything has changed. It's too hard." She grazes her hand across her cheek, trying to mask the obvious tears that are slowly slipping out of her eyes.

"What are you going to do for a job? I know you can't afford where you live now, even if you are splitting rent with Rachel. And what about your screenplay? I thought you wanted to get into this business so that you can work your way up. I can help you do that, Hales."

"I will figure it out," she responds curtly.

"Please, Hales, I don't want to lose you," I plead.

"I wasn't yours to lose in the first place and you weren't mine to lose either," Haley says.

I grab her face between my hands. "That's not even remotely true. Don't do this. Don't run away. You promised."

She pushes away and just like that, she is out of my reach again. "I made that promise when I thought that you were everything to me. When I thought I'd finally found the guy who was it for me."

"Haley, I am still that guy. I'm the same guy."

She shakes her head. "I am not running away, Aidan."

"Yes you are, because you are scared."

"No, I am getting myself out of a situation I shouldn't have been in the first place. I am *not* running."

"You are. Just like you did three years ago." I feel her delicate hand make its way across my face.

She points a finger at me, infuriated, "That's not fair and you know it." Tears start rolling down Haley's cheeks again.

That does it. I have become the thing she is running away from and I don't know how to salvage this.

"I'm sorry," I say. "That wasn't fair."

"I am not running. I am simply abiding by the contract we established. According to our contract, this–" She points back and forth between the two of us. "–is over."

33

Aidan

I haven't seen Haley since she walked out my trailer door on her last day.

That was almost four months ago.

After I return from my European tour for my latest movie, I try everything to get back into her life. All the press wants to see Haley next to me.

Join the club.

Once I land, my car is waiting for me. I head to Haley and Rachel's apartment straight away, but Rachel answers the door and says that Haley is taking a nap and it's probably best that I don't bother her. I try explaining what happened, or *didn't* happen, between me and Natasha.

"Look Aidan, I believe you, but I gotta support my girl. She is really going through it right now. I mean, look at it from her perspective. She literally risked everything to fake-date you, you both caught actual feelings for each other–which let's face it, duh–and then when you promised her that she was your forever, she saw you and Natasha, who was wearing practically nothing by the way, making out and then heading into your house."

"Nothing happened." I nearly growl, still pissed-off that this is the way Haley is going to remember me. She is probably replaying that kiss over and over in her head, inevitably haunting her.

"Natasha shouldn't have been *near* your door, let alone going *into* your damn house, Aidan. Even if Haley wasn't on her way there–it's the trust factor she has an issue with. I bet memories of what she walked in on with Robert and that homewrecker flooded her consciousness. She felt like she was burned twice."

All I can do is nod. I am at a loss at what to say.

"Hey, for what it's worth, I think you are a stand-up guy. And I know you couldn't control the circumstances with Natasha. I get it. But when you're heartbroken, you can't see past certain things. Just give Haley some space. Maybe she'll come around once she's done being depressed about the situation. See you on set, Aidan."

Their green door slams in my face. It guts me that Rachel used the word "depressed" when talking about my girl. I don't want any space between us anymore. I guess I'd been naively hoping that after I returned from Europe, Hales would run back into my arms like they do in the movies.

Reality is different.

Reality fucking sucks.

Months pass, and I throw myself into work. Trying to distract myself with memorizing lines and strength-training. I run on the beach every single morning, even if I have an early call time, hoping that maybe, just maybe, I will see the woman of my dreams running toward me and I can scoop her up, throw her over my shoulder, and take her home with me.

But that never happens.

I could probably compete in an Iron Man competition at this point, given how immersed I am in working out these days.

———

December 30th. I am back in New York for the holidays to be with my mom. She has a new boyfriend and I actually like him. I know this man is important to my mother because she hasn't let anyone in her life since my dad. I could tell that he really likes my mom and respects her. I've never seen my mom so happy, and so I am in effect happy.

I am mindlessly scrolling my Instagram reels when a knock on my door knocks me out of my trance. *I didn't buzz anyone in. What the hell is going on?*

The knocking becomes incessant.

"Aidan Stone, answer your damn door! I know you're in there!"

I look through my peephole and see none other than Anna and Dan.

Dan turns to Anna and says in a low voice, "What if he's not home, honey. We are going to look like lunatics to his neighbors and then security is going to kick us out of this building. The doorman was already suspicious of us when we snuck in after that delivery man."

"I know he's in there," Anna growls.

What the hell are they doing here and how did they know where I live? Actually scratch that, I don't want to know. Anna probably has some scary ways of finding out information.

I open the door. *Here we go.*

"I'm assuming you are here to kick my perfect little ass?" I say, looking directly at Dan.

Confused, he looks back at me. "What? No. What the hell are you talking about?"

Anna chimes in: "Damn right he is!" She charges into my apartment and Dan follows suit, looking dumbfounded and quite honestly a little scared. He was completely out of the loop on this promise that Anna made months ago on his behalf.

"Wait, no Anna, I am not going to kick Aidan Stone's ass. Are you joking me? I am half his size. He would snap me like a twig." A flash of panic enters Dan's eyes as he glances back and forth at me and his fuming wife.

"Well, if you're not going to, I will." She marches over and slaps me across my face. So hard that it stings. *Okay. I was expecting way worse than that from the best friend of the woman I love.* "You promised me that you wouldn't shatter her again and there you went and did it anyway! How could you do that to Hales? She is seriously the sweetest person on this whole fucking planet and you broke her! Aidan, did you know that all she did for a month after your whole situation, deal, whatever the hell you want to call it, ended? Hmm? She sat in her room and cried. Barely ate. Barely slept. It was like a Bella in *New Moon* level of depression. I called her twice a day and texted Rachel constantly to make sure she was okay. To make sure she didn't fall further into her own intrusive thoughts of not being enough for someone." She slaps me again, on the other cheek this time. "How dare you cheat on her with your ex!"

Wait, what the hell?

"Is that what she told you?" I ask incredulously.

Anna nods vigorously.

"That's not true at all. Natasha kissed me. That's all that happened."

"Why should I believe you? According to Haley and the various tabloids and social media posts, you were in love with Natasha at one point. I am Team Haley all the way." Anna crosses her arms and stands with one hip out. A classic pissed-off stance.

Rubbing my cheek, I respond, "I thought I was in love with

Natasha. I didn't know what real love felt like until Haley. I know what you are about to say, that that sounds like a line from one of my movies and that I am bullshitting you right now. But I swear I am not, Anna." I look her deep into her eyes, hoping she will see the truth in mine. "I love Haley so much that it is killing me that she is not by my side every second of every day. If I knew what it would take to win her back, I would. You don't think I've also been fucking depressed? Hell, it has been a million times worse this time than my very public breakup with Natasha. Only this time, instead of parading around with women and drinking until the early morning and having hangovers and regrets, I've been throwing myself into my work. Distracting myself. Trying not to think about the woman who made me feel alive again, who made me feel like a normal guy and didn't treat me special because of what I do. Except the distraction doesn't work. It's a terrible type of purgatory I can't escape. Every aspect of my job reminds me of Hales. She was such an important part of my world for over three years. These past months have been terrible. And even when I come home, I've been lighting her favorite scented candle and making coffee non-stop because it reminds me of her. I hate myself every day for allowing Natasha into my home four months ago. I should've slammed the damn door in her face the moment I saw it was her and not the love of my life." I put my hands on my hips and look down at the floor, feeling defeated as ever but I have to make one more important point: "And just to make it clear, I will always be Team Haley, too."

Finally, I see a flicker in Anna's eyes. A shift from rage to understanding.

"Anna," Dan says, "I think he's telling the truth. I can tell when someone is lying and telling the truth. I see the pain in his eyes and I could only imagine that would be what my own eyes would look like if I lost you."

I knew I always liked Dan.

"I know he is, too." Anna breathes out and steps back to allow some sort of distance between us. "I can tell you love my best friend, Aidan. But why would Haley tell me that you cheated on her?"

"I don't know. Maybe she thought that would be an easier excuse to tell people as to why things ended between us. That narrative is unfortunately what she has gotten used to. Things just got complicated and she wanted a way out." I fall onto my couch and cover my eyes. "She wanted to protect her heart."

I get it. If I saw Robert at Haley's door, kissing her and she let him in, my mind would wander too and make assumptions. I would be hurt too. Actually, I would grab him by the shoulders and throw him the hell out of her house, but that's besides the point.

Anna and Dan make their way over to my couches and slowly sit down.

"Please tell me that she is doing okay." I clasp my hands together and let them fall between my knees, looking down at the floor.

"Well I think that 'okay' is relative but yes, she is doing a lot better than when things first went south. She actually called me the other night and told me some good news."

My heart drops. She started dating another guy. Someone who wouldn't let her slip away like I did. Someone who would hold onto that delicate hand of hers and never let it go. This is what I deserve.

"It's not that," Anna quickly reassures me. It's scary how this woman can read people's minds. "Her manuscript got picked up by some executives at Netflix. They want to make it into a mini-series. I guess it's true what they say: if your personal life is going to shit, then your professional one will be on the rise. That's kind of why we are here, plus we haven't spent New Year's Eve in New York in years. We are here to celebrate with her."

She's in town? I smirk because she's been right here in New York. She isn't 3,000 miles away. I'm so relieved those executives actually listened to me and legitimately read the script like I asked them to.

It is time to confess. "I did that."

"You did what?" Anna and Dan ask in unison.

"A few months ago, Rachel handed me a manuscript with

instructions to read it and told me that if I wanted even the smallest chance to be in with Haley again, that I needed to use my influence as a possible producer on the project to get this greenlit. She said that Haley submitted it already but it might get lost in the slush pile. I read the whole script but I knew after the first ten pages that it was something great. I haven't read a manuscript for a romantic comedy like this in a long time. I knew it was something special. And I was so fucking proud of her for finishing it in the first place. She finally figured out her happy ending and I realized that what went on between us, especially our time on that beach after the wedding, meant something to her. She used that as her happily-ever-after in her screenplay. I realized that she still cared, but I was and am still on the outs with her. I knew that if I couldn't get her back because of who I am in the industry, I at least needed to use my power in Hollywood for good, especially since I'm now seen as the Golden Boy again. All thanks to Haley."

I smile for the first time in months because I could only imagine Haley dancing around in her room, probably blasting Taylor Swift and genuinely dancing like a goof in celebration of this news. I would've gladly watched her do that for hours. Unfortunately, the only look on Haley's face seared into my brain is the one she gave me as she left my trailer for the last time. "I helped greenlight her manuscript. I knew being a screenwriter has always been her dream. I wanted her dreams to come true. That was the least I could do."

"Oh my god. Aidan, this changes things."

"This doesn't change anything."

"Of course it does. You know Haley almost as well as I know Haley. She'd want to know who the man behind the curtain is. She'd want to know that you fought for her to have her dream as much as she wanted it. She'd want to know that no matter what shitty things happened between you both or how complicated things got, that you were always on her side and that you stood by her." I see the wheels in Anna's brain turning, and then she stands up and points at me. It is like I am able to see a lightbulb actually turn on above her head. "I think this is how you can get her back."

My ears perk up at that last statement. "What do you mean?"

"I think you need to tell her what you did for her. It may be the thing that pierces through that thick wall she rebuilt these past few months."

Dan chimes in, "Yeah, but how is he going to do that? Haley isn't returning any of his calls or texts, and she would kill us if she knew that we told Aidan she's in New York. We are basically dragging Haley to this party tomorrow night just so she can get out. She doesn't really want to go out in the first place."

I know exactly how to win Haley back. "I need y'alls help. Are you with me?"

34

Haley

"How much longer do I have to stay? I really just want to go back to the Airbnb, open a pint of Ben and Jerry's cookie dough ice cream and a bottle of wine, and watch Anderson Cooper and Andy Cohen get drunk on national television."

This is torture. Everyone around me is coupled-up. Most people at this party are happily drunk, wearing those silly glasses with the year on the front and party hats. *Why did Anna and Dan drag me to this stupid New Year's Eve party?* Granted, I've been lying on my bed most nights for the past four months, going over and over in my head about how stupid I was for getting into bed, literally and figuratively, with Aidan Stone.

How I hated myself for still wearing his stupid oversized UConn shirt that I found in my suitcase while I was unpacking. I hate that I want to keep him close by wearing it, as if it is some magical shirt that would send a damn signal saying *come back to me*. I hate that I can still smell the rain pounding the streets of New York, that I can still smell the candle that was burning when Aidan almost kissed me in his apartment during the blackout. I hate that I can still feel his hands all over my body and all the sweet kisses he has given me. It's like they are imprinted on my body forever.

I hate that I scroll through Instagram and stop on whatever news item mentions Aidan's name. I am watching his life through pictures now, rather than being in his life. I can feel him forget me. He stopped trying to call and text months ago. He probably thinks I'm not worth it.

Yet again, I wasn't enough.

The only silver lining during these months of torment was that call I got from the studio about how they got a hold of my script– that I finally and bravely submitted –and they loved the story. They want to make it into a miniseries, which is huge right now with all the major streaming services and entertainment in general. I jumped around in my room in excitement, blasting Taylor Swift and singing at the top of my lungs, knowing that all of my dreams were coming true and that moving out to L.A. was not a waste. The only problem was that the silver lining was attached to a dark gray cloud: the daily reminder that I can't share my excitement with the man I truly still loved more than anything. He started to become a big part of my dream. Now he was probably making dreams with someone else.

I hate that I don't know how to live my life without missing Aidan. And he's probably moved on with someone much hotter than me. Someone who looks great next to him with no effort at all. He's probably at some fancy L.A. party right now, canoodling with the next hot, up-and-coming actress, one who won't run away when she gets scared that it's turning into something real. I hate that Aidan was right: I was running away out of fear.

If only he knew how much I want to run back into his strong arms and stay there forever.

"We have thirty minutes until midnight. Just stick it out, okay?" Anna and Dan are standing together, both drinking champagne. They also are wearing those silly hats and glasses. They look annoyingly cute together, as always.

"Why? So I can watch everyone else share a kiss with their date while I stand alone in the corner, miserable?" I cross my arms and lean against the bar.

"No, because I don't know, maybe someone will want to kiss you at midnight. You never know, Hales. You might be surprised." Dan weirdly clears his throat and nudges Anna's side. They exchange looks like they know something I don't.

But that only happens in fairy tales. In romantic comedies. This is real life and there is no Harry coming to get Sally back. I lost my Harry months ago. There is only one person who I want to kiss me at midnight. But it's never going to happen. No one is going to walk through that door professing his love for me.

———

Fifteen minutes later, I am still standing at the bar, this time with a drink in my hand.

"Hi. I'm Zach."

I gulp down my drink and turn toward the man next to me. He is really handsome, tall and with a cute smile. Eyes like emeralds, complimenting his olive skin. Despite all of those things, my heart doesn't leap one bit nor do shivers make their way through my body. That's the other thing about dating the sexiest man alive–no other man compares.

"Hi." I give a quick smile.

"Aren't you going to tell me your name?"

Did I seriously revert back to my awkward social self in only four months? "Oh, sorry. Yes. I'm Haley."

"It's nice to meet you, Haley. Would you like to dance with me?"

Why the hell not? I have no other prospects. At this rate, I'm going to end up like Charlotte from *Pride and Prejudice*, marry someone like Mr. Collins just so I won't end up an old maid. It's not like Mr. Darcy is going to walk through that meadow and tell me how much his sentiments have not changed.

"Sure."

Zach flashes a smile and leads me out to the dance floor. We haven't been dancing long when someone bumps into me. I turn–it's Anna.

"Oh sorry. Haley, who is *this?*" Anna's eyes look panicked, crazed, as if I am the one acting crazy. This woman desperately needs to look into a mirror. She's been acting strange all night.

"Um, this is Zach." I give her *what the hell are you doing?* eyes.

"Uh huh, and what are you doing with *Zach?*" Her eyes dart from Zach to me and then to the door.

What the hell is going on?

I gave a courteous smile to Zach and say, "Zach, can you hold on for just one second?"

"Sure."

"Thanks." My smile disappears as I grab Anna's hand and pull her away from Dan and into the hallway.

"Okay. What the hell is going on? First you wanted me to stay so that maybe some guy would come and kiss me at midnight, and then when that guy comes along, you act like I am crazy to be dancing and making conversation with him. What if Zach is the love of my life? You are getting in the way of that!"

"Yeah he's a guy, but he's not the *right* guy."

"What are you talking about? What do you mean he's not the *right* guy?" This was ridiculous. I shake my head and say, "I am going back out there to continue dancing with Zach and hopefully he will kiss me at midnight because I need him to, Anna. I need to get over Aidan. I need the memory of Aidan's lips on mine to be erased; otherwise, I won't be able to fully breathe ever again. Just let me have this, okay?"

"Okay," she says, clearly deflated. She sighs and looks down at her Apple watch and then back down the hallway.

Gosh she is acting strange.

I make my way back to the tall drink of water waiting patiently for me in the middle of the dance floor. He really is handsome. Kind of a Jackson Avery look to him. At the very least, I am going to be kissed at midnight. At the very best, this man could be the one for me. He reaches out his hand and grabs mine, pulls me in and glides me across the dance floor.

Five minutes left until midnight and for some reason, something feels off. I don't want to be here. In another man's arms. Dancing to Frank Sinatra. TVs are broadcasting Dick Clark's New Year's Rockin' Eve with Ryan Seacrest. The ball is about to drop and ring in the new year. One of new promises. New hopes. New resolutions that are most likely not going to be fulfilled by next December. This all feels wrong. There is something in the universe pulling me away from this man.

Two minutes.

I grab Zach's arms and stop our movements altogether. "Zach. I'm sorry. You seem like a really sweet guy. Thank you so much for dancing with me tonight and making me feel special. You are going to make some woman very happy. You are such a gentleman. I just need to leave."

"Really? It's almost midnight."

"I know, but I just can't be here. I'm sorry, I have to go."

I start walking away. Anna runs up to me and grabs my hand. "Wait, Hales, where are you going?"

"I'm sorry, Anna. I can't do this. I seriously just want to go back to the Air BnB and put on sweats and watch a movie or something until you both get back."

"No you have to stay! Please."

"I can't. You guys have fun, okay? I'll see you in the new year." I kiss her on the cheek and turn around, making my way through the crowd of people.

One minute.

I glance back at the dance floor. Zach already has a new woman in his arms. *Great.* Anna and Dan are talking to each other and shrugging, probably agreeing that I am a lost cause and they tried their best.

The next thing I know, I run into a rock-hard chest. "Oh my God, I am so sorry."

"Why is it that you are always running into me, Hales?"

My heart starts to beat wildly. The butterflies that have been dormant for months now are fluttering again in my stomach. *It can't be.* But every fiber of my being knows that it is him.

The deep teal color of his eyes is all I need as confirmation. Those eyes have haunted me in the best and worst ways every time I've closed my eyes these past four months. My body becomes tingly and hot and my head starts spinning.

"What are you doing here?"

"I'm here for you."

My insides turn to mush, but my head stubbornly wants to win this fight. Self-preservation mode engaged. "Well, I am on my way out, so if you'll excuse me."

Aidan blocks in my path.

"Aidan, move out of my way."

"Not until you agree to listen to what I have to say."

"I don't really have any interest in what you have to say." I can feel the smallest crinkle between my brow. I am half-angry and half-wanting to just bawl in front of the most beautiful man I've ever known. Hell, the world has ever known. But this is the kind of emotional limbo I've been trapped in for months now.

"Then I'm not moving," Aidan says with a small, smug grin. Does he think that ridiculously attractive smirk is going to change my mind? Well, maybe. But that's besides the point. I absolutely am not going to let it. Maybe in the past those tactics would have worked on me, but not today. Not after everything that's happened. I am channeling an Amazonian woman now and will bulldoze my way out of this situation. I do wish I had a lasso I could throw around him to make sure I'm getting the truth. The truth is hard to come by these days, even with all the "transparency" of social media. If I learned anything from "dating" Aidan, it's that what you see in the pictures certainly does not tell the whole truth.

Despite all of this, I know deep down that Aidan will let me go. He isn't a psycho. But for the life of me, I can't get my feet to lift off the ground and walk away from him. That magnetic force is back and stronger than ever.

I cross my arms to come off like I am annoyed, which don't get me wrong–I am. Annoyed that he came back into my life, right when I finally felt like I was on solid ground. Why does this man have the innate ability to simultaneously make the world crumble at my feet and be my fricken world? "Fine. Proceed. You have thirty seconds before I walk right past you and go..."

"Home, put your pajamas on, eat Ben and Jerry's and watch *When Harry Met Sally* for the thousandth time?"

Damn he's good. My jaw drops and eyes narrow. "How do you know I don't have a hot date waiting for me at another location? You don't know me, Aidan Stone."

He steps forward, dangerously close, and stops when we are mere inches from each other. The familiar scent of sandalwood and musk infiltrates my senses. My heart quickens at the sheer masculinity permeating from Aidan. I didn't realize how much I missed him standing next to me. He isn't even touching me and my body is on fire again. I look around and thankfully everyone's eyes are on the TVs, watching the ball drop in Times Square, and not plastered to us.

He steps a little closer and my core heats up and does that stupid flippy thing again. "I beg to differ, Haley Swann. I feel like I know you like no one does. I know that you are a Swiftie, even though you pretend you're not. I know that you love creamer more than you love coffee in your mug every morning. I know that you are the most talented writer I've ever met. I know that you get a cute little crinkle between your eyebrows when you are upset. I know that you bite your lower lip while you are contemplating something that's important to you or when you are too afraid to say what you're thinking." *He shouldn't know that look yet.* "I know that you hate being the center of attention, and you are willing to sacrifice your own peace for the peace of others. I know that you love your family unconditionally, even the ones who aren't blood." His eyes avert for a millisecond over to where Anna and Dan are standing. Then something clicks in my brain. *Of fricken course.* No wonder Anna was acting weird all night and saying things like the *right guy.* She was waiting for the guy in front of me. They planned this out.

I look back up at Aidan and start saying, "Unbeliev...."

Before I can finish the word, he then brushes his finger across my lips. "I still have twenty seconds, Swann." And there is that smirk again–only this time, he leans down a little closer to my face, so our noses almost touch. My knees are starting to buckle. Even my own body is revolting against my will. *Amazonian woman my ass.*

"I know that you always put others first, even when you don't have to. I know that you love to sing, even though you pretend like you have the worst voice in the world. That's right, I heard you in the shower."

My cheeks turn bright red at that observation.

"I know you bring out the best in people. You certainly have with me."

I am about to protest, but his finger finds my lips again.

"And even though you think I am saying all this to win you back or you think I am lonely or it's a cliche time to do this, and even though you pretend like you don't want to hear it, the truth is that all the things I know about you...I also love about you, Hales."

My heart pounds uncontrollably, so loud that I swear that the entire room can hear it over the countdown.

Ten seconds.

"You were my rainbow in the storm that was my life, Haley Swann. And I love you."

Five seconds.

Aidan Stone just said he loves me. He never stopped loving me.

Three.

Me. Haley Swann.

Two.

The girl who wasn't enough for anyone.

One.

The girl who only wrote about happily ever afters, and never got one of her own.

"Happy New Year!"

As fireworks go off in Times Square, some are exploding in my belly, desperately wanting to reveal themselves to the man who just professed his love for me.

And yet, my defenses shut down every firework like water to flames. Who does he think he is?

I shake my head and halfway scoff, trying to reconstruct my walls in mere seconds, walls that I worked so hard to rebuild since he broke them down the last time. "Classic Aidan Stone, thinking you can walk in here on New Year's Eve and expect to win me back. Just tell me that you love me and think that will work? Well I have news for you, Stone, it's going to take a lot more than that to ever win me back. This isn't the movies." I cross my arms once more and hope he won't see through my bullshit. At this moment I wish I were the actor, convincing the audience that what I am saying is true.

But that's the thing about Aidan. He could always see right through my pretenses.

Aidan inches even closer to me. His lips are almost touching mine as Auld Lang Syne plays in the background.

Stay strong, Haley. Stay strong.

"No, babe," Aidan says softly. "This is real life. I want everything that happens after the happily-ever-after. I want to be the man your dad told you to be with. The one who regards you as his whole world. And just for the record, I plan to remind you of all the ways that I adore the ground you walk on until you forgive me. I plan to love every part of you...no matter how long it takes, because you are worth fighting for. You are more than enough for me. You are my entire universe, Hales."

I can feel his lips slightly brush against mine. That is it, I am done for.

"Dammit Aidan, you say things like that and..." I look up at his pleading, blissfully hopeful eyes, trying to blink away tears in my eyes in the process.

"And what, beautiful?" Aidan places his hand on my jaw and lightly runs the tips of his fingers through my hair. He has me and he knows it.

"...you make it impossible for me to not love you, too."

And there it is. The radiant smile I've desperately missed all of these months of being apart. The smile that lights up my world, no matter what is going on any given day. The smile of the man I am irrevocably and unreservedly in love with.

Aidan closes the miniscule gap between us and presses his lips to mine. And my god have I missed his warm, soft lips on mine. Even though we have kissed so many times before, this one feels different. It is loaded with so many I'm sorry's on both ends, so many unfiltered desires, so many hopes for the future. This kiss isn't for a show. This kiss isn't for the cameras.

This kiss is for us.

I try to pull away so I can look at Aidan, but he doesn't let me. He grasps the back of my head and pulls me in closer, making it near impossible to escape his lips. It was stupid of me to even try because it is finally our turn to have the fairytale kiss. The kiss all the little girls and teenagers see and wish they would have one day. The kiss that makes you melt with every movement. The kiss that signals to your heart that this is it. The kiss that makes you think you are in the best dream ever and you don't want to wake up. This is a kiss that writers write about in romances. Except I am about to wake myself up for another realization that flashes in my brain. I reluctantly break our kiss and say, almost breathlessly, "It was you."

That mischievous smirk returns, only this time, Aidan's teal eyes are on fire, hungrily awaiting my lips to return to his. After he doesn't respond, I add, "You were the one who greenlit my manuscript."

"No, Netflix greenlit your manuscript. I was simply the messenger." Then he squints his eyes like he is trying to remember something difficult. "And maybe I said a thing or two about how it would be the biggest mistake of their lives if they didn't give you a shot. And I told them to never mention that I brought them the manuscript or else I would back out as a producer indefinitely."

Producer? Suddenly it is all making sense. He worried I wouldn't accept the offer if I knew it was because of him. But now, knowing that he played a major part in getting my script into the right hands—it makes all of it so much sweeter. He knew why I moved out to L.A. in the first place. Other than escaping my past, it was to start a future as a writer. He literally made my dream come true.

"I don't know what to say or do to repay you. I don't deserve you."

"You don't have to say or do anything, Hales. And when are you going to get it through that stubborn head of yours—it's not that you don't deserve me. It's quite the opposite, baby girl—it's me who doesn't deserve you. And I will live out the rest of my days wondering why the universe conspired with me to find you. I'm just so grateful that it did."

Even though at this point I sense that cameras are flashing, videos are being taken, and eyes are glued to our scene, I don't care. I realize that no matter how many people are yelling our names to look at them for a picture, no matter how many exes try to weasel their way back into our lives, no matter what the tabloids claim, I have found my home with Aidan. He is my safe space. He is the one who grounds me when I feel like spiraling out of control with my anxiety and intrusive thoughts—he silences them.

He is the one I want to call mine.

I slide my arms up around Aidan's neck and tiptoe slightly to reach his lips. I squeal when Aidan cups my ass and lifts me into his arms. I wrap my legs around his immaculate torso, and he grabs the back of my neck to ensure that my lips never leave his—so passionate, so demanding. I want to get completely lost in his kisses for the rest of time. His lips, his tongue, the sounds he makes when I kiss him with equal measure all consume me.

And I will happily let his kisses consume me, because I'm not planning on leaving behind this man ever again.

Whether he knows it or not, he is my rainbow in this crazy storm of life, too.

Haley

I feel the slobber from Ginny's tongue on my nose, which unfortunately wakes me up from one of the best dreams I've probably ever had. I am too scared to say it outloud for fear of jinxing it away. I want it to happen in real life someday and hopefully Aidan does, too.

I walked over to the windows and open the blackout curtains that Aidan installed for me when I moved in, and take in the sight of skyscrapers and tons of cars and people down on the street.

Yep, that's right. We moved in together.

Aidan is still in the hunt for a new assistant. He is so stubborn about choosing someone he can trust, especially since the person he trusted most in the world is now his steady girlfriend of almost a year.

Aidan decided that he wanted to take a hiatus for a few months and be back in New York until he was ready to return to work in L.A. He has been getting non-stop offers after his last film and honestly, since we started dating the press hasn't shut up about it.

Butterflies flutter in my stomach and I smile a huge smile at the thought of how long Aidan and I have been together, and the fact that it is starting to snow outside. Today is Thanksgiving and the official start of the Christmas season. Everything seems possible and magical and I am here for it. I am in such a bliss bubble–I never want it to pop. Even though it has been the craziest year of my life, dating the hottest guy on the planet and having my life offered up on a silver platter to the public to gobble up at their leisure, it's all been worth it because the man who is making me breakfast right now, is the best human being I've ever met.

"C'mon Ginny. Let's go eat. I'm sure he'll give you a piece of bacon. He always does."

I don't bother changing out of my pajamas, which consist of Aidan's oversized UConn shirt that I wore when I first spent the night here, pajama bottoms, much to Aidan's dismay, and cozy socks. I make my way down the hallway to the kitchen, where to my delight, Aidan is flipping bacon and sipping coffee. From the TV I hear Savannah Guthrie, Hoda Kotb, and Al Roker announce the performers and upcoming balloons to look out for in the parade. I can see the small flurries descend upon them through the screen. Aidan remembered how much I love watching the parade, relaxing with coffee and cozying up on the couch. I told him this fun fact on one of our real dates a few months ago.

This whole scenario is a sight I never want to forget. It is getting banked as a core memory.

Ginny jumps on her hind legs and places her paws on the granite countertops. As I predicted, Aidan takes a piece of bacon that is already cooling on the plate next to him and gives it to Ginny. I know this man too well. In so many new ways that I never thought possible.

I stand there admiring the man who tells me he loves me multiple times a day, every single day. Every single one of those I Love Yous ruin me in the best way. In the way that I don't know what I would do if I ever lost this person in my life. In the way that makes my heart ache. In the way that makes me fall even more madly in love with him. And if that seems cliche, I don't care. I know I was made for loving this magnetic force of a man. A man who put aside his pride and helped out his dying father when he needed it, and although Aidan turned out not to be a match, it was a first step toward healing that relationship for him. A man who, I might add, is cooking me my favorite breakfast in light-gray sweatpants and a fitted heather blue shirt, which will no doubt bring out those teal eyes.

I grab one of the many throw blankets I brought into this apartment to make it more homey. Aidan has the candle department down, a little fun fact I like to tease him about on the regular, but that I secretly love. I plop onto the massive couch...the very one that we slept together on for the first time. Ginny jumps up and curls next to me, so close I can't really move my feet. "Umph," I let out.

Aidan finally turns around and smiles. "Good morning, babe! Between the TV volume and the sizzling bacon, I didn't even hear you walk into the room. Coffee?"

I snort. "Um, of course. I actually take offense that you asked me that question." I pet Ginny's side, causing her to pant with her tongue hanging out dubiously and in utter bliss. I feel Aidan's soft lips come into contact with my forehead and my insides melt. Handing me the coffee, Aidan says, "Morning, beautiful. Happy Thanksgiving."

I smile just like Ginny, dubiously and gleefully. "Happy Thanksgiving."

And as I predicted, his shirt does bring out his eyes. Remembering that the bun on top of my head is probably all over the place and I am literally in oversized pajamas that are drowning my entire body, I suddenly feel self-conscious. "If you think I look beautiful now, you must think I look like a pure goddess when I am actually ready for the day." I shake my head and sip the heavenly coffee. "Seriously, Aidan. How can you think I look beautiful right now? I have no makeup on. My hair is probably full of knots. I have mismatched clothes on. Shall I continue?"

"Haley Swann, you are always beautiful. In all your forms. You're beautiful when your hair is a ratty mess. When you are in oversized, mismatched pajamas. All the time." I smirk a little. He really must love me. "Actually, I have a solution if you really feel insecure in those pajamas."

I raise one eyebrow. "Oh yeah? Shoot."

"Not wear anything at all. That is my number-one preference." Aidan heads back toward the kitchen, winking back at me, grinning that devilish grin of his. It is truly lethal.

"Well unlike some people, I don't have a perfectly sculpted body where I can just walk around without anyone judging me."

"Oh Hales, you definitely can't see what I see, which is a damn shame if you ask me. You don't realize how gorgeous you are."

No matter how many times Aidan has told me that I am beautiful, or rather gorgeous, I still can't process in my brain that this is real life. That someone like Aidan —an absolute dreamboat in every possible definition of the word – can find someone like me on the same level as him. Before I can protest his claim, my phone dings. Apparently when we were out running errands like any normal couple, some paparazzi took it upon themselves to snap photos of us holding hands and walking around Bryant Park.

That's another aspect of our relationship I don't think I will ever get used to. Always being in the spotlight. Always being under a microscope. Always exposed to the world's scrutiny. "Aidan, have you seen this?"

Aidan doesn't answer me right away and when I look over at him, he is staring down at his phone, distracted by whatever is on his screen. He is probably looking at the picture of us and realizing how far out of my league he is. I get extra nervous because I feel like there is a sense of momentary disconnect between us. There's something about Aidan's demeanor that is off, I just can't figure out what it is. My heart starts racing and not in the giddy way it has been for the past year; right now, it is racing out of panic.

"Aidan?"

"Hmm?" he responds, finally breaking his attention from the small screen on the countertop. He clicks the side button to blackout his screen. Why is he acting so weird? "Oh, no I haven't seen the picture."

So he wasn't looking at the picture. Then what is making him so frazzled? He leans over from the back of the couch and we both look at my phone together and read the caption underneath the photo of us:

"Aidan Stone and girlfriend Haley Swann spotted in Bryant Park looking extra cozy together. The couple has been a steady item since last winter."

"Hmm..." Aidan says as he straightens back up. His hands are lodged in his pockets and he has the smallest inkling of a furrowed brow. He starts walking around the couch toward where I am sitting. "I think there is something wrong with that caption though."

"What?" I zoom in on the caption so I can read it closely and don't spot anything wrong with it. It is actually a good picture and caption about the two of us. No judgment. Just facts. "I don't know what you're talking about. Everything is spelled right."

"Are you sure?" Aidan motions for Ginny to get off the couch and he sits right next to me. How does this man feel like a furnace in a short-sleeve shirt in the winter? I am struggling to feel warm and I am underneath the softest, warmest blanket we own.

"Aidan, I'm sure. I am the writer, I should know."

"Interesting because I could've sworn that it says *girlfriend*."

"Yeah...so? How is that wrong?" I am so confused right now. We've been boyfriend and girlfriend for a while now, especially when I count the time we were fake dating. Why is that word wrong?

"Hold on, I think I might have something that might fix it." Aidan adjusts slightly, reaches into his back pocket, and pulls out his wallet. He opens his it and retrieves a napkin from one of the compartments.

And not just any napkin.

The napkin.

There is no way he kept it all this time. I would've thought at some point, it would have fallen out, gotten destroyed, got torn to shreds after our four-month hiatus. Any option would have been more believable than what I am witnessing right now.

He hands it to me. "I added a little addendum to our contract, Ms. Swann."

How is this happening right now?

"You kept this? For a year and a half, you've had this with you every day?"

He nods and gestures to look at the napkin. The only change I notice is that Aidan crossed out the word "not" that followed the word "absolutely" as it pertained to our condition about sex. I let out an exhale and laugh. "Seriously Aidan? I think we've already unofficially made this amendment, but thank you for pointing this out."

"Oh I made that change a long time ago, you goof." He winks at me, satisfied with himself. "Turn it over."

The jingling of bells and cheers fill the background as Santa is making his appearance along 34th street. I turn over the wrinkled-up napkin and see the words:

Marry Aidan.

My mouth turns dry and my pulse starts racing. Time stands still and all I can hear is Ginny panting as her tongue is hanging out of her mouth, almost as if she is also anxiously awaiting my answer. The sound of the parade is fading away and suddenly it's just us. In our living room. With one lingering question – well more like, request – hanging in the balance. I look up at Aidan and finally say, "What?"

He scoots a little closer to me on the couch and gestures toward my phone. "I think the word that they misspelled in that caption was girlfriend. I think, well I hope, that what it's really supposed to say is *fiancée.*"

I keep blinking at an uncontrollable rate. I am in such a state of shock that I can't form any other word except, "What?" I feel like I am back in Samantha's office the day that Aidan suggested we essentially start a romantic relationship out of the blue. This certainly is out of the blue.

Aidan continues, "I know that I may have been acting weird earlier. Both our moms texted me Happy Thanksgiving and asked if I had proposed yet. Anna and Rachel have also been blowing up my phone incessantly. I didn't want you to see."

The air feels like it has been knocked out of me. In the best way. In the absolute best way. I've never seen Aidan so flustered. Nervous. I thought I was the one who spewed out the word vomit. It seems like right now the roles have reversed. Then he pulls out a little black box from his pocket as if out of thin air. I inhale sharply. My body starts tingling all over from the excitement of the contents of that little black box. If I thought I knew what breathlessness felt like, I was sorely mistaken. He lifts the top half of the box, revealing the most gorgeous ring I've ever seen: a solitaire cushion-cut diamond set in a thin rose-gold band. It is classic, stunning and perfect. Just like the man of my dreams who is kneeling in front of me.

Aidan grabs my left hand and holds it in his. "It's an absolute privilege to love you, Haley Swann. You're the best thing I've ever had and I know I was made for loving you. Completely. Unconditionally. And if I had an infinite amount of days like today, the everyday where you wake up with your hair a mess, dressed in oversized shirts, *preferably mine,* and a smile so pure and gorgeous, I would die a happy man. You are like coming home and I've never had that before."

I usually am the one who can't stop talking, and now it is Aidan's turn to get flustered. I have to put this poor, devastatingly handsome and amazing man out of his misery. I place my finger to his lips, causing them to pucker slightly.

He chuckles, running his hand through his hair. "Sorry I'm so nervous. You aren't saying anything and oh my God this is too much, just like when I had you agree to fake-date me except this is worse because we are actually together and you're freaking out. Oh gosh Haley please don't break up with me, I should have talked to you about it first. I mean I did ask your mom and Anna for their blessing... yes, I asked Anna too because I figured she would probably kill me if I didn't...anyway you can seriously say no. I will love you no matter what, you know that right?"

I know exactly what to do. Without saying anything I take the napkin from his hand, stand up and make my way toward the junk drawer in the kitchen. I pull it open and get out a black pen. I scribble on the napkin and return the pen, then walk over to Aidan and hand him the napkin.

He looks down at the napkin and sees what I wrote:

YES!

"Yeah?" He lets out a sigh of relief.
"Yes. Of course!"
Smiling, Aidan takes the ring out of the box and slides it onto my finger. It fits perfectly.

I love that he proposed in the comfort of our own home, while it is snowing, in my favorite city in the world, as bacon sizzled in the kitchen. This moment is perfect, just like Aidan. Just like us.

I take his face in my hands and kiss him like it is for the last time. That's how I am going to kiss him for always because tomorrow there is no guarantee and when you love someone, *truly* love someone, you want them to know just how much every day. He sits back on the couch and pulls me on top of his lap so that I am straddling him. His hands slide underneath my shirt. His hands are so hot to the touch in comparison to my cold skin. He lit a fire inside of me the day I met him, and I am convinced it will never diminish as long as he is mine. And now he is going to be mine forever. My hands are running through his hair and his lips are just as hungry as mine. I pull back just for a moment and say, "You know something?"

Breathless, Aidan responds, "What's that?"

"I am truly the luckiest girl in the world. You destroyed all my walls, Aidan. You found your way into my heart and took up permanent residence. I can't imagine living my life with anyone else."

Aidan stands up, carrying me with him. "See, that's where you are wrong, Hales."

I can feel the crinkle on my nose start to form. He pushes our breakfast back on the stove and moves the bacon on top of the toaster oven to deter Ginny from inhaling it in one bite. Before I can challenge him, Aidan continues as he carries me toward our bedroom, "*I'm* the luckiest *man* in the world. You *are* my world. There's no contesting that."

He lays me down on the bed and hovers over me. "Haley, will you forgive me?"

Uh oh. *For what?*

"For what?" I say as calmly as humanly possible.

"For not talking to you about this proposal either." His dimples are on full display. My heart leaps out of relief. "I suck at communicating with you about any proposal you are directly involved in."

I playfully push against his rock-hard chest with my left hand, and that is when I notice how truly gorgeous my ring is. He knocked it out of the park, like he does in all aspects of his life. He needs to take off this shirt immediately if he knows what's good for him. I decide to play along, "I think I can forgive you. On one condition."

"Oh yeah what's that, *fiancée?*" he says in the sultriest voice I've ever heard come out of his mouth. I will never tire of hearing him say that word... until he replaces it with a new word. *Wife.* He plays with the tendrils surrounding my face and brushes them behind my ears, a practice I am gladly allowing him to perfect.

"That this proposal has no expiration date." I bite my lip and wait for his response, slightly tugging at the bottom of his shirt. "Other than our wedding date, of course."

Aidan finally takes off his shirt and leans down to kiss me. A kiss that almost sends me into oblivion. "Deal."

AFTERWORD

Dear Reader,

I hope you enjoyed Aidan and Haley's love story. It was so much fun writing these characters and their story. Fake dating has always been a trope that I loved reading about and loved watching on screen, especially when the guy falls first. I also wanted to explore how heartbreak can happen in many different ways and how everyone's journey of recovering from that heartbreak is unique. I always wanted Aidan to be the confident one in their relationship and for Haley to be the one to doubt it, especially as she struggles with anxiety and being so guarded.

I love films so I always wanted to write a book about that industry: the exciting and difficult parts. I wanted to explore how what you see on social media and the tabloids is not the whole story and that movie stars are people first and foremost. Ultimately, I wanted Aidan and Haley's love story to illustrate that what people see on the surface isn't exactly the truth, and for them, what's behind the curtain is so much better than they could both ever imagine.

What did you think about it? I would love to hear!

It would mean so much to me if you take a couple minutes to

leave a review on Amazon or Goodreads. You can also follow me on my socials and join my mailing list to find out about upcoming books and bonus content. My debut novel, *Stuck with Me,* is also available now on Amazon. Thank you!

XO, Leslie

Terms

Holding hands

Hugging

Kissing ?
(only when necessary)

~~S~~ ABSOLUTELY
NOT

ACKNOWLEDGMENTS

Thank you to my readers. I wouldn't be a writer without knowing there are people like you, who take the time to read my story and hopefully fall in love with Haley & Aidan as much as I have. I appreciate the time you took to read this love story and I hope that it left you smiling.

Thank you to my book doula and editor, Dallas Woodburn. You believed in my art and I will be forever grateful for your support and guidance. Thank you for seeing that my art truly does matter and for making my book the very best version it can be!

Thank you to the incredible team at Breakthrough Books. I am honored to be a part of this publishing family. You made my book come to life in ways that I couldn't have done myself.

Thank you to my fellow, amazing, group of thriving women authors. I could not have finished this book without you all. You all gave me the strength and encouragement to move forward with my book. You all saved me from thinking I wasn't good enough.

Thank you to my beta readers: Gracie, Anahi, Natalie, Aziz, Juan, and Gennesis. Without you, I wouldn't know if this book would be worth publishing. Your insights and feedback are so invaluable to me; I do not take that for granted.

Thank you to my parents, sisters, and in-laws for your unending support. You all have always fostered the creative spirit and I am lucky to come from a family where my dreams were never squandered but nourished. Thank you for being in my corner, cheering me on.

Thank you to my sweet boys for always being my motivation in everything I do. You both are my personal rainbows.

And to my Hawaiian pizza loving husband—thank you for being my weirdo. Always & forever.

XO, Leslie

BOOK CLUB DISCUSSION QUESTIONS

1. What is the significance of the title? Did you find it meaningful? Why or why not?
2. What did you think of Aidan and Haley at the beginning of the story?
3. Were there any quotes (or passages) that stood out to you? Why?
4. What did you like most about the book?
5. How did the book make you feel? What emotions did it evoke?
6. Who was your favorite character? Why?
7. What did you think about the female relationships in the novel? What was your favorite?
8. Who would you cast to play Aidan in a movie? Who would you cast to play Haley in a movie?
9. Were you rooting for the couple to get together all along? Why or why not?
10. If you could talk to the author, what burning question would you want to ask?

IMMERSIVE READING KIT

SMELL: Cashmere & Rain (Native), Sandalwood & Pomegranate (The Hamptons Candle or Diffuser by Life in Lilac)

EAT / DRINK: Hawaiian Pizza or Pepperoni Pizza, Waffles, Ben & Jerry's Chocolate Cookie Dough Ice Cream, Popcorn, Coffee with Oatmeal Cookie Oat Milk Creamer, LaLa Land LaLa Latte

WEAR: Cardigan, blue blocker glasses, oversized UConn basketball shirt

LISTEN:

The Expiration Date Playlist
(in no particular order)

"You Are in Love (Taylor's Version)," by Taylor Swift
"Everything Has Changed (feat. Ed Sheeran) (Taylor's Version)," by Taylor Swift & Ed Sheeran

"Fallin for You," by Colbie Caillat

"Like No One Does," by Jake Scott

"Beyond," by Leon Bridges

"Why Can't I?," by Liz Phair

"What If," by Colbie Caillat

"I Was Made for Loving You," by Tori Kelly & Ed Sheeran

"Let You Love Me," by Jervis Campbell

"Thinking 'Bout Love," by Wild Rivers

"Incredible," by James TW

"Tell Me That You Love Me," by James Smith

"Tuesdays," by Jake Scott

"Magic," by Colbie Caillat

"Fall into Me," by Forest Blakk

"Sparks Fly (Taylor's Version)," by Taylor Swift

"T-Shirt," by Thomas Rhett

"New York," by Ed Sheeran

"The Middle," by Jimmy Eat World

"Demons," by Imagine Dragons

"Dirty Little Secret," by The All-American Rejects

"august," by Taylor Swift

"If You Love Her," by Forest Blakk

"Favorite T-Shirt," by Jake Scott

"Delicate," by Taylor Swift

"Cornelia Street," by Taylor Swift

"How Long Will I Love You," by Ellie Goulding

"It Had to Be You," by Harry Connick, Jr.

"Lover," by Taylor Swift

"This Love (Taylor's Version)," by Taylor Swift

"Look What You Made Me Do," by Taylor Swift

"Rainbow," by Kacey Musgraves

"Enchanted (Taylor's Version)" by Taylor Swift

"Lavender Haze," by Taylor Swift

"Beautiful Things," by Benson Boone

"Lavender," by Jake Scott

"Dandelions," by Ruth B.
"Be," by Garrett Kato
"invisible string," by Taylor Swift

For the full playlist, search for "The Expiration Date Playlist" on Spotify

ABOUT THE AUTHOR

Leslie McElroy was raised in Santa Fe, New Mexico but currently resides in Dallas, Texas. She loves her family, cozying up with a good book and coffee, and watching sports. Leslie has always dreamed of becoming a writer since she was a teenager, but she finally wrote her first novel, *Stuck with Me*, after being inspired from reading other contemporary romance novels and knowing that she had a story to tell. Leslie loves watching movies, listening to music, and is an introvert at heart. She is a mom of two boys and is married to her college sweetheart. Leslie hopes that through her writing, she can connect with people around the world and spread happiness with the characters and stories she creates.

Follow Me on Socials & Let's Be Friends
authorlesliemcelroy.com
Instagram: @authorlesliemcelroy

each other. The fear of admitting their true feelings aren't the only obstacles that stand in their way. Lucy is intrigued by a new fling and Jamie is tied down with his new fiancée. Are these two characters willing to reopen old wounds or move forward in their lives? Lucy and Jamie have to face the reality of the choices they made and find out if true love really finds a way.

www.ingramcontent.com/pod-product-compliance
Lightning Source LLC
Chambersburg PA
CBHW070446300726
48975CB00007B/2056